WILLIAM MANN

The Long Way Home

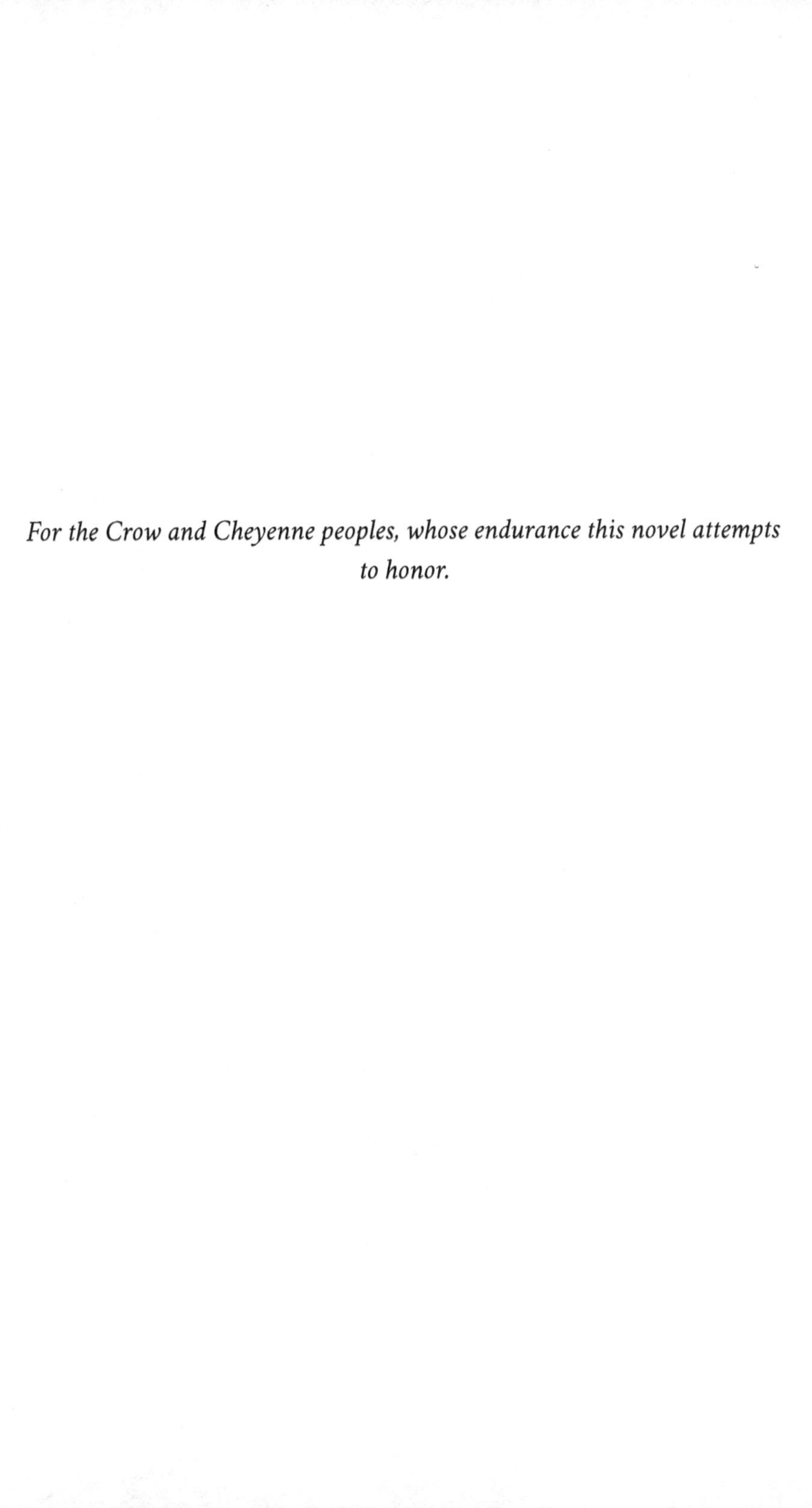

For the Crow and Cheyenne peoples, whose endurance this novel attempts to honor.

"Up north the pines make a rustling sound in the wind, and the trees smell good."

— Iron Teeth (Mah-i-Ti-Wo-Nee-Ni), Northern Cheyenne woman, Darlington Agency, Oklahoma, winter 1877–78. Recorded by Peter Powell, Sweet Medicine, 1969.

Contents

Author's Note

The Long Way Home is a work of fiction. Watches Twice never existed. Emėškeha'e never existed. But the march south to Darlington did. The fever that killed children in Oklahoma did. The Fort Robinson breakout did. The women who sewed rifle parts into their clothing and walked north through Kansas and Nebraska did. The Ghost Dance did. Wounded Knee did. The Tongue River reservation, established by executive order in November 1884, does, and the Northern Cheyenne Nation endures on it today.

The historical figures in this novel — Little Wolf, Dull Knife, Two Moons, Porcupine, Wooden Leg, Goes Ahead, Plenty Coups — are rendered as faithfully as the documentary record and the demands of fiction allow. Where their documented words exist, I have used them. Where the record is silent, I have tried to be consistent with who they were.

The Crow and Cheyenne language in this novel was constructed from attested lexical sources, primarily the Cheyenne Dictionary compiled by Wayne Leman, Laird Fisher, and the Cheyenne Language Committee at Chief Dull Knife College in Lame Deer, Montana, and Randolph Graczyk's *A Grammar of Crow* (University of Nebraska Press, 2007). The names and phrases are documented in the appendix. I am not a speaker of either language. Any errors are mine.

The history covered in this book is not distant history. The Dawes Act dispossessed Native nations of approximately 90 million acres. Boarding schools separated children from their families and their languages within living memory. The descendants of the people in this novel are still here, still fighting for sovereignty, still refusing to be erased.

Eméškeha'e's act — reading the letters, correcting the errors, writing back, refusing to accept what she is told cannot be changed — is the novel's central argument. Memory is not passive. In the face of erasure, remembering is resistance.

The historical notes and sources in the appendix are offered for readers who want to follow this story beyond the final page. This novel is my attempt, imperfect as it is, to contribute to the work of honest remembering.

William Mann, 2026

1

Héšenovéhe

The ridge wasn't much, a rise in the broken country, just enough to see the valley without being seen if he kept still and kept his horse still and did not let the last of the afternoon light catch the metal of anything he carried.

Watches Twice had been still for a long time.

Below him, the village moved the way villages moved at the end of a day. Women working at fires that had just been coaxed to life, the smoke rising thin and pale against the darkening tree line along the creek. Children doing what children do, chasing, falling, being called back. A man moving between the horses, checking legs, running his hand along a shoulder. The ordinary work of people who had survived another day and were now preparing to survive the night.

He had seen this before. Not this village. Not these people. But this.

He shifted in the saddle, and the cold moved with him, finding the gap between his collar and his neck, settling there. The dampness had been in everything since morning, in his blanket when he rose, in the ground under his horse's feet, in the air itself, which carried the smell of wet earth and new grass and the distant smoke from those fires below. Fall in this country came without apology. The grass had gone pale and dry, and the cold had an edge to it that arrived early and stayed.

He would not have a fire tonight.

He thought about that, the cold camp waiting for him somewhere behind this ridge, away from any line of sight to the valley. The jerky that had been in his pouch too long. Water from a creek that tasted of snowmelt and clay. He had slept in worse conditions and would sleep in worse again, and thinking about it would not improve any of it, so he stopped thinking about it and looked back down at the valley.

* * *

A woman was speaking to a child. He could not hear the words at this distance, but he could see the shape of it, the way she bent toward the child, the child's face turning up toward hers. His mother had bent toward him that way once. He did not remember her face clearly anymore. He remembered the bending. He remembered the quality of its attention, the way it made a small person feel like the only thing in the world worth looking at.

He did not let himself stay with that.

The fires were building now as the light continued to fail. More women moving. The faint, uncertain smell of something cooking reached him on the air, and his stomach acknowledged it before he could stop it. He had not eaten since morning.

Below him were people who were hungry. He understood this the way he understood the cold; not as an idea but as a thing present in the body. They had been walking since the previous September. They had fought the Army in Kansas and Nebraska, and they had buried their dead along the way and kept walking. What was in that valley was what was left.

He should go back.

The column was three hours behind him, maybe four. The captain was waiting for his report. The man had a particular way of waiting that made the air around him feel pressurized, and Watches Twice had learned to move quickly to avoid prolonged exposure. He had found the village. That was his job. He had done it. He should go back and say what he had found and let the Army decide what the Army decided.

He gathered the reins.

Then from below, carried up on the cold air, a sound, a man's voice, low and unhurried, speaking to a horse. A low murmur, the kind a horse leaned toward. The same sounds his father made. The same patience in it.

He did not go back.

* * *

The last light was almost gone now. The fires below were the brightest things in the valley, and the shapes of people moved between them, and the horses had settled, and somewhere in the village a child was crying. Not from any specific pain but from the accumulated weight of being alive and tired and small.

He had made that sound once. He barely remembered making it. He remembered the silence that came after his father's hand found the back of his head, the warmth of it, the steadiness.

His father's hands.

He sat with that for a moment and then put it away in the place where he kept things that could not be looked at directly, and he looked instead at the fires, and at the people moving between the fires, and at the horses standing quiet at the edge of the firelight, and he felt the cold working into him from the saddle and from the air and from the ground his horse stood on.

These were Cheyenne.

He had known this before he rode out this morning. He had known it for months, since the Army came to the reservation looking for men who could track and read country and keep their mouths shut. He had known it the way he knew his own name, as a fact that sat at the center of everything and did not require thinking about because it was always already there.

These were Cheyenne.

And in that village below, moving between those fires, were women who had fed boys who had grown into men who had ridden into a Crow camp on a cold morning and done what men did when they came to kill, and one of those men had held a seven-year-old child by the arms and made him watch, and the watching had taken something out of the boy that the man had never gotten back.

Watches Twice sat on his horse on the ridge in the cold and the dark, coming down, and he did not go back to the column.

Not yet.

2

Watches Twice

The morning his mother died, she had braided his hair.

He did not remember much from that time, he was three years old, and the world was still mostly sensation, mostly warmth and smell and the particular quality of voices, but he remembered that. Her hands were working through his hair with the patience she brought to everything, the slight pressure of her fingers against his scalp, the sound of her humming something low and without words while the camp moved around them in the early light.

Iiláxxe Baa. Kind-Hearted Woman. That was what people called her, and it was what she was. Not as a performance, not as something she worked at, but simply as her nature, as elemental as cold water and warm fire. He would not understand this until he was much older, until he had met enough people to know that her particular quality of attention, her gift for making whoever she was speaking to feel like the most important person in the camp, was not common. He would not understand it until it had been gone long enough that he could feel its shape by its absence.

That morning, she finished his braid and turned him around to look at him and said something he could not later remember, something that made him laugh, and then she sent him to find his father.

Bíawakshish, Red Bear, was at the edge of the camp where the horses were kept, doing what he did every morning, moving among them with the unhurried attention of a man who understood animals and did not need to perform that understanding for anyone. He was a large man, broad through the chest, with hands that seemed too big for the careful work they did, checking a leg here, smoothing a palm along a neck there, speaking low words that the horses leaned into.

The boy ran to him across the wet grass. Red Bear caught him without looking up from the horse he was tending, one arm swinging out and scooping the boy against his side, the gesture of a man who had always known exactly where the boy was.

This was spring. The grass was new. The air smelled of mud, the creek running fast with snowmelt, and somewhere behind the camp, a meadowlark was doing what meadowlarks did in the morning as if it were the most important work in the world.

There were butterflies.

Not many, it was still early in the season for them, but enough. Yellow ones, small and uncertain in the cool air, lifting from the grass and settling again. The boy saw them, pulled away from his father's side, and went after them, without plan or hope of success, running through the wet grass with his arms out.

Red Bear watched him.

He stood with his hand still resting on the horse's neck and he watched his son chase butterflies across the meadow in the early light, and his face had the expression it sometimes had when he did not know anyone was looking, open, unguarded, the love in it so plainly present that Búuwatisshish, passing at the edge of the camp with his medicine bundle over his shoulder, paused to look at it.

The old medicine man stood and watched Red Bear watching his son, and said nothing, and moved on.

Iiláxxe Baa went into labor that afternoon.

The boy knew something was happening because the women came, two, then three, then four of them moving in and out of the lodge with the particular purposefulness that meant adults were managing something children did not need to see. He was put outside with a piece of dried meat and told to stay near the fire.

He stayed near the fire.

Red Bear stood outside the lodge. Not pacing, Red Bear did not pace. He stood as he did with the horses, very still, his weight settled, his hands at his sides. But his hands were not right. The boy watched his father's hands and knew something was wrong before he knew anything else.

The sounds from inside the lodge were not right either.

He did not know what right sounded like, having never been present for a birth, but he understood wrongness the way children understood things. Not through reasoning but through the body, through the sudden cold that had nothing to do with the air temperature, through the way the women's voices had changed from purposeful to urgent.

He went to his father and stood beside him, and Red Bear put his hand on the back of the boy's head and held it there.

They stood together outside the lodge while the light failed, the fire burned down, and the sounds inside changed again, this time not to urgency but to something worse than urgency. A particular quality of silence, not the absence of sound but the presence of something that had no sound.

One of the women came out.

She looked at Red Bear, and Red Bear's hand tightened briefly on the back of the boy's head, and then he went inside.

The boy stood alone by the dead fire.

Búuwatisshish came and sat beside him. The old man did not speak. He put his hand on the boy's shoulder, and they sat together in the dark, and the boy did not cry because he did not yet fully understand what had happened, only that his father was inside the lodge and his mother was not going to come out and braid his hair again in the morning.

The baby did not come out either.

***

Four years is a long time when you are young, and it is the only time you know.

The boy grew up in his father's shadow, as plants grew toward light, not by deciding to, but because that was where the warmth was. Red Bear was not a man who spoke much, but when he did, the boy listened, and when he did not, the silence between them was comfortable and full of things that did not need saying.

Red Bear taught him to ride before he could walk well. Taught him to read the ground, to look at what grass said about what had passed over it, to understand the difference between a trail made by men moving fast and men moving slow. He taught him the names of things. Not just the Crow words but the meanings beneath the words, why the hawk was called what it was called, why the river had its name, why a man's name was not given to him but grown into him through what he did and what he saw and who he was in the world.

The boy was good at watching.

Red Bear noticed this early, the stillness in his son that most children didn't have, and how he looked at things with a completeness that suggested he was not just seeing but understanding. He would watch a spider build its web for an hour without moving. He would sit at the edge of the creek and watch the water run over rocks until Red Bear called him twice before he heard.

Búuwatisshish noticed it too.

The old medicine man had watched the boy since the night his mother died. Not intrusively, Old Hawk was not a man who intruded, but with the patient attention of someone who had seen something and was waiting to understand what it meant. He would find reasons to be where the boy was. Would sometimes stop and speak with Red Bear while the boy played nearby, his old eyes moving between the father and the son with an expression no one thought to read because Old Hawk's expressions were not easy to read.

* * *

The boy turned seven in the spring.

The Cheyenne came on a morning in early summer when the grass was tall, and the camp was not expecting trouble.

They came fast and from the east, where the light was still low and difficult, and the first warning was the horses. That particular sound horses made when something was wrong, a sound every person in the camp knew and responded to before they were fully awake. Then shouting. Then the sound that was not shouting.

Red Bear had his weapons in his hands before the boy understood what was happening.

What happened next, the boy would spend the rest of his life not thinking about directly, approaching it only sideways, as you approached something that would blind you if you looked at it straight. He remembered it in pieces that did not always come in order. His father's voice telling him to run, the ground under his feet, a hand catching his arm from behind, the smell of horse and sweat, the sounds of the fight moving through the camp.

The man who held him was not interested in the boy. He held him facing forward with one arm across his chest and a knife at his side, where the boy could feel it, and what was in front of him was his father.

Red Bear fought as he did everything, without waste, without performance, with complete attention to what was in front of him. He was not a young man, but he was not old either, and he fought well and for a long time, and the boy watched every moment of it with the terrible clarity of a child who has no choice but to see.

His father was winning.

The boy understood this even at seven, that Red Bear was better than the men around him, that the fight was going one way and not the other, that the Cheyenne had not expected this particular man to be this difficult to kill. There was a moment when the boy felt something close to relief move through him, something that said, *my father, my father is going to be all right.*

Then the man holding him tightened his grip and said something in a language the boy did not speak, and one of the other Cheyenne turned to look at the boy, then at Red Bear.

Red Bear looked at his son.

The boy watched his father understand what was happening. Watched him take it in, the arm across his son's chest, the knife at his son's side, the meaning of it. Watched Red Bear's face do something it had never done before in the boy's presence, something that was not fear exactly, but was the thing that lived next to fear when the thing you feared was not for yourself.

Red Bear's tomahawk was in his hand.

He looked at his son for a long moment. The fight had gone still around him. That brief held breath before a fire went out.

Then Red Bear lowered the tomahawk.

He did not drop it in surrender. He lowered it slowly, deliberately, with the same care he brought to everything, and he stood straight, and he looked at his son, and his face was open as it was only when Red Bear thought no one was watching, the love in it so plainly present that it was almost unbearable to see.

The boy understood what his father was doing.

He did not have words for it at seven years old. He would not have words for it for a long time. But his body understood it before his mind caught up, a comprehension that started in the chest and moved outward, like falling and being caught at the same time.

Don't, the boy tried to say. Nothing came out.

The Cheyenne moved.

Red Bear did not look away from his son. Through all of it, through everything the Cheyenne did in the next few moments, Red Bear looked at his son. His eyes did not leave the boy's face. Even at the end, even when the boy wanted to look away and could not, his father's eyes were steady and present and full of the thing that had no name.

The man holding the boy released him.

The boy did not move. He stood where he was and looked at his father on the ground, and the world had gone very quiet, a quiet that was not peaceful but was the shape left by something that had been there and was not there anymore.

He had been seen. In the last moment of his father's life, he had been the only thing Red Bear looked at. He did not know yet whether that was a gift or a weight. He would spend a long time not knowing.

He walked to his father and sat down beside him in the grass and put his hand on his father's chest as his father had put his hand on the back of his head outside the lodge four years ago, and he sat there while the camp came back to life around him, while the women moved and the men accounted for the living and the dead, while the smoke from two burning lodges rose into the summer sky.

Búuwatisshish found him there.

The old man sat down beside him in the grass without speaking and they sat together as they had sat together outside a lodge four years ago and the boy understood that Old Hawk had been here before with him, in this particular country of loss, and that the old man was not going to try to move him from it or tell him it would be all right because Old Hawk did not say things that were not true.

They sat together until the boy was ready to stand.

* * *

In the weeks that followed, Old Hawk watched him.

The boy moved through the camp present, continuous, going about what needed to be done without complaint or visible grief. He ate when food was given. He slept. He did the things boys did. But there was something in him that had changed, some quality of stillness that had deepened past what was ordinary for him, past what was ordinary for anyone.

He did not talk about his father.

He did not talk about his mother either, but that had always been true. Iiláxxe Baa was a presence in the camp that everyone felt and no one mentioned directly, as you did not mention a wound that had healed clean but left a scar.

Old Hawk watched and waited and said nothing.

* * *

It was late summer when the boy found the wolf den.

He had been out past the edge of the camp, farther than he was supposed to go alone, following the creek east through the cottonwoods to where it bent south toward the open ground. He found the den in a cutbank above the creek, a hole in the earth under the roots of a fallen cottonwood, and from it came sounds that stopped him where he stood.

He crouched in the grass and watched.

There were four of them. Maybe five, it was hard to count because they moved over and around each other without stopping, tumbling, biting, and making the small urgent sounds of animals that had not yet learned what the world required of them. Their eyes were open but uncertain. They smelled of earth and milk and something wild underneath.

He watched them for a long time.

He did not hear Old Hawk come up behind him. The old man moved quietly for a man of his age, another thing about him that people noticed and did not comment on.

Old Hawk crouched beside him, looked at the pups, then at the boy, and said quietly, "The mother will come back. She will kill you if she finds you here."

The boy looked at him.

"Come," Old Hawk said.

The boy went.

* * *

Two days later, Old Hawk did not see the boy in the camp.

He was not alarmed; the boy often moved at the edges of things, just inside the boundary of where he was supposed to be. But something made the old man walk east along the creek through the cottonwoods to where it bent south toward the open ground.

The boy was there.

Crouched in the same place, in the same stillness, watching the den.

Old Hawk stood behind him for a long moment without speaking. The pups were there, moving, tumbling, making their small sounds. The boy was watching them with the complete attention he brought to everything he decided was worth watching, which was most things, which was everything.

Old Hawk looked at the boy's face.

He saw what he had always seen there, the watchfulness, the stillness, the quality of attention that was not ordinary. He saw the boy who had stood at the edge of a lodge at three years old while his mother died inside it and had not looked away. He saw the boy who had been held by a Cheyenne warrior on a summer morning and made to watch his father fall, and had not closed his eyes.

He saw a boy who went back.

Who always went back.

Who looked at the hard thing once and then looked at it again because once was never enough to understand it fully.

Come, Old Hawk said again.

The boy rose from his crouch and came without argument, and they walked back through the cottonwoods together toward the camp. Old Hawk did not speak on the way back, and the boy did not speak, and the creek ran beside them, and the cottonwood leaves moved in the late summer air.

* * *

Old Hawk called the band together three days later.

He did not explain what he was doing, Old Hawk rarely explained. He simply said there was a naming to be done, and the people came because when Old Hawk said there was a naming to be done, you came.

The boy stood in front of the band, did not fidget, and did not look at his feet. He looked at the faces of the people around him with the steady attention that was already his most recognizable quality, already the thing people noticed first about him and remembered longest.

Old Hawk stood before him.

The old man looked at the boy for a long moment, long enough that some of the people shifted, long enough that a child younger than this boy might have looked away. The boy did not look away.

Then Old Hawk spoke.

He told the band about the wolf den. About finding the boy there once, bringing him back, and finding him there again two days later. He told it plainly, without drama. He told them what it meant for a boy to go back into danger, not out of recklessness but out of the need to see clearly. To look again. To understand.

He said the boy had watched twice and had not flinched either time.

He said the boy's name was Bíalish Dúua.

Watches Twice.

The people received the name with the understanding that it meant something, had been considered, and was true.

What they did not know, what only Old Hawk knew, and the boy in some unspoken way perhaps understood, was that the name was true in more ways than he had told them.

That it had been earned not twice but four times.

That there was a lodge at night and a father's hands and a summer morning in the grass, and that the boy standing before them had looked at all of it and had not looked away.

Old Hawk looked at the boy one more time.

The boy looked back.

3

The Soldier's Flag

The ceremony had been over long enough that the fire at its center had gone to coals and the people had drifted back to their own lodges and their own fires, carrying the name with them, carefully, turning it over, feeling its weight.

Goes Ahead did not drift.

He was eleven years old, standing at the edge where the fire had been, watching the boy move through the dispersing crowd. Not obviously, Goes Ahead was already learning not to be obvious about the things he watched, but steadily, with the patience of someone who had decided this was worth understanding.

The boy was seven. Goes Ahead had seven-year-olds in his life, younger cousins, the children of his father's friends, and he knew what seven looked like. Seven looked like movement, like noise, like the inability to be still for more than a few moments before something pulled you away from it.

This boy was not that.

He stood in the middle of the people moving around him, as a stone stood in a current. Not resistant exactly, not performing stillness, just genuinely still in a way that made the movement around him more visible by contrast. He was looking at nothing in particular. Or he was looking at everything. Goes Ahead could not tell which, and his inability to tell was part of what held him.

Old Hawk had just given this boy a name in front of the entire band.

Goes Ahead had been at namings before. He knew what they looked like: the child receiving the name with the particular self-consciousness of someone being looked at by everyone at once, the shuffling, the downcast eyes, the visible effort to be worthy of the moment. That was what seven looked like at a naming.

This boy had looked back at Old Hawk.

Not defiantly. Not performing courage. Just back. Steady and present and complete, the way Old Hawk himself looked at things, and Goes Ahead had watched Old Hawk his whole life and had never seen anyone look back at the old man that way. Had never seen anyone meet that gaze without something shifting in them, some adjustment, some concession to the weight of it.

The boy had not adjusted.

Goes Ahead stood at the edge of the dead fire and watched Bíalish Dúua, Watches Twice, walk back toward the lodges, and he felt something he did not have a name for, something that was not admiration exactly because admiration required understanding what you were admiring, and he did not yet understand this. He only knew he had seen something. That it would stay with him. That he would be thinking about it still when the boy was a man, and Goes Ahead was something other than what he was now.

He did not speak to the boy that evening.

He was not ready yet. And the boy, he suspected, would not have been interested in being spoken to. The boy was already somewhere inside himself, already in that country he seemed to inhabit, the one Goes Ahead could see from the outside but could not enter.

He watched him go.

Then he went home.

* * *

The mixed blood came into camp two hours before dark.

He came from the south on a horse that had been ridden hard and not recently rested, and he wore the clothes of a man who moved between worlds, part this, part that, belonging completely to neither. He had a trader's eyes, the kind that assessed everything they landed on out of long habit, and he had been riding for days and had the look of a man carrying something he wanted to put down.

Watches Twice was at the edge of the camp when the man rode in. He was doing what he often did at the edge of camp, watching the open ground to the south, watching how the light moved across it, learning its moods as his father had taught him to learn a horse's moods before you ever put a hand on it.

He heard the man before he saw him. Hoofbeats coming in from the south at a pace that said urgency without saying panic, a distinction Watches Twice already understood at nine years old, having been taught it by a man who was no longer alive to teach him anything else.

The mixed-blood rode in and pulled up, and people came to him with the particular attention they gave riders who arrived from the south with that particular look on their faces. He talked as he dismounted, talking before he was fully off the horse, because the news wanted out and he had been carrying it alone for too long.

Watches Twice drifted closer.

He caught pieces of it— a word here, a phrase there, the emotional shape of it before the content. He heard *soldiers*. He heard *Cheyenne*. He heard a place name he did not know, Sand Creek, spoken in a tone that made the not knowing feel like mercy.

He heard *many dead*, and the way the man said it told him that many was not a number he wanted to know.

The mixed blood was moving through the camp now, walking toward Old Hawk's lodge, still talking to the people around him, and Watches Twice followed at the edge of it, close enough to hear the fragments, far enough that no one thought to send him away. He heard *women* and *children.* He heard something about a flag, the soldier's flag, and he did not understand the flag part, but the women and children part he understood.

He understood it in his chest before he understood it anywhere else.

The man ducked into Old Hawk's lodge.

The people outside stood for a moment and then dispersed—carrying it away with them to their own fires, where it would be turned over, examined, and added to the larger picture people were always assembling from fragments, rumors, and things seen from a distance.

Watches Twice did not disperse.

He sat down cross-legged in the grass outside Old Hawk's lodge, and he waited. The camp settled into its evening rhythms around him. Fires building, the smell of food, children being called in, horses moving at the picket line with the particular restlessness horses had at dusk. He sat in the middle of all of it, and he was still, and he waited.

The mixed blood came out while there was still light. He looked at the boy sitting in the grass and said nothing, just looked, with those trader's eyes, the assessment happening quickly and then releasing, and walked back through the camp toward wherever his horse was.

Watches Twice watched him go.

Then he looked at the lodge entrance for a moment.

He went in.

Old Hawk was at his fire. He did not turn when the boy entered. He waited while Watches Twice came around the fire and sat down across from him, and when the boy was settled, Old Hawk looked at him across the flames with the expression that was not quite a question but left room for one.

The boy looked at the fire for a moment.

"I heard the man talking," he said. "As he walked."

Old Hawk said nothing.

"He said soldiers killed Cheyenne. At a place called Sand Creek."

"Yes."

"Many dead."

"Yes."

The fire moved between them. Outside the lodge, the camp sounds continued, voices, children, the ordinary music of people living their lives in the early dark.

"Women," the boy said. "And children."

"Yes."

Watches Twice looked at the fire for a long time. When he looked up, his face had the quality it always had, that stillness, that completeness, but underneath it something was moving that Old Hawk could see because Old Hawk had been watching this boy's face for two years and knew its weather.

"Were they the ones?" the boy said. "The ones who killed my father."

Old Hawk looked at him steadily.

"I don't know," he said. "The man didn't say which band."

The boy looked back at the fire. His hands were on his knees, and he was very still.

"But maybe," he said.

"Maybe," Old Hawk said.

They sat with that for a moment. The fire moved. Outside a child called out something and was answered and then went quiet.

"Let me tell you about Sand Creek," Old Hawk said.

* * *

He told it as he told everything, without hurry, without drama, building it from what was small, adding carefully until it had heat enough to sustain itself. He told the boy about Black Kettle. About a chief who had chosen peace when peace was the harder choice. Who had brought his people to Sand Creek because the Army had told him they would be safe there. He told him about the American flag Black Kettle flew over his lodge, given to him by the government itself, as a sign that anyone sheltering under it was under the government's protection.

The boy was listening. Old Hawk could see the resistance in him, the particular stillness that meant the boy did not want to be receiving what he was receiving, but he was listening. He had always been constitutionally unable not to listen.

Old Hawk told him about the morning of November 29th. About the soldiers riding in before dawn. About the flag still flying in the gray light. About Black Kettle standing outside his lodge holding it up because he could not believe what he was seeing.

The flag did not stop it.

He told him what happened then without telling him everything. He was a medicine man, and he knew what a nine-year-old boy could carry. He told him enough. He told him about the women. The children. The ones who ran and hid in the river's cut banks, in the freezing water, and listened.

Then he stopped.

The fire had burned lower. The camp outside was quieter.

Watches Twice had not moved through any of it.

After a while, the boy said, "Black Kettle had the flag."

"Yes."

"And they still came."

"Yes."

He was quiet for a long time. Old Hawk did not fill the quiet.

"They killed my father," the boy said finally. Simply. The words placed down in front of another person after a long time of carrying them alone.

"Yes," Old Hawk said. "They did."

Another long quiet. The fire between them.

Then the boy looked up at him with those eyes, that complete attention, and asked the question Old Hawk had been waiting for, the one that told him the seed had found ground even if it hadn't yet broken surface.

"Why did Black Kettle trust the flag?"

Old Hawk looked at him across the fire.

"Because he wanted his people to live," he said. "And it was the only thing he had left to trust."

The boy looked at that for a moment. Turned it over carefully, completely.

Then he looked back at the fire and said nothing more.

Old Hawk did not say anything else either.

They sat together in the quiet until the boy was ready to go.

When Watches Twice finally rose, Old Hawk did not say anything. The boy ducked through the lodge entrance and was gone, and Old Hawk sat alone at his fire and listened to the boy's footsteps move away through the camp and then stop.

He knew without looking that the boy had stopped and turned back toward the lodge.

Had stood there for a moment looking at it.

Then the footsteps moved away again and did not stop.

Old Hawk sat with his fire and said nothing, and the night settled around him.

4

Eighty-One

The world did not stay still while the boy grew.

He would understand this later, that the years between nine and seventeen were not simply time passing but time accumulating, how a river accumulated silt, each thing deposited quietly on top of the last until the bottom was something different from what it had been. At nine, he was a boy sitting at Old Hawk's fire, asking why Black Kettle trusted the flag. At seventeen, he was something else. The distance between those two things was not measured in years but in what the years had put in him.

***

The soldiers came through in the summer, when he turned ten.

There were six of them, riding in from the east on horses that were good horses but not as good as Crow horses, and they carried themselves with the particular authority of men who believed the ground beneath their feet belonged to them regardless of where they were standing.

The camp received them with the watchful stillness of people who had learned that how you received a thing often determined what the thing did next.

Old Hawk went out to meet them.

Watches Twice observed this from a distance that was close enough to see and far enough to be unremarkable. He watched the old medicine man walk out to the soldiers with his hands open and his face arranged in a welcome that was not quite warmth but close enough to it that a man who did not know Old Hawk's face well would not notice the difference.

There was talking. There were goods exchanged. The soldiers had things the camp could use, and the camp had things the soldiers wanted, and the exchange happened with the practiced ease of people who had done this before and expected to do it again. There was something that looked, from a distance, like friendliness.

Watches Twice watched Old Hawk laugh at something one of the soldiers said.

He had seen Old Hawk laugh before, genuinely, at things that were genuinely funny, a rare event that transformed the old man's face briefly into something younger. This laugh was not that. This laugh lived in the right place on the face but did not reach the eyes, and Watches Twice cataloged the difference, filing it without yet knowing what file it belonged in.

The soldiers left before dark. Old Hawk watched them go, then turned back toward the camp, and his eyes found Watches Twice standing at the edge of things, and something passed between them that was not quite acknowledgment and not quite a question, but contained elements of both.

That evening, Watches Twice came to Old Hawk's fire.

He sat down and looked at the flames for a while, and then said, "You laughed at what the soldier said."

Old Hawk looked at him.

"Was it funny?" the boy said.

Old Hawk considered this with the seriousness he brought to questions that deserved seriousness.

"No," he said.

The boy looked at the fire. "Then why?"

Old Hawk picked up a stick and turned it in his hands. "When a man laughs at what you say," he said, "he is telling you that you are safe. That you are understood. That there is no reason to be careful." He set the stick down. "A man who believes he is safe and understood stops watching."

Watches Twice looked at him.

"And you want them to stop watching," the boy said.

"I want them to leave," Old Hawk said. "And go back to where they came from. And tell the people who sent them that the Crow are friends." He looked at the fire. "Friends are not watched the way enemies are watched."

The boy sat with that for a long time.

"But they are not friends," he said finally.

Old Hawk looked at him across the fire with the expression that was not quite a smile.

"No," he said. "They are not."

He did not say anything else, and Watches Twice did not ask anything else, and they sat together until the fire burned low and the boy went home carrying something he did not yet have words for.

* * *

The news of the Fetterman Fight came in the deep cold of that December.

Watches Twice was eleven years old. The winter had been hard. The camp was settled in the river valley where the cottonwoods broke the wind. The horses stood close together at the picket line with their heads down. The rider who brought the news came in from the east, looking tight in the shoulders, deliberate in the face, the body already braced for the reaction.

Eighty-one soldiers dead.

A whole column. Gone. Red Cloud's warriors had drawn them out of the fort in the manner of how you drew an animal out of its den, with something that looked like prey moving in the right direction, and then closed around them on a ridge north of Fort Phil Kearny and killed every one of them before the light changed.

The camp took this in.

It was not a simple thing to take in. The Crow were not mourning eighty-one soldiers, these were not their men, this was not their loss. But the Lakota and Cheyenne who had done this were the same Lakota and Cheyenne who raided Crow horse herds and pushed at Crow territory and had been doing so for longer than anyone in the camp could remember. Red Cloud's victory was not a simple thing. It was a dangerous thing and a remarkable thing simultaneously, and the camp held both of those at once, quietly, without resolution.

Watches Twice went to find Old Hawk.

The old man was already outside his lodge, standing in the cold, looking at nothing in particular, which meant he was looking at everything. His breath made small clouds in the frozen air. He did not turn when the boy came to stand beside him.

They stood together in the cold for a while.

"Eighty-one," Watches Twice said.

"Yes."

"Red Cloud did that."

"His warriors. Yes."

The boy looked at the frozen river bottom, the cottonwoods stripped bare, the horses standing in their patient misery at the picket line.

"The Cheyenne fought with him," the boy said.

"Yes."

"The same Cheyenne."

Old Hawk did not ask which Cheyenne. He knew which same Cheyenne.

"Some of them," he said. "Probably."

Watches Twice stood with that for a moment. He was eleven years old. His father had been dead for four years. The Cheyenne had just helped kill eighty-one soldiers. Part of him felt something about that which he did not want to examine too closely because he was not sure he would like what he found.

"Was it right?" he asked.

Old Hawk was quiet for a long time. Long enough that the boy thought he might not answer. Then…

"The soldiers were building forts on land the treaty said was Lakota land," Old Hawk said. "Red Cloud told them to stop. They did not stop. Red Cloud fought them." He paused. "That is what happened."

"But was it right?" the boy said again.

Old Hawk looked at him. "That is your question to answer," he said. "Not mine."

Watches Twice looked at him.

"I'm asking you," he said.

"I know," Old Hawk said. "And I am telling you that it is your question."

He went back inside his lodge.

Watches Twice stood alone in the cold for a long time.

* * *

The talk about Red Cloud started after that and did not stop for years.

It was everywhere, at the fires, among the warriors, among the boys who were becoming warriors and needed something to measure themselves against. Red Cloud was the measure. You could not agree about him, could not land anywhere stable when you thought about him, and that instability was part of what made him impossible to stop talking about.

Goes Ahead was fourteen that winter, and he had opinions about everything, which carried the full force of recent discovery, as if the thought had occurred to no one before him.

Watches Twice was eleven, and he mostly listened.

They were at the edge of the camp one afternoon, a loose group of boys, the cold not quite cold enough to drive them inside, Goes Ahead holding court how he did sometimes, not performing exactly, but thinking out loud, which for Goes Ahead amounted to the same thing.

"He beat them," Goes Ahead said. "That is the true thing. Whatever else you say about him, he beat them."

One of the other boys, older, a warrior's son who wore that fact like clothing, said that Red Cloud fought Crow too, that Crow horses had been taken, that Crow warriors had been killed, that this was not something to admire.

"I didn't say admire," Goes Ahead said. "I said beat." He looked at the other boy with the particular steadiness that was already his most recognizable quality. "Those are different things."

Watches Twice watched Goes Ahead say this and thought about what it meant that a Crow boy of fourteen could hold those two things at the same time, Red Cloud is our enemy and Red Cloud beat them, without needing to resolve them into something simpler.

He thought about Old Hawk laughing at the soldier's joke.

He thought about his father's hands lowering the tomahawk.

He thought about Black Kettle's flag.

He did not say anything. He was eleven, he was still mostly listening, and the listening was doing something in him that talking would have interrupted.

"Why does he fight the Crow?" someone said. "The whites are the ones taking the land. The whites are the ones building the forts. Why fight us?"

Goes Ahead looked at the horizon for a moment. "Because we let the Army build the forts," he said. "Because we signed the treaty. Because—" He stopped. Seemed to be working on something. "Because we are in their way."

Nobody said anything for a moment.

"Old Hawk says the Army will do to us what they did at Sand Creek," Watches Twice said.

He had not meant to say it. It came out of him, not chosen, just present.

The boys looked at him. He was the youngest there, and he had just invoked Old Hawk, which was the equivalent of placing a large stone in the middle of a conversation. Nobody argued with Old Hawk directly. They just went quiet around whatever he had said until they could find a way past it.

Goes Ahead looked at him for a moment with something that was not quite assessment and not quite recognition but lived somewhere between them.

Then the moment passed. The conversation moved elsewhere, and Watches Twice went back to listening.

But Goes Ahead looked at him once more before they drifted apart, a brief look, the kind that said, *I heard that. I am thinking about that,* and then it was gone.

* * *

In the spring of 1867, three of the older boys went out with an Army patrol.

They were not called scouts. Nothing was formalized, nothing was official. The soldiers needed men who knew the country north of the Yellowstone. The older boys knew that country. There were things the soldiers had that the older boys wanted. The arrangement agreed upon as when both parties had something the other needed.

They came back six days later with Army blankets and a rifle between them and the particular quality of young men who have done something they are not entirely sure how to feel about.

The camp received this with the watchful stillness that was the Crow's great collective gift, the ability to observe without immediately reacting, to let a thing be what it was before deciding what it meant.

The older warriors said nothing directly.

The older women said nothing directly.

Old Hawk said nothing at all.

Watches Twice watched the three boys move through the camp with their Army blankets and their shared rifle, and he felt something that was not quite envy and not quite contempt, but pulled toward both. He was twelve years old, and he knew the country north of the Yellowstone as well as any of them. He had been reading ground since his father taught him to read it, and he had been refining that reading every day since, the same way he refined everything, by going back, by looking again, by not accepting the first interpretation of a thing when a second look might show him something the first had missed.

He could do what those boys had done.

He could do it better.

He went to Old Hawk that evening.

"The boys went with the soldiers," he said.

"Yes."

"To scout."

"To show them the country," Old Hawk said. "There is a difference."

Watches Twice considered this. "What difference?"

"A scout finds things," Old Hawk said. "A man who shows the country walks beside someone who has already decided where he is going." He looked at the boy. "One chooses. The other follows."

"And the soldiers," Watches Twice said. "Where are they going?"

Old Hawk looked at him steadily. "Where they always go," he said. "Further."

The boy sat with that.

"Would you go?" he asked. "If you were me."

Old Hawk was quiet for a long moment.

"I am not you," he said finally. "And you are not ready to answer that question yet." He looked at the fire. "When you are ready, you will not need to ask me."

* * *

In the summer of 1868, the Army burned its forts.

Not in the camp's sight, Fort Phil Kearny was miles to the south and east, but the news came, rider to rider, each telling carrying the weight of something that had not been expected. The soldiers were leaving. Red Cloud had won. The government had signed a new treaty. The terms were Red Cloud's terms, and the forts were coming down.

Watches Twice heard this in the camp and went to find Old Hawk.

The old man was outside his lodge in the long summer light, sitting on a robe with his medicine bundle beside him and his eyes on the middle distance, which was where Old Hawk's eyes went when he was watching something nobody else could see.

Watches Twice sat down beside him.

"They burned the forts," he said.

"Yes."

"Red Cloud made them."

"Red Cloud fought for his people," Old Hawk said. "And the government moved." He paused. "That is what happened."

The boy recognized those words. They were the same words Old Hawk had used in the cold after the Fetterman Fight, not judgment, not instruction, just the fact of the thing placed in front of him like a stone on the ground.

"You do that," Watches Twice said.

Old Hawk looked at him. "Do what?"

"Tell me what happened," the boy said. "Not what it means. Not what I should think about it. Just what happened."

Old Hawk looked at him for a long moment.

"Yes," he said.

"Why?"

The old man turned back to the middle distance. The summer light was long and golden across the grass, and somewhere in the camp a child was laughing.

"Because what it means," Old Hawk said, "is yours. It was always yours." He was quiet for a moment. "I have watched you since you were three years old. I have watched you look at hard things and not look away. I have watched you go back to look again when anyone else would have been satisfied with what they saw the first time." He paused. "You do not need me to tell you what things mean. You need things to look at. That is all I have ever given you."

Watches Twice sat beside the old man in the long summer light and looked at the middle distance with him and thought about Red Cloud burning the Army's forts with his victory and thought about his father lowering the tomahawk and thought about Black Kettle holding up the flag that did not stop anything and thought about the boys who had come back from the Army patrol with their blankets and their shared rifle and their uncertain faces.

He did not arrive at any conclusion.

He did not expect to.

He was thirteen years old, and Old Hawk had just told him that the conclusions were his, that they had always been his, and he understood that this was both a gift and the loneliest thing anyone had ever said to him.

He sat with it anyway.

5

Heávohe

He had been riding the eastern approaches since morning.

He did this most days now, rode out alone, early, following the ground the way his father had taught him. Not hunting exactly. Not scouting for anyone. Just riding and reading, trying to understand. The grass. The birds. How the light moved across a draw at different hours. He had been doing it long enough that the riding itself had become a kind of language he was teaching himself, one word at a time.

This morning, he had ridden further than usual. Further east than he generally rode, past the place where the elders said the line was, the line the white chiefs had drawn across the land in Washington, the line that existed on paper and nowhere else. He had crossed it without ceremony because there was nothing to cross. The grass did not change. The sky did not change. The ground continued east, indifferent to what any paper said about it.

He was off the reservation. He knew it, and it felt like nothing but further.

* * *

That was when he heard the shot.

He pulled up and sat on his horse and listened. The echo moved across the flats and died. Then another shot. Same direction. East and slightly south, maybe half a mile, coming from a low place in the ground where a creek drainage cut through the grass.

He rode toward it.

He came up on a rise and stopped.

Below him, maybe a hundred yards to the east, a horse and a mule stood tied to a clump of sage. The horse was a good animal; he could see that from here, a big roan, well-muscled, standing with the patience of a horse that had been left many times and knew what waiting meant. The mule stood beside it with the indifference mules brought to everything.

Beyond them, maybe thirty yards further, a man lay prone in a shallow hollow in the ground. Large man. Larger than most, and even prone, even at this distance, the size of him was apparent. He had a rifle laid across his saddle, which he had placed in front of him in the hollow, and he was completely still, not the stillness of waiting but the stillness of having already decided everything and now simply executing it.

In front of the man, two hundred yards out, the herd moved among the fallen animals. Stepping around, stepping between, heads down, grazing on, not understanding the stillness of the ones that lay among them.

The man shifted slightly. Settled. The rifle moved a fraction.

The shot came flat and hard across the grass.

Another animal went down.

The herd milled. Did not run.

Watches Twice sat his horse on the rise, watched, and tried to make sense of what he was looking at. Eight animals down. The man was already reloading with the same unhurried precision he brought to everything, not rushing, not pausing, just working, in the manner of a man who worked at something he had done so many times that the doing of it required no thought at all.

* * *

He can't use that much meat, Watches Twice thought. *No man can use that much meat.*

He looked at the fallen animals. At the herd moving around them. At the man in the hollow reloading.

He did not understand what he was seeing. Not the fact of it, he could see the fact of it plainly enough. But the why of it. A Crow hunter killed what he needed and used what he killed. He killed with ceremony and with intention and with an understanding of what the killing cost and what it gave. This man was killing as fire burned, not because it needed what burned, but because the burning itself was the goal.

The rifle settled again.

Another shot.

Nine animals down.

Watches Twice turned his horse to go.

It was that movement, the horse shifting on the rise, the small disruption against the skyline, that caught the man's eye.

The man in the hollow turned his head.

He did not reach for anything. Did not call out. Did not move his body at all. He simply turned his head and looked directly at Watches Twice across the hundred and thirty yards between them with the same stillness he brought to the rifle and the hollow and the fallen animals, and he looked at the boy completely, without hurry, without alarm, with the flat total assessment of a man to whom the world was a series of things to be read and responded to and nothing more.

Watches Twice had been looked at before. He had been looked at by warriors and elders and by Old Hawk himself, who looked at things with more completeness than anyone he had ever known.

This was not that.

This was something else. Something that had no warmth in it and no cold either. No hatred, no friendliness, no recognition of the boy as a person who mattered or didn't matter. Just seeing. A hawk's seeing. Complete and indifferent and utterly without mercy, not because it wished harm but because mercy required caring about the outcome, and this man's eyes said that he had been doing what he did for long enough that outcomes had stopped mattering to him.

Watches Twice did not run.

He turned his horse and rode back in the direction he had come.

He could feel the eyes on him. Not threatening, that was the wrong word for it. Just present. On him, without preference, without malice, simply there, like sunshine.

He looked back.

Declan had not moved. Had not reached for anything, had not called out, had not shifted his body in the hollow. Only his head was turned, watching the boy ride away with the same expression he used with the rifle, complete, unhurried, utterly without heat.

Watches Twice faced forward and rode.

He felt those eyes on his back until the rise took him, and then he heard the shot come flat across the grass behind him, and then nothing.

He rode back to camp.

* * *

He tended his horse at the picket line, taking his time with it as his father had taken time with horses, and then he went to Old Hawk's lodge and ducked inside and sat down across the fire.

Old Hawk looked at him and waited.

"I heard a shot," Watches Twice said. "East and south, half a mile maybe. I rode toward it."

Old Hawk said nothing.

"A horse and a mule tied. A hundred yards from where the man was. Maybe more." He paused. "The man was prone in a hollow. A rifle was across his saddle in front of him. He was shooting into the herd."

"How many animals down?" Old Hawk said.

"Nine when I left. Maybe more by now."

Old Hawk looked at the fire.

"He didn't use the meat," Watches Twice said. "He didn't move toward the animals when they fell. He just kept shooting." He paused. "I don't understand what I saw."

"Tell me the rest," Old Hawk said.

"I turned to go. He saw me. Turned his head." Watches Twice stopped.

Old Hawk waited.

"I have seen men look at things," the boy said carefully. "I have seen warriors look at an enemy. I have seen hunters look at game." He stopped again, working on it. "This man looked at me as he looked at the herd. Like it was all the same to him. Like I was something to be read and then set down."

Old Hawk was very still.

"The horse," Watches Twice said. "The roan, it had a scabbard on it."

Old Hawk looked at him.

"Cheyenne work," Watches Twice said. "Patterned. Good work."

Old Hawk sat with that for a moment. Something moved across his face that Watches Twice had not seen there before, not surprise exactly, Old Hawk was not a man who was surprised by things, but a particular quality of recognition, the face of a man who has been waiting for something to arrive and has just heard it knock.

"Tell me about the man," Old Hawk said. "Was he a big man? How did he move?"

Watches Twice told him. The size of him, even prone. The stillness. How he reloaded without looking at his hands. The shot came, and he settled again afterward as if the shot and the settling were one continuous motion.

Old Hawk listened to all of it without interrupting.

When the boy finished, Old Hawk looked at the fire for a long moment.

"I know this man," he said.

Watches Twice waited.

"He came through our camp. Three, maybe four years ago. He traded fairly." Old Hawk paused. "I sat across a fire from him. I looked at him, trying to understand." He was quiet for a moment. "Those eyes you are describing. Yes. I know those eyes."

"Who is he?" Watches Twice said.

"The Cheyenne call him Heávohe," Old Hawk said.

The boy did not know the word.

"Demon," Old Hawk said. "Evil spirit."

Something moved in Watches Twice.

"Why," he said.

"Because he kills them," Old Hawk said. "Not because he hunts them. Not from hatred. He does not hate the Cheyenne." He looked at the fire. "But they have hunted him for years, and when they find him, he kills them. And when the next ones come, he kills those, too. By now, he has killed dozens of them."

Watches Twice was very still.

"It started with a woman," Old Hawk said. "A Crow woman. Ashkáale. The daughter of Daxpitcheehísshish." He paused to let the name land. "He pulled her from danger, and Cheyenne died that day. They did not forget. They hunted him afterward. He proved difficult to kill." He paused. "He does not go looking for them. But he will not die for their convenience."

The fire moved between them. Outside the lodge, the camp went about its evening business: voices, horses, the smell of food, and children being called in.

Watches Twice was aware of the thing in him that wanted to feel something clean and satisfying about the Cheyenne, fearing this white man. The people who held a seven-year-old boy by the arms and made him watch. Afraid of this large, still man with the flat eyes and the Cheyenne scabbard on his roan horse.

It is not yours, he thought. *That feeling does not belong to you.*

"What I saw today," he said. "The nine animals. The herd still milling. He wasn't hunting."

"No," Old Hawk said.

"Then what?"

Old Hawk looked at him steadily. "What is it the Army wants?" he said. He paused. "What is it the white men back east want. The men who buy the hides. The men who run the machines." He looked at the fire. "The white man takes what he wants until it is gone. The buffalo, gone, the hides for their machines, the meat left to rot. And when the buffalo are gone, the people who lived by the buffalo are gone too. No fight needed. No soldiers needed." He paused. "Their problem solves itself."

Watches Twice looked at the fire.

The buffalo and the people, he thought. *The same problem.*

He did not say it aloud.

"The scabbard," he said instead. "A Cheyenne made it."

"Yes," Old Hawk said.

"He carries it anyway."

"Yes."

Watches Twice sat with that. A man who had killed dozens of

Cheyenne riding with Cheyenne work on his horse. Not as a trophy.

"The woman," he said. "The chief's daughter. Is she still living?"

"Yes, she lives. Still near him."

"He protects her."

"Yes."

"And kills the Cheyenne who come for him."

"Yes."

"And kills the buffalo."

"Yes."

Old Hawk said nothing more. He looked at the fire and left the boy with what he had given him, not a lesson, not a verdict, just the shape of a thing placed in front of him to be looked at from whatever angle the boy could manage.

Watches Twice sat there for a long time.

When he rose, Old Hawk did not look up.

* * *

He went out into the evening and walked through the camp and past the picket line and out into the grass and kept walking east until the camp was behind him and the dark was coming down and the plains opened up around him, wide and indifferent and full of a silence that was larger than it used to be.

He stood in the grass.

Somewhere out there, the man was still working. Or had finished working and was making camp. Or was riding east with the hides on the mule and the roan stepping out well in the last light and the Cheyenne scabbard moving with the horse's motion.

The same hands, he thought.

He stood there until the cold moved him.

Then he turned and walked back and did not stop outside Old

Hawk's lodge and did not look back at the dark.

He lay down and looked at the smoke hole above him, listened to the camp settle into sleep around him, and thought about a large, still man turning his head on a rise and looking at him with eyes that saw everything and were moved by nothing.

He did not sleep for a long time.

6

Further

Old Hawk found Watches Twice in camp and walked up to him, stopping close. He looked at him with those guarded eyes.

"I am going to a council," he said. "You will come."

That was all.

Watches Twice packed what he needed, brought the horses around in the morning, and helped Old Hawk mount, standing close, ready without making his readiness visible. Old Hawk had not asked for this. He had simply become slower in ways that were nobody's fault, and Watches Twice had adjusted to the slowness without discussion, without acknowledgment from either of them.

They rode east and south through country Watches Twice knew like he knew his own hands. He read it as they moved through it, the grass, the birds, how the draws ran, and where the water was, and what the ground said about what had moved across it recently. He did this without thinking. It had become as natural as breathing, continuous, below intention, simply present.

Old Hawk rode beside him and said nothing and watched him read the country with the expression that Watches Twice had never been able to fully interpret. Something between satisfaction and sorrow.

Something that had both of those in it without being reducible to either.

They rode for two days.

On the second evening, they made a dry camp on a rise, and Watches Twice built a small fire. They ate without much talking. The stars came out over the plains, completely, all at once, as if they had been waiting just behind the light.

Old Hawk looked at the stars for a long time.

The old man's face in the firelight was a face Watches Twice had been looking at his whole life, and he knew every line of it. There were more lines now than there used to be. The lines were deeper, and the fire found all of them. He thought, not for the first time, but more clearly than before, *he is old. He has always been old to me, but now he is old in a different way.*

He did not say anything.

Old Hawk did not say anything.

They slept.

* * *

The council was larger than Watches Twice expected.

He had known it would be significant. Old Hawk did not travel two days for things that were not significant, but the size of the gathering told him something before anyone spoke. More Crow in one place than he had seen in years. The various bands together, the chiefs and warriors and medicine men, the whole weight of the nation assembled in one camp on the flat ground beside the river.

He did not sit with the men.

He sat where he always sat, at the edge, far enough back to see without being seen, close enough to read faces if not always hear words. Old Hawk moved forward to take his place among the medicine men and the elders. Watches Twice watched him go, then turned his attention to the assembly.

Plenty Coups spoke for a long time.

Watches Twice caught pieces of it, the voice carried unevenly across the open ground, and the wind took parts of sentences and left others, but he did not need every word. He had learned long ago that the meaning of a thing lived in the faces of the people receiving it more fully than it lived in the words themselves.

He watched the faces.

He saw the men who were already there. The men who had done the mathematics before the council began and arrived at the same place Plenty Coups was leading them, and were simply waiting for it to be said aloud so they could act on it. Their faces were settled. Decided. The faces of men who had made peace with a hard thing and were ready to move.

He saw the men who would never be there. The men who heard the argument and understood it and rejected it, not because the logic was wrong, but because some things were not about logic. Their faces were closed like men who had decided to absorb what was coming without conceding it. They would go along because going along was what the nation needed. They would not pretend it was anything other than what it was.

He saw the men in between. The majority—the ones whose faces moved through several things at once, who worked on it in real time, who looked like Watches Twice felt most of the time—carried contradictions without resolution and found a way to move forward anyway.

He found Old Hawk's face in the assembly.

Old Hawk was nodding slightly. Not in agreement, not the way a man nodded when he heard something he believed. More like how a man nodded when he heard something that confirmed what he had always known was coming. *Yes. This. I have been watching this approach for a long time.*

Watches Twice watched Old Hawk's face and understood something about the two days of riding and the silence and the stars and how Old Hawk had looked at them, that Old Hawk had not come to this council to influence it or to learn from it. He had come to witness it. To be present for the moment when the thing he had spent forty years watching finally arrived.

He had brought Watches Twice so that Watches Twice could witness it too.

This, Old Hawk's presence said. *Remember this. You will need to know you saw it.*

* * *

They rode home in the same silence they had ridden there in.

It was the same silence, and also not the same silence. The same absence of words. A different weight in the absence.

On the first night riding back, they made camp beside a creek, and Watches Twice built the fire. They ate while the stars came out, and Old Hawk looked at them again.

Watches Twice looked at the fire.

"Plenty Coups is right," he said finally.

Old Hawk looked at him.

"Isn't he?" Watches Twice said.

Old Hawk looked at the fire for a long moment.

"He is doing what he believes will keep the people alive," Old Hawk said. "Whether he is right, we will not know for a long time."

Watches Twice sat with that.

"But you came," he said. "You traveled two days to hear it."

Old Hawk looked at the stars.

"I traveled two days so that you could hear it," he said. "And so that I could see your face when you did."

He did not say anything else.

Watches Twice did not ask anything else.

* * *

Goes Ahead found him at the picket line in the early spring.

He was not looking for Watches Twice specifically, or he was, but he came at it sideways, Goes Ahead's habit, as if he had simply arrived in the same place by coincidence, and whatever happened next was incidental.

He stood beside Watches Twice and looked at the horses for a moment.

"The Army is putting together scouts for the spring campaign," he said. "Men who know the Powder River country." He paused. "Men who can read ground."

He did not look at Watches Twice when he said it.

"Pay is fair," he said.

Then he moved on.

Watches Twice stood at the picket line and looked at the horses and held what Goes Ahead had placed in front of him, carefully, turning it over, feeling its weight.

He rode out that afternoon. East, past the line that wasn't there, into the country that continued indifferently beyond what the paper in Washington said. He rode until the camp was a long way behind him and the country opened up and the silence that was larger than it used to be settled around him.

He thought about the council. About the faces of the men who had already done the mathematics.

He thought about Old Hawk's nod in the assembly. *Yes. This is what it comes to.*

He thought about a large, still man in a hollow with a rifle, turning his head, looking at a boy on a rise with eyes that were moved by nothing.

He thought about his father's hands.

He rode back before dark and went to find Goes Ahead.

"All right," he said.

Goes Ahead looked at him for a moment, that look, the one from the naming ceremony fifteen years ago, the one that said *I heard that, I am thinking about that*, and nodded once.

That was all.

* * *

The morning of June 17th, the country was ordinary, the grass moving in the early wind, the creek running, the light coming flat and gray off the ridgelines to the east. The column moved north with the scouts ranging ahead and the birds doing what birds did in the morning as if it were the most important work in the world.

Watches Twice ranged ahead.

He was doing what he was born to do, and he knew it. The reading, the watching, the ground speaking to him in the language he had been teaching himself since he was fifteen years old, riding east past invisible lines. This part was right. This part had always been right. Whatever else was complicated about being here, this part was not complicated.

He read the country, and the country told him things, and he brought those things back to the officers who needed them, then went out again. The morning was cool. The creek drainage ran clear and cold where he crossed it. A hawk was working the thermals above a ridgeline to the north.

Then everything happened at once.

The attack came from multiple directions simultaneously. There was no useful warning because the warning and the thing itself arrived together, the sound of the first shots already part of the reaction to them, the country that had been empty suddenly full of movement and noise in a way that made the emptiness before seem like something that had never been real.

Watches Twice was in the middle of it before he understood he was in the middle of it.

He did what he did.

He read. He watched. He moved to where the ground told him to go and away from where the ground told him it was wrong. He brought what he saw back to the men who needed to know it and went out again. He did not draw his weapon except to hold it because the holding of it was what his hands wanted to do, and he let them do that much.

But he saw everything.

He saw a Cheyenne warrior not twenty yards from him, young, his own age or younger, the face under the paint just a face, frightened and determined and completely human in a way that hit Watches Twice somewhere he had not expected to be hit. He had imagined this moment many times in the years since he was seven. He had imagined what he would feel when he first saw a Cheyenne warrior close enough to read his face.

He had not imagined this.

The warrior did not see him, or saw him, assessed him, and moved on, already past him, already on to something else. And then he was gone into the dust and noise. Watches Twice was already moving, and the moment was over.

But the face stayed.

He looks like me, Watches Twice thought. *He is what I am on the other side of this.*

He did not have time to stay with that. The fight moved, and he moved with it. There was no time for anything except the next thing and the next thing after that.

He heard the pleading.

Then, he saw the man. He was in the dust and the noise, close, the voice carrying above everything else, finding him, like a child crying finds you. The pleading had no language he understood. It did not need one. The sound itself was the language, and the language said *I know what is happening, and I cannot stop it, and I am not ready.* Watches Twice understood it completely and moved away from it because there was nothing else to do, and carried it with him anyway.

He saw Goes Ahead kill the man.

It was not dramatic. That was the thing about it, the complete absence of drama in it. Goes Ahead moved with the efficiency of a man doing something he had decided he could do, had practiced doing, and was now simply doing. The Lakota warrior was there, and then he was not. Goes Ahead was already turning, already assessing the next thing, his face during and after exactly the same face, focused, present, undisturbed.

Not cold. Not cruel. Just resolved. A man who had resolved something in himself that Watches Twice had not yet resolved and was operating from that resolution, from solid ground, from something settled.

This is who he is, Watches Twice thought. *This is who he has chosen to be.*

The question underneath that thought sat in him like a stone and did not move.

* * *

The fight lasted six hours.

Crook held the field. Did not advance. The column made camp on the ground where the fight had happened. The scouts came in, and the wounded were counted. The dead were counted, and the evening came down over all of it, without distinction, without acknowledgment of what the day had been.

Watches Twice sat apart from the others.

The ground around him still held the evidence of the day, the torn grass, the dark patches, the particular silence that came after violence. The silence after a storm was different from the silence before it. He sat in it and looked at nothing in particular, which meant he was looking at everything, and what he was looking at held the shape of something he had not expected to find here.

He was twenty-one years old. He had been moving toward this place since he was seven years old, standing in summer grass with his hand on his father's chest. He had imagined many times what it would feel like to finally be here, to finally be riding against the people who had taken everything from him.

It felt like nothing he had imagined.

The Cheyenne warrior's face. Young. Human. Looking back at him from the other side of the same fight with the same fear and the same determination and the same desperate need to survive the next five minutes.

Goes Ahead's face. Undisturbed. Resolved.

The pleading man's voice. The language he didn't speak and didn't need to speak to understand.

No one wins, he thought. *That is the true thing. No one here wins. The killing is just the means. The end is always the same, one person or one group of people controlling another. Taking what they want and holding it. That is what this is. That is what it has always been.*

He sat with that until the camp slept around him.

He did not sleep.

* * *

He rode back to the Crow camp in late summer.

The grass was longer than when he had left. The light was different. The camp was in its summer place on the river. The horses were fat on the good grass, and the children were doing what children did in the long warm evenings. Nothing about it looked like a place that needed what he had been doing for the past months.

He tended his horse, and then he went to Old Hawk's lodge.

Old Hawk was at his fire.

He was older.

Not dramatically, just the accumulation of the months Watches Twice had been away, the small daily additions that you only saw when you had been gone long enough. He sat differently than he used to sit. The fire was built lower than he used to. The medicine bundle beside him was in the same place it had always been, but something about how it sat there was different. Watches Twice looked at it for a moment before he looked at Old Hawk's face.

He sat down across the fire.

Watches Twice looked at the fire.

"No one wins," he said. "The killing is just a means to an end. The end is always the same. One people controlling another people. Taking what they want. That is all it is. That is all it has ever been, and that is all it will ever be."

He stopped.

He looked at Old Hawk.

Old Hawk looked at him across the fire for a long moment.

He said nothing.

He nodded.

Once.

Watches Twice looked at the nod and felt the weight of it, not the agreement in it, not the confirmation, but what was underneath both of those. The tiredness. The long work of watching the world become what you always knew it would become. Twenty years of placing stones on the ground in front of a boy and stepping back and waiting for the boy to find his way to the truth that the stones were pointing at.

"I wondered when you would see it," Old Hawk's face said. His mouth said nothing.

They sat together at the fire for a long time.

The camp moved around them in the warm evening, voices, children, horses, the smell of food. The ordinary life of people living as well as they could in the time they had.

When Watches Twice finally rose to go, Old Hawk did not look up.

At the lodge entrance, Watches Twice stopped.

He stood there for a moment with his back to the old man and the fire.

Then he stepped out into the evening and did not look back.

* * *

He rode out the next morning.

East. Past the line that wasn't there. Into the country that continued indifferently beyond what any paper said about it.

He rode until the camp was behind him and the country opened up and the silence settled around him, wider than it had been the last time he rode out here, the herds thinner, the sky larger above the emptying grass.

He sat his horse on a rise and looked east.

The country continued. Indifferent. Patient. Older than anything that had happened on it or would happen on it.

He sat there for a long time.

Then he rode on.

Not back. Forward. East. Further than the line. Further than he had been before.

Reading the country.

Watching.

7

Silver

He told himself it was the work.

That was what he said when Goes Ahead asked him, sideways, in the manner Goes Ahead asked things. Not quite a question, standing at the picket line looking at the horses, the invitation implicit in the silence he left open after mentioning the escort mission.

"I know the country," Watches Twice said. "South through Nebraska. Into Kansas."

Goes Ahead looked at the horses.

"It's a long ride," he said.

"Yes."

Goes Ahead said nothing else. He did not need to. The silence he left had a shape to it, not disapproval exactly, not warning, just the shape of a man who understood something that the other man had not yet finished understanding.

* * *

That evening he went to Old Hawk's lodge.

The old man was at his fire. Watches Twice sat down across from him and said nothing, and Old Hawk said nothing. The fire warmed his face.

After a while Old Hawk spoke.

"You know why they are going south," he said. It was not a question.

"The Army won the war," Watches Twice said.

Old Hawk looked at the fire. "One man agreed," he said. "Standing Elk. He spoke for the band when the band had not asked him to speak. He told the soldier chief, the one they call Crook, they would go." He paused. "Dull Knife said no. Little Wolf said no. The people said no. But Standing Elk agreed, and the government heard what it wanted to hear and called it settled."

Watches Twice looked at the fire.

"Crook told them they can return if they are unhappy," Old Hawk said. "After a year. If the place does not suit them, they can come home." He was quiet for a moment. "Washington had already decided before Crook made that promise. The promise was not his to make."

The fire moved.

"Nearly a thousand people," Old Hawk said. "Walking south because one man agreed and the government saw it as settled." He looked at Watches Twice. "That is what happened."

He did not say anything else.

Watches Twice sat with it for a long time. Then he rose and went to the lodge entrance and stopped.

Old Hawk looked at the fire.

"Daxpitcheésh awáala," he said.

Watches Twice went out into the night.

* * *

Watches Twice rode out the next morning.

Old Hawk was standing at the edge of camp when he left. Not

waiting, Old Hawk was not a man who waited visibly. He was simply there. Present for things that required witnessing, absent for things that didn't. His medicine bundle over his shoulder. His old eyes on the middle distance.

Watches Twice rode past him.

He did not stop. He did not look back.

He felt Old Hawk's eyes on him until the camp was out of sight, and then he felt them still.

* * *

The column assembled at Red Cloud Agency on a morning in late May.

Watches Twice had seen large gatherings of people before. The council where Plenty Coups spoke, the camps that formed after a successful hunt, the bands coming together for the Sun Dance. He thought he knew what a thousand people looked like.

He did not know what this looked like.

They came out of the agency in a long, slow line, men, women, children, elders, horses, dogs, the accumulated material of a people's life packed onto travois and carried on backs and balanced on heads. They came out organized, which surprised him. He had expected something closer to chaos, or to defeat's particular disorganization. What he saw instead was a people who had decided how they would do this. Who had looked at what was being asked of them and determined that they would do it with whatever dignity the asking left them.

Dull Knife walked at the front.

He was not a young man, in his sixties, moving with the careful deliberateness of age, but he walked like a chief, which meant he walked like a man who understood that how he carried himself was the only thing left entirely in his control. The people behind him watched how he walked and walked the same way.

Little Wolf was further back in the column, moving along its edges, his eyes on everything at once. A war chief's habit, reading the country, reading the people, reading the soldiers surrounding them for anything that required a response. He saw Watches Twice and looked at him, a problem already categorized and set aside.

Watches Twice looked back.

Then he rode to his position at the column's flank and did not look back again.

* * *

The first days went south through the Nebraska country he knew.

He rode the flank and read the ground, not because the ground needed reading for this mission, there was no enemy to find, no ambush to anticipate, but because reading the ground was what his mind did when it had nothing else to do, and here it had nothing else to do. The grass. The draws. The light moving in the late afternoon off the ridgelines to the west.

Behind him, the column moved.

He did not look at the column more than he needed to. He told himself this was professional, a scout watched the perimeter, not the thing being escorted. He rode the flank, watched the country, listened to the sound of nearly a thousand people moving through the grass, and told himself he was doing his job.

In the evenings, the column camped, and the soldiers made their fires. Watches Twice made his apart from both. He ate his jerky and drank his water and listened to the camp sounds from the Cheyenne side of the perimeter.

They were not the sounds he expected.

He expected silence, or grief, or the particular suppressed noise of people who had been defeated and knew it. What he heard instead was ordinary. Voices. Children. The sound of fires being built, food being prepared, and people talking about the ten thousand ordinary things people talked about at the end of a day. Someone laughing. A woman singing something low and without words while she worked.

He had heard those sounds his whole life.

He lay on his bedroll, looked at the stars, and listened.

When he closed his eyes, the sounds from the Cheyenne side of the perimeter moved through the dark, the voices, the fire sounds, the low singing, and it felt almost as if he were home.

He did not open his eyes for a long time.

*　*　*

The country changed as they moved south.

Not all at once, gradually, each day's landscape almost indistinguishable from the day before but the accumulation undeniable. The grass shorter. The air heavier. The sky a different color, not worse exactly, just different, the blue of it deeper and more relentless than the sky over Crow country.

He watched the Cheyenne feel it.

Not dramatically, they were not people who expressed things dramatically, at least not here, not now. But he watched the elders move differently in the heat, their bodies working harder to cover the same ground. He watched the women shade the youngest children with whatever cloth they had. He watched a man stop at a creek crossing and stand in the water for a long moment, his face turned up toward the sky, before the column's movement pulled him forward again.

He was forty days into the march when he saw the girl.

She was perhaps three years old, young enough that the walking was still an effort, old enough that she was doing it herself rather than being carried. She was at the edge of the column, near enough to her mother that the tether of attention between them was visible even at a distance, far enough that she moved with a small child's illusion of independence.

She stopped.

In the middle of the moving column, she simply stopped and looked at something in the grass. A yellow butterfly, its wings opening and closing in the Kansas heat. The column moved around her, and she stood still and watched the butterfly in the grass with the total absorption of a very small person who has not yet learned that some moments are not appropriate for wonder. The butterfly took flight as she watched it, and she ran to catch it, laughing.

Her mother came back for her without breaking stride, one arm swinging out, scooping the girl against her side, the girl going without protest, and then craning her neck to look back at the butterfly as they moved forward.

Watches Twice sat on his horse, watched this, and did not move for a long moment.

His father catching him without looking up from the horse he was tending, one arm swinging out and scooping the boy against his side in the way that suggested he had always known exactly where the boy was.

He rode on.

He did not look at the Cheyenne column for the rest of that day.

* * *

Fort Dodge sat on the Arkansas River in the flat heat of a Kansas summer.

The column stopped there for two days for resupply, the soldiers rotating through the fort's amenities, the Cheyenne camped on the flat ground outside the walls, in the heat that came off the Kansas plains like something alive and intentional.

On the second day, the quartermaster set up his table in the shade of the fort's wall and paid the scouts.

Watches Twice stood in the line. When his turn came, the quartermaster counted coins into his hand without looking at him. Thirteen silver dollars, the weight of them surprising every time, heavy for their size, the metal warm from sitting in the sun.

He closed his hand around them.

He put them in his pocket.

He walked back out into the heat and took his position at the column's flank and felt the weight of the coins against his leg and did not reach for them again.

The column moved south.

The coins moved with it.

*　*　*

Indian Territory announced itself before it was visible.

Something in the air changed. The smell of it, the particular flatness of the light, how the horizon extended further than it should have, and offered nothing at the end of its extension. The grass was sparse and dry, and a different color from any grass he had ridden through. The sky was enormous and indifferent, and the heat came from it and from the ground simultaneously as if the land itself was participating in the work of wearing a person down.

He watched the Cheyenne enter this country.

He watched Dull Knife's shoulders.

The chief had been walking for seventy days with the bearing of a man who understood that bearing was the last sovereignty. His shoulders had not changed through Nebraska or Kansas, through the creek crossings and the heat and the nights camped on ground that was not their ground. They had not changed.

They changed now.

Not dramatically. Not visibly unless you were watching closely, and Watches Twice was always watching closely. Just a settling. A fraction of an inch. The bearing still present, but something underneath it, acknowledging what the body already knew and the mind had been refusing.

This is where we are going.

This is what it is.

Watches Twice felt the coins in his pocket.

He did not reach for them.

* * *

They arrived at the Darlington Agency on August 5, 1877.

Fort Reno sat adjacent to the agency, its buildings low and practical in the heat, the soldiers who came out to receive the column moving with the efficiency of men completing a transaction. The column was counted. Numbers were recorded. The Northern Cheyenne were delivered to the agent, John Miles, who welcomed them with the practiced warmth of a man who believed he was doing them a service.

Watches Twice sat his horse at the edge of it and watched.

He watched the Cheyenne look at what they had been brought to. The agency buildings. The flat treeless ground extending in every direction. The absence of everything that had shaped them, the mountains, the Powder River country, the cold, clear water, and the short grass of the high plains. The presence instead of this, this flat-baked Oklahoma earth, this air that tasted of something wrong, this sky that pressed down rather than opening up.

He watched Dull Knife stand in the middle of it.

The chief stood still for a long time. He did not look at the soldiers, the agent, or the buildings. He looked at the horizon. At the flat featureless distance that had nothing in it that belonged to him or ever would.

Then he turned and walked toward wherever his people were making camp.

He did not look back.

Watches Twice sat his horse.

He rode to where the Army officer was processing the scouts' dismissal. He gave his name. The quartermaster counted the final wages into his hand, more coins, added to what was already there.

He turned from the table with the coins still in his hand.

Across the flat ground, the Cheyenne were making their camp. He watched them do it, the automatic competence of people who had made camp ten thousand times, who knew without thinking how to arrange a space, how to orient a lodge to the wind, how to make something that resembled home out of whatever the ground offered.

The ground here offered very little.

At its edge, near where the women were working, the girl stood still.

She was not looking at something in the dirt this time. She was not absorbed in the small wonders that had carried her through Nebraska and Kansas. She was standing with her hands at her sides, looking at the Agency, at the low buildings, the flat treeless ground, the sky that pressed down instead of opening up, and her face had something in it that three-year-old faces should not have. Not understanding. Not yet. But the body's knowledge arriving before the mind. The particular stillness of a small person who has walked a very long way and arrived somewhere that does not feel like the end of walking.

Her mother came to her.

She took the girl's hand and walked her forward into the camp, and the girl went without protest, not looking back.

Watches Twice looked at the coins in his hand.

They were heavier than they had been at Fort Dodge. He did not know how that was possible, but it was true.

He put them in his pocket.

He tied his horse to a post, walked to the edge of the agency, and looked south.

There was nothing to the south. More of the same, the flat ground, the relentless sky, the heat that came from everywhere at once. Somewhere beyond his sight, the Southern Cheyenne were living on this land as best they could, which was not well. Somewhere behind him, the Northern Cheyenne were beginning to understand what their year here would be.

He stood there for a while.

Then he untied his horse and rode north.

* * *

The ride north took three weeks.

He did not hurry. The horse needed rest and water, and he gave it both, stopping at the creeks and the rivers, riding in the early morning and the late afternoon, and sitting out the worst of the heat in whatever shade the country offered, which was not much.

He was alone in a way he had not been alone in months. Not the comfortable solitude of his daily rides out past the invisible line, this was heavier than that, more present, like a second rider who kept pace with him and said nothing.

He passed back through Kansas. Through the country the column had walked.

The ground still held it, the thousand-yard swath of compressed grass where nearly a thousand people had moved through. The fire rings. The places where the column had camped, and the ground still bore the evidence of it. He read these signs as he read all signs, completely, the information arriving before he could choose not to receive it.

A child's moccasin, small, worn through at the heel, left behind or dropped and not retrieved. He rode past it without stopping.

He kept riding north.

* * *

The Crow camp was in its late summer place on the river when he returned.

The grass was longer than when he left. The horses were fat. Children ran between the lodges in the long August evening, doing what children did. The fires were being built. The smells of food moved through the camp, and everything was ordinary. He had been away long enough that the ordinary was remarkable.

He tended his horse at the picket line.

Then he went to Old Hawk's lodge.

The old man was at his fire. The fire was built lower than it used to be. He had noticed this before the march, and it was more true now, the fire smaller, the lodge dimmer. Old Hawk sat with his medicine bundle beside him and his eyes on the flames, and he did not look up when Watches Twice ducked through the entrance.

He was older.

The months Watches Twice had been gone had done what months did to old men, quietly, without announcement, the accumulation of small diminishments that added up to something undeniable. He sat differently. He breathed differently. His hands on his knees were the hands of a man who had decided to rest them there and might not move them again soon.

But he was there.

Still there.

Watches Twice sat down across the fire.

He did not speak. Old Hawk did not speak. The fire moved between them, and outside the camp went about its evening, and the light failed, and the stars came out.

After a long time, Watches Twice reached into his pocket.

He took out the coins.

He looked at them for the first time, really looked at them, in the firelight, the silver of them catching it, the faces on them belonging to a government that had decided what to do with nearly a thousand people, had done it, and considered the matter settled. He looked at them for a long time.

Then he set them on the ground between himself and Old Hawk.

He did not say anything.

Old Hawk looked at the coins.

He looked at them for a long moment. Completely. Without hurry. Then he looked at Watches Twice.

He did not say anything.

The fire moved.

Outside, a child laughed at something, the sound of it carrying through the camp and then gone, and the night settled around them, completely, without asking.

They sat together until the fire burned low.

When Watches Twice finally rose to go, he left the coins on the ground.

Old Hawk did not look up.

At the entrance, Watches Twice stopped.

He stood there with his back to the old man and the dying fire and the coins on the ground between them.

Then he went out into the night.

8

Home

Watches Twice was standing near Old Hawk's lodge when he saw the child. She was chasing butterflies through the long summer grass, her arms out, her laughter rising without effort.

A yellow butterfly lifted from a stem and drifted just out of reach. The girl followed it, laughing, hopeful, without a plan or a chance of catching it, only the joy of the movement itself. Her mother called something to her from the fire, and the girl turned, smiling, and ran back.

Watches Twice watched all of it.

He watched the girl's small hands. He watched the butterfly rise. He watched the ordinary happiness of it settle into the afternoon.

The butterfly lifted again, caught a current of warm air, and drifted upward until it was only a flicker of color against the sky.

* * *

Seven hundred miles south, a yellow butterfly landed in the dust.

It settled on a blade of dry grass beside the Cheyenne camp at Darlington, its wings opening and closing in the heat. No footsteps came toward it. No small voice rose in delight. The air was still except for the sound of flies and the distant coughing from the barracks.

A woman sat outside her lodge.

Her hands were in her hair. She was braiding it, slowly, without the absentminded rhythm of someone doing a familiar task, but with the careful attention of someone who needed her hands to be doing something. The braid was uneven. She did not seem to notice.

Beside her, a pair of small moccasins lay in the dust.

They were clean. The leather, soft from use. The heels were worn down from walking. They sat where they had been placed, toes pointed toward the lodge, as if waiting.

The woman's hands moved through her hair. The butterfly lifted. The moccasins did not move.

* * *

To the north, the girl laughed again, a bright sound, carried on the late-summer air. Watches Twice turned his head slightly, listening, without hurry.

The butterfly was gone. The girl was still running. The world, for this moment, was intact.

* * *

Emėškeha'e was young when they left the Red Cloud Agency. Twenty, perhaps twenty-one. Her face still carried something the months at Darlington had not yet finished taking.

She had noticed the Crow scout on the march south.

Not because she was looking for him, she had not been looking for anything except the ground in front of her feet and her daughter's position in the column. But he was always there, at the flank, and when you walked for seventy days, you learned the geography of everything around you, including the men assigned to watch you. He was quiet in the way men were quiet when they were actually watching rather than performing watchfulness, and he watched the column with a completeness she felt without being able to say exactly why.

Emėškeha'e did not look at him directly. She had enough to carry.

She remembered arriving.

The Crow scout had been at the edge of the Agency when they came in. She had registered him there the way you registered anything that had accompanied you on a long journey and was now present at its end. He was on his horse. He was watching. That was what he did.

She had not looked at him. She had looked at what she had been brought to.

She remembered the ground. The flatness of it, the particular quality of flat that was different from the flat of the northern plains, this was not the flat of open distance and long sight lines, and the sense that you could see everything that mattered. This was the flat of enclosure, of a horizon that offered nothing, of a sky that pressed down rather than opened up. She had stood in the middle of it while the column sorted itself around her, and she had understood something in her body before she understood it in her mind.

Her daughter had stood beside her, holding her hand, looking at the same horizon with the serious attention of a child who was trying to understand what the adults around her were understanding.

Emėškeha'e had taken her hand and walked her forward into it.

* * *

The first weeks were not the worst weeks.

There was the strangeness of the place, the wrongness of the air and the light, and the smell of the river. There was the inadequacy of the rations, the Southern Cheyenne sharing what little they had, which was not enough for themselves and certainly not enough now, and the particular humiliation of hunger among people who had never been hungry by policy before. There was the heat, which came from the sky and the ground simultaneously, with no relief in the evening, unlike the heat on the northern plains, which had relief at night. Here, the heat simply continued through the night and remained in the morning as if it had never paused.

But her daughter was well.

She ran in the evenings when the sun went low, through the dry grass at the edge of the camp, after the insects and the small movements that caught her eye. Eméškeha'e watched from outside the lodge, braided her hair in the evening light, thought about what needed to be done tomorrow, and tried not to think about the mountains.

Váváhke would come back when she was called. She always came back.

The fever came in October.

It arrived suddenly, completely, the small body going hot between one moment and the next as if a fire had been lit inside it. The mother had seen fever before. She knew what to do. She cooled the child's forehead with water from the river, kept her covered when the shaking came, and held her through the nights that were longer than they should have been.

The fever went away.

Then it came back.

This was the nature of this fever. The particular cruelty of it, the way it left long enough to allow hope and then returned to take the hope back. The other women in the camp knew it. They had watched it move through the lodges since the first weeks of arrival, the fever that came from the air of this wrong country, from the mosquitoes that bred in the river bottom, from something in the Oklahoma dark that the northern people had no defense against because they had never needed a defense against it.

The mother learned the pattern of it.

She learned when it would rise, when it would drop, and when the shaking would come, and she learned to be ready for each of these things. She did not leave her daughter's side during the worst of it. She did not sleep during the nights when the fever was highest. She sat beside the small body, and her hands did what a mother's hands did, cooling, covering, holding.

Between the fevers, her daughter ate what there was to eat, which was not much. The rations were inadequate and arrived irregularly. What arrived was often wrong for small children, not the food her body knew, not the food that had built her through three years of northern plains winters. The mother gave her daughter what she could from her own portion, ate what remained, and told herself this was enough.

It was not enough.

The fever came back a third time in November.

This time it stayed.

The mother's hands did not stop moving through those days, cooling, covering, holding, the same motions repeated because the repetition was the only thing she could offer, and she would offer everything she had for as long as it was needed. She did not sleep. She did not eat more than she had to. She watched her daughter's face and waited for the moment when the fever would break the way it had broken before, and she would feel the small body cool under her hands and hear the breathing slow into something that sounded like rest.

The moment did not come.

* * *

She placed the moccasins outside the lodge on a morning in late November.

She placed them carefully, the toes pointed toward the entrance, the leather soft from use, the heels worn down from walking. She smoothed them with her thumb. She arranged them so they were even, parallel, waiting.

Then she sat down beside them, put her hands in her hair, and began to braid it.

The braid was uneven. She did not notice.

Around her, the camp went about its morning, the fires, the voices, the ordinary sounds of people doing what they did because there was nothing else to do. A child ran past the edge of her vision. She did not look up.

Her hands moved through her hair.

The sun rose higher.

The flies came.

* * *

The dying continued through the winter.

Not dramatically, nothing about it was dramatic, which was part of what made it unbearable. People went to sleep and did not wake. People who had been warriors and hunters and mothers and elders, who had survived the Dull Knife Fight and the march south and the first months of this wrong country, died of a fever that the right country would never have given them. Forty-one dead by the end of that first winter. The number recorded in the agent's ledger with the practiced efficiency of a man who filed such things under the category of expected outcomes.

John Miles wrote to Washington that the situation was difficult but manageable.

Washington wrote back that the situation was being monitored.

The Cheyenne buried their dead in the Oklahoma ground and waited for the promise that had been made to them, that if the place did not suit them, after a year, they could go home. The year passed. They asked. Miles said no. They asked again. Miles said no again. Dull Knife went to Miles and said that his people were dying. Miles said the situation was being monitored.

Little Wolf said nothing to Miles.

Little Wolf was watching.

* * *

By the spring of 1878, he had been watching for seven months.

He watched the rations arrive in short, irregular amounts. He watched the medical supplies fail to arrive at all through the worst of the winter. He watched his people get smaller, not just in number but in themselves, the particular diminishment that came from being in the wrong place for too long, from being people without the things that made them who they were. No buffalo to hunt. No mountains to navigate. No cold, clear water. No sight lines that extended far enough to see what was coming.

He watched Dull Knife petition Miles.

He watched Miles refuse.

He did not petition Miles himself. He had understood something about Miles in the first weeks that Dull Knife had taken longer to understand, that the agent's refusals were not obstacles to be argued around but walls built by men in Washington who had already decided what would happen here and had sent Miles to administer the decision. Arguing with Miles was arguing with a tree. The tree did not care about the argument.

Little Wolf went back to his camp and thought about trees.

* * *

The young men had been watching the horses.

Not the Agency horses, those were counted and accounted for, and any interference with them would bring soldiers from Fort Reno before the sun moved. The horses of the settlers and ranchers in the surrounding country. The horses that grazed on the open ground beyond the Agency boundaries were tended by men who did not expect the people at Darlington to be paying attention to what was beyond the boundaries.

The people at Darlington were paying attention to everything.

Through the spring and summer of 1878, the young men slipped out of camp in the nights. Not many at a time, never enough to attract notice, moving through the dark with the particular competence of men who had grown up in a world where moving through dark without being noticed was a survival skill. They found horses. They moved them to places that were not the Agency. They noted the locations. They did not bring the horses in.

Not yet.

The women had been watching the guns.

When the Army had processed them at Fort Robinson the previous year, the soldiers had taken their weapons, the rifles, the pistols, anything that could be used against the men who were escorting them south. What the soldiers had not taken were the pieces. A rifle disassembled is not a rifle. The barrel of a rifle is a piece of metal that could be anything. The stock is wood. The mechanism is a collection of small components that could be worn as decoration, sewn into clothing, or attached to moccasins as an ornament.

The women sewed.

They sewed through the summer evenings when the light lasted and through the early mornings when the air was briefly cool, and they talked about ordinary things while their hands did what their hands were doing, and anyone watching would have seen women sewing, which was what women did, which was unremarkable.

* * *

In August, Little Wolf went to Miles one more time.

He said what he had said before, that his people were dying, that the promise had been made and not kept, that they wished to return to their home in the north. He said it plainly, the way he said most things. He was not a man who argued or pleaded. He stated what was true and waited to see what would be done with it.

Miles said no.

Little Wolf looked at him for a moment.

Then he went back to his camp.

He did not speak to Miles again.

* * *

The night of September 9th, the fires burned at their usual heights. The voices moved through the camp in the usual patterns. The children who were left, fewer than there had been, the winter and the fever having done their work, were put to sleep in the usual way, the mothers' hands doing what mothers' hands did at the end of a day.

Eméškeha'e sat outside her lodge for a while, looking at the dark.

Then she went inside.

Around midnight, the camp began to move.

Not loudly. Not with the noise of panic or the noise of celebration. With the particular quiet of people who had decided something and were now doing it, each person knowing their part, the whole thing assembling itself in the dark with the competence of a people who had been preparing for this for months without anyone saying aloud what they were preparing for.

The horses came in from where the young men had been keeping them.

The guns came out from the clothing and the moccasins and the bundles where they had been living since Fort Robinson, assembled now, piece by piece, in the dark, by hands that knew exactly what they were doing.

Dull Knife walked to the front of the column that was forming.

He stood straight.

Little Wolf moved to where he needed to be.

The people moved with them, 353 of them, less than a third of the thousand who had walked south fourteen months before, the rest dead or too sick to travel or unwilling to risk what this would cost.

They walked north.

They left their fires burning.

* * *

The agent's clerk discovered they were gone at three in the morning.

He stood in the empty camp for a moment, the fires still burning, the lodges still standing, the ordinary evidence of habitation arranged so convincingly that for a moment he thought he had miscounted, that they were simply asleep, that in the morning everything would be as it had been.

Then he understood.

He rode for Fort Reno.

* * *

Seven hundred miles north, in the Crow camp on the river, Watches

Twice was asleep.

He did not know yet what had begun in the Oklahoma dark. He did not know that the people he had escorted south fourteen months ago were walking north through the night with their horses, their reassembled guns, and their 353 remaining bodies, pointed toward home.

He did not know that the Army would begin looking for scouts who knew the country in the morning.

He did not know that he would say yes before the question was finished.

He did not know that Vávàhke was not among them.

He slept.

Outside Old Hawk's lodge, the fire had burned to coals. The old man was inside, breathing in the way he breathed now, carefully, with the attention of a man who had decided not to take anything for granted. His medicine bundle was beside him. His hands were on his knees.

The night was quiet.

The stars were out.

Seven hundred miles south, 353 people walked north through the dark toward everything the Army was going to throw at them, and they walked anyway, because the alternative was to stay in the place where the fever came from the air and the moccasins sat outside the lodge with their toes pointed toward the entrance as if waiting.

They walked.

9

Sanctuary

The officer came to the camp on the morning of September 10th.

He was not a man Watches Twice had worked with before. Still, he knew the type, efficient, direct, the economy of movement that distinguished officers who had been in the field long enough to stop performing authority and simply exercise it. He asked for Watches Twice by name. He did not ask through anyone.

"The Northern Cheyenne left Darlington last night," he said. "All of them. We need men who know the country north of the Arkansas."

Watches Twice said yes.

The officer nodded once, told him where to report, and rode out.

Watches Twice went to pack what he needed.

He had been to Old Hawk's lodge the night before and had sat across the fire from the old man for an hour without either of them speaking. The silver still lay where Watches Twice had left it. When he had risen to go, Old Hawk had not looked up. Watches Twice had stopped at the entrance. Then he went out into the night.

He packed his kit, brought his horse around, and rode out before the light had fully arrived.

He did not look back.

The country between the Crow camp and the Pine Ridge of Nebraska was ten days of hard riding, the Yellowstone behind him, the Powder River country opening south, Wyoming rolling toward the North Platte, and then the broken ground of the Nebraska panhandle where the plains folded into ridges and cedar canyons and the White River cut through it all.

He rode south and east, thinking about what he knew.

353 people had left Darlington. He had escorted them there fourteen months ago. He knew how they moved, knew the chiefs who led them, knew the country they were trying to reach. The Army had columns converging from multiple directions. The forts in Kansas and Nebraska all mobilizing. Ten thousand soldiers, according to the reports, which seemed impossible, but the country felt that way. He was not part of the pursuit. He was riding to where the country said they would come.

He arrived in the Pine Ridge country in the first week of October.

The Cheyenne were still in Kansas.

He read the country they would move through and waited.

* * *

The column crossed the Arkansas River on the night of September 23rd.

They crossed where the river ran shallow and wide, west of Dodge City, the horses swimming the current, and the children carried on their parents' backs. The water was cold enough that it took something from every person who entered it and never gave it back. They came out onto the north bank in the dark, shook the water from themselves, and kept moving because the north bank was not a place to stop.

Little Wolf was already reading the country ahead.

He had been reading it for two weeks, the draws and the ridges and the places where the Army would set up and the places where they wouldn't bother, the ground that favored movement and the ground that favored ambush. He had been right about Turkey Springs. He had been right about Punished Woman's Fork. He would be right again because being right was what had kept them alive this long.

He looked north at the dark country and understood what it was asking of them.

More. It was always asking for more.

He went back to the column and led them north.

* * *

The hunters came back empty on the third day in Nebraska.

They had gone out before dawn as they had always gone, moving into the country, reading the grass and the wind and the light. They came back at midday with nothing.

The plains were silent.

Not the silence of animals that had been startled and moved away. That silence held potential, the sense that the animals were nearby and would return. This was different. The silence of absence. The silence of something that had been here longer than anyone could remember and was not here anymore.

Little Wolf stood at the edge of the camp and looked at the country around him.

He had known this was coming. The word had traveled north for years, rider to rider, fire to fire. But knowing a thing was coming and standing inside the arrived thing were different in a way that no amount of knowing prepared you for.

He did not say anything about it.

He told the people to eat what they had and keep moving.

* * *

They crossed the Platte on a cold morning in early October.

The river was wide, wider than anything they had crossed in Kansas, the channel braiding across a broad sandy floodplain, the cottonwoods along both banks gone to yellow in the October cold. But it was shallow. It spread itself thin across the sand, running in multiple channels that shifted as you moved through them, the water rarely above the horses' knees.

They crossed in the early morning light, the cold of the water finding every person who entered and reminding them of the season and what was coming.

Little Wolf crossed last.

He stood on the south bank for a moment before he entered the water, looking north at the far side. The cottonwoods there. The sandhills began their long roll beyond the tree line, pale and open under the October sky.

North of the Platte.

He had not been north of the Platte in fourteen months.

He rode his horse into the water and crossed without looking back, and came out on the north bank and kept moving because the north bank was not a place to stop either, not yet, not until they were through the sandhills and into the Pine Ridge country and further still, always further, until they reached the place that had their name on it.

The people came out of the water behind him, shook the cold from themselves, and kept moving.

North of the Platte.

Almost there.

Almost.

* * *

The split happened in the last week of October.

They were in the sandhills of northwestern Nebraska.

The country was big and open in a way that surprised people who expected Nebraska to be flat. The hills rose and fell in long dune-shaped swells, some of them climbing high enough to hide a column of people on the move, others dropping into comparatively flat ground where the sand lay pale and exposed, and the wind worked it constantly. Trees grew only where water collected, cottonwoods in the creek bottoms, the occasional clump of cedar on a protected slope, and everywhere else the country was open grass and sand and sky, the sky enormous over all of it, the barrenness of it feeling less like emptiness and more like age, like a country that had been here long before people arrived and was indifferent to their presence.

Little Wolf had chosen this country deliberately. A pursuing force struggled in the sandhills. The terrain confused direction, the loose sand swallowed tracks, the hills blocked sight lines. His people struggled in it, too, the sand making every step harder than it should have been, the cold coming off the hills at night with nothing to break it. But his people were used to struggling. He was counting on the Army being less so.

Dull Knife came to him in the evening.

The chief sat down, and Little Wolf sat with him, and neither of them spoke for a while. They had known each other for a long time. They had fought together and led together and buried their dead together, and now they were here, in the sand hills of Nebraska, and they were not going to agree about what came next.

Dull Knife said what he had been thinking for days, that he was tired, that his people were tired, that Fort Robinson was two days northwest and Red Cloud was there, and the Army at Fort Robinson had always treated the Cheyenne with some measure of decency. That they could surrender there and be safe for the winter and negotiate from a position of survival rather than running.

Little Wolf listened.

Then he said what he had been thinking, that he did not trust the Army's decency, that the only safety was distance, that he intended to put as much distance between his people and the Army as the country allowed.

They looked at each other.

There was nothing more to say. They had each stated the true thing. The true things did not agree, and no argument could resolve it.

Dull Knife's people would go to Fort Robinson.

Little Wolf's people would go north.

They did not say goodbye in any formal way. They had been together too long for formality. Dull Knife rose, and Little Wolf rose. They looked at each other once more in the evening light, and then they went back to their people.

That night, the column split in the dark and moved in two directions, and the sandhills received both of them without comment.

* * *

Watches Twice came up on the first rise in the broken country east of the Pine Ridge and stopped his horse.

Below him, moving through a canyon drainage, was the column.

He counted.

He counted again.

Something was wrong with the numbers. He had escorted 937 people to Darlington fourteen months ago. 353 had left. The column below him was not 353 people. He could read the size of a moving column as he read everything, by the width of it, the spacing, and the number of horses on the outside. What was below him was not 353 people.

It was roughly half that.

He sat on the rise and watched them move through the canyon below and thought about what half meant.

Two possibilities. Either they had lost half their people in six weeks of running and fighting, possibly, the Army's pursuit had been designed to make it so, or they had split. Two bands moving in different directions.

He needed to know which.

He rode down from the rise and circled wide around the column, staying to the high ground, and came in behind them. He picked up their trail where it entered the Pine Ridge country from the southeast and began to backtrack.

He rode southeast for two hours through the sandhills.

The country worked against him in ways that flat ground didn't. The sand held tracks differently than grass or hardpan. Footprints, preserved with strange clarity in sheltered places, completely erased by the wind in others, the trail appeared and disappeared as the ground changed beneath him. The hills rose and fell without pattern, dune-shaped swells giving way to flat open ground and then rising again, the cottonwoods along the creek bottoms the only fixed points in a landscape that seemed designed to disorient. The sky was enormous and pale, offering nothing.

He found it anyway. A scout learned to read sand as he read everything else, completely, without hurry, letting the information arrive before deciding what it meant.

The trail coming north from Kansas was wide and clear, 353 people, the full band, and then, in a flat between two sand hills where the wind had not yet worked the ground, the trail split.

He stepped down from his horse, crouched, and read it.

One trail bearing northwest. Toward the Pine Ridge. Toward Fort Robinson.

One trail bearing north. Into the sandhills. Toward nothing.

He stood up and looked at both trails for a long time.

Two decisions. Two directions out of the same impossible place.

He thought about what he knew. Two bands splitting. One was going north into the sandhills, where the Army would lose them until spring. One was going northwest toward Fort Robinson.

His mind went to the military question first because it was the one he had come to answer. If this were a coordinated attack on Fort Robinson, one band circling from the north, one approaching directly, then the band heading directly for the fort would arrive first. He needed to know what that band's intentions were before the Army was caught unaware.

He needed to follow Dull Knife.

He mounted his horse and rode northwest.

He followed them for three days.

Not close. He stayed to the high ground, the ridges above the canyon drainages, reading their movement from above—a scout's distance. Far enough to be invisible. Close enough to read what the movement said.

The first day, he watched for the signs of a war party preparing to fight, a column tightening before engagement, scouts ranging ahead looking for ground to hold rather than ground to pass through, the particular energy of people moving toward something they intend to attack.

He did not see those signs.

What he saw was different.

The column moved at the pace of its slowest members. An attacking force moved at the pace of its fastest; you left your weakest behind when you were going to fight. This column left no one behind. It moved together, the healthy helping the sick, the strong carrying what the weak could no longer carry.

The second day, he circled behind them and read the trail they had left.

What they shed told him more than what they carried.

A heavy iron cooking pot, set carefully beside a fire ring. Not dropped. Placed.

A blanket, folded. The folding told him something. You did not fold a blanket you were abandoning carelessly.

A warrior's shirt, quilled, the kind worn for ceremony or for the last fight, left on a rock.

Medicine bundles. Two of them in a mile of trail. The last things a person carried. Left because whoever carried them could not carry them anymore or was no longer there to carry them.

A cradleboard. Empty. Leaning against a cedar beside a creek.

He read all of it without stopping.

He remounted and rode ahead of them again, back to the high ground, and watched them move through the Pine Ridge country below.

* * *

The third day, he understood.

It was not any single thing that told him. It was the accumulation of three days of reading the pace, the trail, how the column held together, the direction of it, the quality of the movement itself. An attacking force had a particular energy that was unmistakable once you had seen it. This was not that energy.

This was the energy of people who had stopped running.

Not because they had given up. Not because they were broken. But because they had made a decision and were living it out. The direction of the column was deliberate. Northwest, toward Fort Robinson, unwavering. They were not looking for ground to fight on. They were not ranging ahead for ambush positions. They were walking toward something they had chosen to trust.

They were going to surrender.

He sat on his horse on a ridge above them and looked down at the column moving through the canyon below and understood what he was seeing.

Dull Knife was not marching on Fort Robinson.

Dull Knife was walking into it.

* * *

On the afternoon of the third day, he came up on a rise in the Pine Ridge country and stopped his horse at the crest and looked down.

Below him, the valley opened, a creek bottom with cottonwoods along the water, gone to fall color, yellow and brown against the cedar ridges rising on the far side. The village was at the bottom. Small. 149 people made a small village, smaller than anything this band had been in its lifetime. But organized as Cheyenne camps were organized, the lodges were placed with intention, the horses on the far side, the fires just beginning to be built for the evening.

Women working at fires that had just been coaxed to life, the smoke rising thin and pale against the darkening tree line along the creek. Children doing what children do, chasing, falling, being called back. A man moving between the horses, checking legs, running his hand along a shoulder. The ordinary work of people who had survived another day and were preparing to survive the night.

He had seen this before. Not this village. Not these people. But this.

He sat very still.

The cold moved with him when he shifted in the saddle, finding the gap between his collar and his neck, settling there. The dampness had been in everything since morning. In his blanket when he rose, in the ground under his horse's feet, in the air itself. Fall in this country came early and meant business.

He would not have a fire tonight.

He looked down at the fires below.

He thought about a pair of small moccasins placed outside a lodge in Oklahoma with their toes pointed toward the entrance.

He thought about a cradleboard leaning against a cedar beside a creek in the sandhills.

He thought about medicine bundles left on the ground, two of them in a mile of trail, the last things left by people who had nothing left to leave.

He thought about thirteen silver dollars counted into his hand at Fort Dodge without the quartermaster looking at him.

He thought about his father's hands lowering the tomahawk.

He sat on his horse on the ridge in the cold, the dark coming down, and looked at what was left of Dull Knife's people in the valley below.

They were not running away.

They were running to.

What they were running to was Fort Robinson, hoping that what waited for them there was the Army's decency. He knew what the Army's decency looked like because he had helped deliver these people to it once already.

He gathered the reins.

He did not move for a long time.

Then he turned his horse and rode back to where the Army column was waiting for his report.

He told the officer what he had found. The location. The direction of movement. The size of the band. The distance to Fort Robinson. Their intention was not hostile; they were moving to surrender.

He told it plainly. Without interpretation. Just what was there.

The officer thanked him and began issuing orders.

Watches Twice rode to the edge of the Army camp and stopped and looked north at the Pine Ridge country in the last of the afternoon light, the ridges and the canyons and the cedar trees dark against the pale October sky.

He sat there for a while.

He unsaddled his horse and tended it and made his cold camp away from the soldiers' fires and lay down and looked at the stars coming out over the Pine Ridge and did not sleep for a long time.

* * *

The Army intercepted Dull Knife's band on October 23rd.

Two companies of cavalry out of Fort Robinson, moving south through the Pine Ridge, found the band two days from the fort. The encounter was not violent. Dull Knife had not come this far to die in a canyon two days from where he was trying to go. He met the soldiers and told them what he had been telling everyone for months: that his people wanted to stay in the north, were willing to surrender, and asked only to remain.

The soldiers gave them food and blankets.

The Cheyenne were ragged, their moccasins were worn through, many were sick, and all were thin from six weeks of running, fighting, and eating nothing.

The soldiers counted them.

The soldiers escorted them north.

On October 25th, 1878, Dull Knife walked into Fort Robinson.

He walked straight. The bearing of a man who understood that how he carried himself was the only thing left entirely in his control. The fort's buildings were low and practical around him. The soldiers watched him come in.

He had been to Fort Robinson before. He remembered it as a place of some decency. He had believed it would be that again.

He walked forward, head up, into the fort.

Things had changed.

10

The Cheyenne Buttes

Watches Twice came back to the Crow camp in early November.

Old Hawk was at his fire.

The fire was built higher than it used to be, higher than the season required, higher than the lodge needed. Watches Twice noticed this and understood what it meant before he sat down.

He sat down across from the old man and looked at him in the firelight.

Old Hawk was older.

His hair had gone from gray to white since the spring. Not all of it, but enough that the change was visible in the firelight, the white of it stark against the darker skin of his face. The face itself was more lined than Watches Twice remembered, the flesh of it sitting differently on the bones beneath, the jaw softer, the eyes deeper set. He was thinner. His hands on his knees were bonier than they had been, the fingers slightly curled how old hands curled when the joints had decided they were done with straightening. Beside him, his meal sat half-eaten and had been sitting that way long enough that it was cold.

He did not look up when Watches Twice came in.

After a moment, he moved his eyes toward his pipe, not reaching for it, just looking at it.

Watches Twice picked up the pipe and brought it to him.

Old Hawk took it without acknowledgment. Not rudely. Old Hawk was not a rude man. But with the economy of someone for whom acknowledgment required energy, he was no longer spending on small things.

He was still there.

Still present. The eyes, when they finally settled on Watches Twice, still had the quality they had always had, the completeness, the unhurried attention. Whatever was leaving him had not yet taken that.

Watches Twice reached into his kit and took out the coins.

He set them on the ground beside the others. The silver from Fort Dodge, still there, still on the ground where he had left it the first time, added to now, the pile grown with each assignment the Army had given him and each time he had come back and sat across this fire and added what he had been paid to what was already there.

The pile was larger than it had been.

Old Hawk looked at it.

He looked at it for a long moment, the silver catching the firelight, the faces on the coins belonging to a government that had been paying Watches Twice to do its work in the world. He looked at the pile and then he looked at Watches Twice and his face did something that was not quite a frown and not quite grief and was not quite anything that had a name.

He did not say anything.

He looked back at the fire.

Watches Twice sat with him until the fire burned low. Then he rose and went out into the November night and stood in the cold for a while, looking at the stars, and did not go back inside.

* * *

At Fort Robinson, the negotiations continued through November and into December.

Dull Knife met with the officers. He met with the agent. He waited for word from Red Cloud, who had been moved to Pine Ridge in Dakota Territory and was himself a prisoner of a kind, his influence reduced to what the government permitted him. In December Red Cloud was brought to Fort Robinson for a council. He and Dull Knife spoke. The word that came back from Washington was not what Dull Knife had been waiting for.

Washington had decided.

The Northern Cheyenne would return to the southern reservation. This was not a negotiation. This was an order.

Dull Knife said no.

He said it plainly, without drama, as a statement of fact rather than defiance. His people would not go back to the place where the fever came from the air and the rations arrived short and the buffalo were gone and the ground held nothing that belonged to them. They had walked five hundred miles through Kansas and Nebraska to escape that place. They would not walk back.

* * *

In late November Dull Knife's son Bull Hump borrowed a horse and rode out to visit relatives living with the Sioux.

He told no one where he was going. He simply went, the way a young man went when he needed to go somewhere, without thinking about how it would look to the men in the fort who were watching every movement the Cheyenne made.

Captain Wessels received his orders and considered what Bull

Hump's departure meant.

He confined the Cheyenne to the barracks.

All of them. For the action of one young man visiting relatives, one hundred and forty-nine people lost what small freedom they had been permitted. The barracks doors closed. The guards doubled. The Cheyenne who had been allowed to move around the fort grounds found themselves inside four walls with bars on the windows and soldiers at the doors.

It was December in Nebraska.

* * *

The barracks had been built to house seventy-five soldiers.

It now held one hundred and forty-nine Cheyenne, men, women, children, elders, in the Nebraska winter that came through the walls and the floor and the gaps around the windows with the patient indifference of a cold that did not need to hurry because it had all the time there was.

They had blankets. Some of them. They had the clothing they had walked five hundred miles in, which was not enough for a Nebraska January. They had each other's warmth, which was something, but it was not enough.

On January 3rd, Wessels informed the Cheyenne leaders that they were formally ordered to return south. The order was Washington's. It was final.

Dull Knife said no.

Wild Hog and Left Hand said their people would not go. Wessels took Wild Hog as a prisoner and put him in shackles.

The Cheyenne did not send anyone to tell Wessels they would go south.

On January 5th, Wessels cut off the food, the water, and the fuel simultaneously.

The cold that had been coming through the walls now had nothing to compete with. The Cheyenne burned what they had: blankets, clothing, and the wooden parts of what furniture the barracks contained. They fed it to the fire, piece by piece, and huddled around what heat it gave; when it was gone, they fed the fire something else. When there was nothing left to burn, they held each other in the dark and waited.

They melted snow for water by holding it against their bodies until it liquefied, until the cold of it had taken more from them than the water gave back, and they drank what they could, held more snow, and drank again.

They did not send anyone to tell Wessels they would go south.

** * **

The children went silent on January 8th.

Not all of them. But enough that the silence was a different kind of silence than the barracks had held before, not the silence of sleep or of exhaustion but the silence of small bodies that had used everything they had and had nothing left to use. The mothers held them, felt the heat leaving them, and did what mothers did, covering, holding, giving what warmth remained in their own bodies to their children's bodies.

It was not enough.

It was never going to be enough.

By the night of January 9th, the young men had endured this longer than they could stand.

They could die here.

Or they could die running.

They chose running. Not because it offered better odds, it didn't. Because dying running was not the same as dying waiting. Because a people who went through the windows of a barracks with what weapons they had left were not the same people as a people who lay down in the cold and waited for it to finish them.

Dull Knife was there. He did not stop them.

He went with them.

At 9:45 in the evening of January 9th, 1879, the first shot was fired.

* * *

They went through the windows.

The men with weapons went first, firing at the guards, trying to clear a path, buying seconds for the ones behind them. The women came next with the children, through the broken windows and into the Nebraska night, the cold hitting them like a wall, the snow deep and the darkness complete except for the lanterns of the soldiers now running toward the sound of the shots.

They ran south across the snow-covered parade ground, reached the White River, and followed its banks west, moving fast. The soldiers coming behind them with torches and rifles, with the particular efficiency of men who outnumbered what they were pursuing by more than they needed to.

Then the Cheyenne turned north.

They scaled the buttes above the river. The cliffs rising dark and steep in the January night, the handholds frozen, the footing uncertain, the women passing children up from handhold to handhold, the men below holding off the soldiers long enough for the ones above to reach the top. The buttes would carry their name after this night. The Cheyenne Buttes. The name given not by the Cheyenne but by the country itself, the country remembering what happened on its face in the dark of January 9th, 1879.

They reached the top.

They ran northwest into the Pine Ridge.

The soldiers came behind them.

The running fight went for miles. Not a battle, not an engagement, not anything the Army's language had a word for that was honest about what it was. It was soldiers pursuing people who had nothing left. No food, no fuel, no adequate clothing, weapons enough for some of them, not enough for most. It was a Nebraska January night, and people running through it with soldiers behind them and the river below them, with nowhere ahead that was going to be safe.

By morning, twenty-six Cheyenne were dead in the snow.

Eighty were recaptured and taken back to the fort.

The rest scattered into the frozen hills.

* * *

The soldiers moved through the valley in the first light of January 10th.

They moved through it, recording, counting, doing what needed to be done. The valley was quiet now, in the particular way that places are quiet after something violent has happened in them, the violence still present in the ground and the air even after the sounds of it have stopped.

At the edge of the river, where the bank dropped to the ice and the mud had frozen in the night, a soldier stopped.

He looked down.

In the frozen mud of the riverbank, preserved perfectly by the cold that had set it like stone, was a child's handprint.

Small. The fingers slightly spread. The palm flat against the mud as if the child had caught themselves there, had put their hand down in the dark and the cold and the running and pushed themselves up and kept going.

The soldier looked at it for a moment.

Then he moved on.

The handprint stayed.

The cold kept it exactly as it was.

* * *

Thirty-two Cheyenne were still moving.

They were led by Little Finger Nail. He was a young warrior, not a chief, not a man whose name the government had on any list of leaders to be negotiated with, pressured, or reasoned with. Just a man who was still alive and still moving and knew how to keep people alive and moving in the Pine Ridge country in January.

He led them northwest for thirteen days.

Thirteen days in a Nebraska January with nothing. No food. No fire. No shelter beyond what the frozen hills themselves provided, which was not much. They moved at night and hid by day and ate what the country offered, which was almost nothing, and they kept moving because moving was what they had left.

On January 22nd, the soldiers found them in a small hollow above Antelope Creek, thirty-five miles northwest of Fort Robinson.

The soldiers surrounded the hollow.

Little Finger Nail's people fought with what they had. Knives, the last of the ammunition, their hands. They were thirty-two people who had survived thirteen days in a Nebraska January and they fought as people fought when fighting was the only thing left that was theirs to do.

The soldiers killed most of them.

The dead were buried in a mass grave, the soldiers called The Pit.

A few escaped into the hills and were not found.

* * *

Dull Knife was not among the thirty-two.

He had been moving since the night of January 9th, himself, his wife, five others from his family, moving through the frozen hills in the dark, hiding by day, moving by night, living on nothing because there was nothing to live on. Seven people. The chief who had walked one hundred and forty-nine people into Fort Robinson now moved through the Pine Ridge with seven.

He moved the way he had always moved, deliberately, understanding that how he carried himself was the only thing left entirely in his control.

He came down out of the hills in late January.

He was still alive.

He did not yet know what that would mean. Whether the government would let his people stay in the north, whether the reservation would come, whether the survivors of Fort Robinson would find something in Montana that resembled what they had lost. He did not know any of that.

He knew that he was still moving.

He walked toward Pine Ridge.

The hills behind him held the winter and the dead and the handprint frozen into the mud of the White River bank and the silence of a place where something had happened that would not unhappen.

He walked.

He was still walking.

11

Broken Country

The fire was built high when Watches Twice ducked through the entrance.

Higher than the season needed. Higher than the lodge needed. The heat of it hit him before he was fully inside. It was not the comfortable warmth of a well-tended fire but the aggressive heat of a fire built by someone who was cold in a way that more wood could not fix, who built it high anyway because building it high was the only response available.

Old Hawk was on his robes.

Not sitting at the fire as he always did, upright, his hands on his knees, his eyes on the flames with the particular quality of attention that made you feel the fire was the one being watched. He was lying down. On his side, facing the fire, his medicine bundle tucked against his chest with the grip of a man who was not going to let go of it. His hair was fully white now. His face in the firelight was the face of a man who had decided to stop holding anything back from what was taking him, not surrender exactly, just done with the effort of resistance.

He was still breathing.

His eyes were open.

When Watches Twice sat down across the fire, Old Hawk looked at him for a long moment. The completeness still there, the unhurried attention, whatever was leaving him had not yet taken that, and then he looked back at the fire.

Watches Twice sat with him.

He did not speak. Old Hawk did not speak. The fire moved between them and outside the camp went about its evening, the light failed, and the stars came out. The fire burned. Old Hawk breathed carefully. Watches Twice sat, watched him breathe, and did not look away.

After a long time, Old Hawk spoke.

His voice was not what it had been. Quieter. The words came with more space between them, as if each one required a small decision. But the quality of the voice was still his, unhurried, precise, placing each word where it needed to go.

"I want to tell you something," he said.

Watches Twice waited.

"A story," Old Hawk said. "A thing I have been thinking about."

He was quiet for a moment. His breathing moved in and out, careful, the attention he gave it visible.

"There was a country," he said. "Good country. You know the kind, the grass long in the valleys, the ridges giving good sight lines, water where it should be, the seasons coming in their order. A country that had been a good country for a long time before anyone who lived in it could remember."

He paused.

"In this country, there was an elk. A bull. Heavy through the shoulders, his rack wide and dark, a bull who had been in this country long enough to know every draw and every water and every place where the grass came in thick in the spring. He knew the country not by thinking about it but by being in it, the knowledge in the body rather than the mind."

Old Hawk's eyes moved to the fire and stayed there.

"And in this same country, there was a mule deer. Also a buck. Smaller than the elk, as mule deer are smaller, but quick in a way the elk was not quick, able to move through broken country, up and over and through, using the land differently. He also knew this country. Had known it as long as the elk had known it. His trails were not the elk's trails. His water was not always the elk's water. But it was the same country. The same grass. The same seasons. The same sky over both of them."

He stopped again. His hand moved slightly on the medicine bundle, not gripping it tighter, just touching it. Reminding himself it was there.

"These two did not love each other. That is not what I am saying."

"The elk was larger. Stronger. When their trails crossed at the water, the elk did not move aside. He came forward, his rack low, his weight behind him, and the mule deer moved. Not always running. Sometimes, just stepping back, giving ground, waiting until the elk had finished at the water and moved on. But always moving. Always the one who gave way."

"This had been true for a long time. Longer than either of them had been alive. The elk came to the water, and the mule deer stepped back. The elk took the best graze in the valley bottom, and the mule deer worked the edges, the slopes, the broken country where the elk didn't bother going because the valley bottom was his and he knew it. The mule deer learned the elk's trails so he could avoid them. The elk did not bother learning the mule deer's trails because the mule deer's trails did not matter to him."

"This was not cruelty. This was just what the country was. The elk was larger, and the mule deer was smaller, and the country organized itself around that fact as water organized itself around stone."

"They had been this way a long time. It was part of what the country was."

Something moved at the edge of his mouth. Not quite a smile. The recognition of something he found accurate.

"There was also a bear in this country. A big male, scarred from old fights, who moved through the valley on his own schedule. The elk knew the bear. The mule deer knew the bear. They had known bears their whole lives. Known how a bear moved, known what a bear's presence meant, known how to read the wind for bear smell, and how to position themselves when a bear was in the country. A bear came from one direction. A bear could be watched, avoided, and waited out. The elk had driven off bears before, had turned and faced them, and the bear had gone, because a bull elk in his prime was not something even a large bear wanted to test. The mule deer could not drive off bears, but he could run, and he was quick, and the bear was heavy and not built for long pursuit. They managed the bear as they had always managed the bear. The bear was a known thing in a country of known things."

He breathed carefully for a moment.

"In the spring, the elk came into his rut, and he fought the other bulls. He gathered his cows. He was what a bull elk is in the rut. Enormous, consuming, the whole world narrowed down to the herd and the fighting, the cows and the ground they stood on. He was not thinking about the mule deer. He was not thinking about anything except the rut and what the rut required of him. This is what the rut does. It takes everything a bull has, and it uses it. There is nothing left over for anything else."

Old Hawk's voice had found a rhythm now. The words were coming more easily, and the spaces between them were still present but less effortful. As if the story itself was doing something for him that nothing else could do.

"And the mule deer in his season did his own version of this. Smaller, quicker, but the same urgency. The same narrowing of the world. His does, his ground, his rivals among his own kind. He and the elk moved through the same country in their separate urgencies. The old arrangement between them was still there, the elk with the valley bottom, the mule deer with the broken slopes, and neither of them had the attention for anything else. They were too consumed by their own seasons."

He paused.

"This went on for a long time. Many seasons. The elk and the mule deer and the country between them. The old arrangement was part of what the country was. The elk at the water. The mule deer stepped back. Neither of them going anywhere. Neither of them stopped being what they were. The country held them both, and that was how it was."

He stopped completely for a moment. His eyes closed. Watches Twice sat very still. Then the eyes opened again and found the fire.

"Then the wolves came," Old Hawk said.

He let that sit for a moment.

"Not one wolf. A pack. Many. And they did not come as the bear came, from one direction, alone. The elk and the mule deer had managed the bear their whole lives. They knew how a bear moved. They knew what a bear's presence meant and what it required of them. A bear was a known thing in a country of known things."

His voice had gone quieter.

"The pack was not a known thing."

"They came from several directions. They were patient with the patience of seasons, of cold, of anything that did not need to hurry because it had enough of everything it needed and could simply wait. The elk and the mule deer, they felt this. They knew something was different. The country had changed in some way they could feel before they could see it. A change felt before clouds arrived. Something in the air. Something in the grass moving or not moving."

He breathed.

"The elk turned and faced the pack."

"This was what elk did. This was what had always worked. The rack, the weight, the fury of a bull in his prime. It had worked against the bear. It had worked against the mule deer. He turned and faced them because turning and facing was what he knew and what his body was built for and what had kept him alive in this country across all the seasons of his life."

"The pack did not come straight at him."

"They spread. They moved to the sides, to the angles, the directions a bull elk's rack could not cover all at once. They were patient. When he turned to one side, they did not press; they simply waited as those on the other side moved a little closer. They had done this before. They knew how it worked. The elk's fury was real. They respected it, and they did not meet it directly. They just kept spreading, kept angling, kept being in more places than he could face at once."

"It took a long time. The elk was strong, and he fought hard. It cost the pack something; the younger ones learned things that day that they would carry the rest of their lives. But in the end, the elk went down. Not from one wound but from the accumulation of them, from the exhaustion of turning and turning and turning and there always being something at the angle he had just turned away from."

Old Hawk's hand moved on the medicine bundle again.

"The mule deer was in the broken country above the valley when it happened."

"He had gone there when the pack first arrived. Not running in panic, just moving, putting the steep ground between himself and what was below. The mule deer knew broken country. His legs were built for it, the hinds longer than the fronts, able to take steep ground at speed where the wolves struggled. He went up and found a ledge and stood on it and watched what happened in the valley below."

"He watched the elk fight."

"He watched the pack spread and angle and wait."

"He watched the elk go down."

"He stood on the ledge for a long time after it was over. The pack fed below him. They did not come up the slope that night; they had what they needed, and they were not hungry enough to work for more. The mule deer stood on his ledge and breathed the cold air and understood something that the elk had not understood or had understood too late."

"The pack was not a bear. You could not face the pack as you faced a bear. The pack did not come from one direction. It did not respond to fury. It was not impressed by the size of a rack or the weight behind a charge. The pack was many. It was patient. It did not fight on your terms. It fought on its own terms, and its terms were always the same. They just kept moving to the places he was not facing. There were always more places he was not facing than places he was."

"The mule deer came down from the broken country in the spring."

"He was careful. He learned the pack's patterns as he had learned the elk's. Where they ran, when they ran, what the wind said about where they were. He used the broken country when he needed to, and the valley when it was safe. He drank at the water at the hours when the pack was elsewhere. He was not comfortable. He was not safe. But he was alive."

"He was still alive."

Old Hawk's eyes moved from the fire to Watches Twice.

"The valley felt different without the elk," he said. "Larger somehow, and emptier, the absence of him a thing the mule deer felt but could not name. They had not loved each other. But the elk had been part of what the country was. Part of the country's meaning. And now that was gone, and the country was the pack's country. The mule deer moved through it carefully, using the broken ground, staying alive."

He looked at Watches Twice for a long moment.

He breathed carefully.

"The pack is still out there."

He did not say anything else.

Watches Twice sat with him until the fire burned low. Neither of them spoke again. Old Hawk's breathing became slower and then slower still. At some point in the long hours of the night, it simply stopped. Fires stopped when there was nothing left to feed them — not suddenly, not with drama, just less and less until there was nothing.

Watches Twice sat with him for a while after.

Then he reached out and took the medicine bundle from Old Hawk's hands, carefully, as you took something from someone who had been holding it a long time, and set it beside him.

He looked at Old Hawk's face in the last of the firelight.

He did not look like a man who had lost something. He looked like a man who had put something down.

* * *

After a while, Watches Twice rose.

The silver was still on the ground where it had always been. The pile of it, the accumulated weight of every assignment the Army had given him, every time the quartermaster had counted coins into his hand without looking at him, every time he had come back to this lodge and added what he had been paid to what was already there.

He looked at it for a long time.

Then he crouched down and gathered it all, every coin, every silver dollar, the whole of it, and put it in his kit.

He did not count it.

He stood up and looked at Old Hawk one more time.

107

Then he went out into the night.

The Crow camp was quiet around him.

He stood outside the lodge for a while, looking at the stars and feeling the particular quality of the dark that came after something irreversible had happened. Not worse than other dark, not heavier, just different. Everything was different on the other side of an irreversible thing.

He did not go to anyone in the camp.

He went to the picket line and tended his horse. Then he went back to his own lodge and lay down and looked at the smoke hole above him and listened to the camp breathe around him.

He did not sleep for a long time.

* * *

In the morning, he packed what he needed.

He did not say goodbye to anyone. There was no one left whose goodbye mattered. He mounted his horse and rode out of the Crow camp and did not look back and felt no eyes on him when he went because the eyes that had always been there were gone now. The going was just going, just movement, just a man on a horse riding away from a place that had stopped being the place it was.

He rode east.

Not with a plan. Not with a destination. He had always ridden east, past the invisible line, further, as his father had taught him to move through country, reading it, letting it tell him what it knew.

The country told him things as he rode.

It told him that the grass was shorter than it used to be. It told him that the sight lines were different. Not the landscape itself but what moved through it, which was less than it used to be, the particular absence of the herds, a thing you felt before you could say what you felt. It told him that the trails he crossed were different. More of them, the wheeled kind, the kind that said settlement and permanence and the white world's understanding of land, which was as something to be divided and owned and held rather than something to be moved through.

He rode through it all and let it tell him what it knew.

He rode for many days.

* * *

The town near the reservation was not much.

A main street with a handful of buildings, most of them raw lumber still pale from the mill. A livery. A dry goods store. A place that sold whiskey without advertising the fact. The street between the buildings was rutted from wagon wheels and pocked with the particular mud that came from too many animals and not enough drainage, and no one caring enough to fix either problem.

Around the edges of the town, the reservation began, not marked by anything official, no line in the ground, just a change in the quality of the settlement. The buildings further apart. Smaller. The particular look of places where people lived because they had been told to live there rather than because they had chosen it.

Watches Twice rode in on a Tuesday morning in the fall.

He tied his horse at the rail outside the dry goods store and went in.

The man behind the counter was white. Middle-aged. The kind of face that had settled into its permanent expression years ago and was not going to change. He looked at Watches Twice with the flat assessment of a man who had decided what kind of place he was in and what kind of people came through it and had organized his expectations accordingly.

Watches Twice looked at the shelves. The goods on them. The prices

109

marked on small cards, in handwriting that had the confidence of a man who knew no one would argue with what he wrote.

The door opened behind him.

Eméškeha'e came in with two other women, Cheyenne, all three of them moving with the purposefulness of people who had come to do something specific. She was older than when he had last seen her; the years had taken from her, but the quality of her was the same. The particular stillness. The competence of someone who had survived things without announcing it.

She did not look at him. He was just a man at the shelves, and she had a purpose.

She went to the counter.

Watches Twice did not move. He kept his eyes on the shelves and listened.

The man's voice had a quality to it that Watches Twice recognized as not exactly hostile, not exactly cruel, just the flatness of someone who had decided what the transaction was before it started and was not going to be moved from that decision by anything the person across the counter said or did. He stated a number. Eméškeha'e said something quietly. The man restated the number. The same number. Not a question either time.

Watches Twice looked at a can on the shelf in front of him and did not look at the counter.

The silence that followed the second number lasted a moment.

Then the door opened and closed.

He turned.

Eméškeha'e and the two women were outside. He could see them through the window, standing on the step, saying something to each other, their hands empty. Then they walked off down the street together, their backs straight, their pace unhurried.

Watches Twice looked at the man behind the counter.

The man looked back at him with the same flat assessment he had given everyone else.

Watches Twice went outside.

He stood on the step and watched the three women walking away until they turned a corner and were gone.

Then he went to his horse.

He reached into his kit.

He took out the silver, all of it, the whole accumulated weight of it, and held the pouch in his hand for a moment.

Then he went back inside.

The man behind the counter looked at him with the same flat assessment.

He set the silver on the counter.

All of it, the whole accumulated weight of every assignment, every march, every ridge above every valley, every report delivered plainly without interpretation, the years accumulated into just what was there.

The pouch made a sound on the wood of the counter that was the sound heavy silver made, specific, weighty.

The man looked at the pouch. Then at Watches Twice.

Watches Twice looked at him steadily.

"The Cheyenne woman who was just in here," he said. "And the others that come in from the reservation. Whatever they owe you, clear it. Whatever they need, they get it. All of it covered by what's on that counter."

The man looked at the pouch again. He was calculating. Watches Twice could see it in his face. The arithmetic happening, the options being assessed, the particular expression of a man who was trying to determine whether the person across the counter from him was someone he could argue with or someone he couldn't.

The man looked at the pouch again, then at Watches Twice.

Something in his face changed. It was not fear, not respect, just the recognition of a man who understood he was not the one deciding how this was going to go.

Watches Twice did not move. He didn't need to.

"And you'll give her full value for every coin," Watches Twice said. "Not what you think it's worth. What it is."

The man looked at the silver one more time.

Then he reached under the counter for his ledger.

He opened it. He picked up his pen. He looked at Watches Twice.

"Name," he said.

"Put it down to whoever needs it," Watches Twice said. "That's the name."

The man wrote something in the ledger. He nodded once, not warmly, not gratefully, just the nod of a man completing a transaction he had decided to complete.

Watches Twice looked at the silver on the counter one last time.

Then he went out.

He untied his horse. He mounted. He sat for a moment, looking down the street in the direction Emëškeha'e had gone.

Then he turned his horse and rode.

* * *

The reservation country moved past him on both sides, the short grass, the sky enormous over it, the particular quality of a landscape that had been remade into something its original inhabitants had not made and did not recognize as their own.

He rode through it without stopping.

Further.

Always further.

12

First Light

The fish weren't moving yet.

Watches Twice stood in the shallows with the line in the water and the early light coming flat across the river and did not mind. The fishing was partly about fish and partly about the state that came before the day started. The particular quality of standing in cold water on an October morning with nothing required of you except attention, which was the one thing he had always had in abundance.

The Tongue ran shallow here, maybe knee deep at the center, the water clear enough that he could see the riverbed, pale sand and flat stones, the occasional dark shape of a deeper pool where the current had worked the bottom into something worth investigating. Cottonwoods along both banks, gone to yellow now, the leaves moving in the small wind that came off the breaks before the sun got to work. Above him on the eastern bluff, the sandstone caught the first light and went orange, the pines along the ridge still dark.

He had been here a year.

Not exactly here, not standing in this specific bend of the river every morning for a year. But here in the sense of this country. The Tongue River drainage. The breaks and the pine ridges and the sandstone bluffs and the small cabin he had built in the draw above the bank where the cottonwoods gave way to the slope and the slope gave way to the first of the sandstone outcroppings that ran south toward Wyoming.

He had stopped here not because he decided to stop but because the country had a particular quality that held him. He had been riding east, and the Tongue River had been in his path. He had crossed it and gone up into the breaks for a while and come back down and crossed it again. At some point, he had understood that he was not going to cross it a third time. Not yet.

He had built the cabin in the fall of the previous year. Not much of a cabin, one room, a fireplace he had constructed from the flat sandstone that lay everywhere on the hillside above, a door that fit well enough to keep the wind out. He had cut the logs from the pine ridge and notched them himself and chinked the gaps with mud and river clay. It had held through one Montana winter, which was sufficient evidence that it would hold through another.

The horse was at the picket outside. The fire was banked. The morning was his.

The line moved.

He lifted the rod. It was a simple thing, a branch he had cut and cured and strung, and felt the weight of it. A cutthroat, from the fight of it. He worked it in without hurrying, took it from the water, and looked at it for a moment. The particular colors of it, the red slash marks along the jaw that gave it its name, the eye clear and untroubled, and then put it in the basket he had set in the shallows.

That was one.

He reset the line and stood in the water, and the morning continued around him.

He was not unhappy here. He had been trying to establish that for himself across the year of being here and had arrived at something close to a conclusion. Not unhappy. Not the opposite of unhappy either, not what he had felt in the Crow camp when Old Hawk was still alive, the fire was built high, and the old man's eyes found him when he came through the entrance with the particular quality of seeing that said you are here, I see that you are here, that is enough.

That was gone. That specific thing was gone. He had stopped looking for it elsewhere because it was not there. It had been one man and one lodge, and it was over.

But the river was here. The breaks were here. The work came when the agency needed him, or the Army needed him. Between the work, the river was here, and the fishing was here. The October mornings were here, and that was sufficient.

He caught two more fish before the sun cleared the bluffs and the morning shifted from early to regular.

He waded out of the water, cleaned the fish on the flat rock he used, wrapped them, and set them in the cabin's cool for later.

He had work today.

* * *

The ride into Ashland took the better part of an hour along the Tongue River road.

He rode south and east, the river on his left, the breaks rising on his right. Sandstone outcroppings and pine ridges, and the occasional draw running down from the high country with a trickle of water at the bottom that would be dry by December. The cottonwoods along the river were past their best yellow now, some of them gone to brown, the leaves coming down in the small wind and settling on the water and moving with the current south.

He had ridden this road enough times to have stopped consciously noticing it, the information in the body rather than the mind.

He passed the place, about four miles out, where the trail came down from the breaks and crossed the river at a wide, shallow ford. He had come down that trail in October of 1878, six years ago, following Dull Knife's band through the Pine Ridge country. He had stood above this drainage on a ridge, looked down at a village in a valley, understood what he was seeing, and ridden back to report it.

He rode past the ford without stopping.

The country was different now. More settled. The trails different, more of them, more defined, the signs of people living in a place rather than moving through it. A Cheyenne family had built a cabin a mile upstream from the ford, smoke coming from it this morning, horses in a rough corral. Further on, a cluster of three or four structures around a bend of the river, washing on a line, a dog that came out to watch him pass without barking.

The people who had walked home were building something in the country they had walked home to.

He noted it without examining it.

* * *

Ashland came into view around the last bend of the river road. It was a small collection of buildings on both sides of the Tongue, the river running through the middle of it. Raw lumber still, most of it, though a few of the older buildings had weathered to grey. The trader's store. The agency office. The post. The saloon that didn't advertise itself as a saloon.

And St. Labre, on the north side of town, set back from the river road, new buildings, pale from the mill, a bell tower catching the morning light. He could hear, faintly, the sound of children, though it was early yet and the day's work at the school had not fully begun.

He rode to the agency office and tied his horse at the rail.

The agent's clerk was a young white man named Hartley who had been in this country eight months and treated everything in it with the provisional tolerance of someone who expected to be somewhere else by spring. He gave Watches Twice a packet of documents to be delivered to the trader and a verbal message to be passed to the Cheyenne headman whose camp was three miles up the river from Ashland.

Watches Twice took both without comment.

He was walking back to his horse when she came out of the trader's store.

He recognized her before he understood that he had recognized her.

That was how it always worked, the information arriving complete before the mind caught up to it. He stopped walking. His horse looked at him.

* * *

She was older. Six years older than the march south, seven years older than Darlington. The years had taken some things, but added others. Her face more settled into itself, the quality of her neither diminished nor softened but deepened, the way the river deepened in certain places where the current had worked the bottom long enough to make something permanent.

She was carrying a wrapped package from the trader's, supplies of some kind, nothing heavy, the kind of errand you did before the school day started. She was alone. She was moving with the particular efficiency of a woman who had somewhere to be and knew exactly how to get there.

She did not look at him.

He was a Crow man standing at the rail outside the agency office. The country occasionally had Crow men in it. She had a package and a direction. He played a part in neither of them.

Then her horse, tied two posts down from his, shifted and stepped sideways into the rail, and the rail caught the lead rope at the wrong angle. The knot that had been good enough for standing quietly was suddenly not good enough for a horse that had decided to be interested in something on the other side of the street.

Watches Twice crossed the distance between them in three steps and had the lead rope sorted and the horse settled before she had finished adjusting the package in her arms.

She looked at him.

Not with recognition. With the ordinary assessment of a person encountering a stranger who has done something useful. The assessment was quick and complete, its quality was familiar to him in a way he had not examined.

"Thank you," she said.

In English. Her English was careful, the words placed with the slight deliberateness of someone who had learned the language as an adult and had not yet stopped thinking about it.

"The knot," he said. He showed her the hitch he had used. "This one holds better."

She looked at the knot. Then at him.

"You work for the agency," she said. Not a question, she had seen him come out of the office.

"Sometimes," he said.

She nodded once in the way of someone filing information and moving on. She checked the knot herself, running her thumb across it, testing it, not taking his word for it, and then she untied her horse and mounted with the package balanced across her knees.

"Thank you," she said again, and rode the short distance to St. Labre's gate and went through it.

He stood at the rail and watched the gate close behind her, a slight upturn to the corners of his mouth.

His horse looked at him again with the patient expression horses brought to waiting.

He went to the trader's and delivered the documents.

* * *

The ride home took longer than the ride out.

Not because he rode slower, he rode the same pace he always rode. But the light was different coming back, the afternoon light hitting the sandstone bluffs from the west and bringing out colors that the morning light flattened. The orange of the sandstone had turned red. The pines above it darkened against a sky that had deepened across the day toward something close to purple at the edges.

He rode the river road. The country told him what it always told him, and he received it the way he always received everything, completely, without hurry.

He tended his horse at the picket.

He went inside, built the fire, and cooked two of the three fish from the morning on the flat iron pan he had acquired from the trader three months ago in exchange for two days of riding.

He ate.

He sat by the fire and listened to the river.

The river made the sound of water moving over stone in the dark, which was a sound he had been listening to his whole life in one form or another, the sound of the country being what it was, regardless of what happened in it.

He thought about the knot.

About the way she had checked it herself without taking his word for it. He smiled again.

He did not think about anything else specifically. The information was there, filed the way he filed everything, available when he needed it.

He banked the fire.

He lay down and looked at the dark above him and listened to the Tongue River moving south through the October night toward Miles City and the Yellowstone and whatever came after that.

He was still here.

13

Recognition

She thought about the knot.

Not first thing, first thing she thought about was the school, which was what she thought about first thing every morning now, the specific inventory of what the day would require of her and whether she had enough left to give it. But after that, in the space between rising and the fire being ready, she thought about the knot.

The Crow man at the rail. Crossing the distance without hesitation, sorting the rope before she had finished adjusting her package. Showing her the hitch, this one holds better, without making anything of it. Not waiting for gratitude. Not extending the moment. Just showed her and stepped back.

She had checked it herself. He had not seemed surprised by that.

She could not remember the last time a man had not seemed surprised by that.

She ate what she had made for breakfast and thought about whether she had room in her life for thinking about a man and concluded that she probably did not. She thought about the knot again anyway.

It was that kind of morning.

* * *

She rode into Ashland in the early light, the Tongue River on her right running shallow and clear, the cottonwoods along the bank still holding some of their yellow, though most of it was gone now, the leaves down and moving in the current. The sandstone bluffs caught the morning light above her, turning orange. The pines on the ridge were dark.

She had been making this ride for three weeks. It had the quality now of a thing done enough times to become automatic. The horse knew the road, the distance known to her body, and the time it took, settled into something she no longer calculated. She arrived at St. Labre, tied her horse at the gate, and went inside, and the day began.

* * *

The day was what her days had become. She did not think about the knot again until she was standing at the trader's store in the middle of the afternoon with a list of things the school needed and the trader telling her which of those things he had and which he didn't, and she was filing the information away when the door opened behind her, and the quality of the room changed. The trader stopped talking.

She felt it before she understood it.

Not a sound. Not a movement. Just something in the air of the room shifted, pressure or temperature, something the body registered before the mind caught up.

She turned.

He was large in the doorway, in a way that made it look as if it had been built for a different scale of person. Not young, she put him somewhere past fifty, the face weathered to something that had stopped changing a long time ago. The kind of face that said whatever was going to happen to it had already happened. He moved through the doorway and into the store with the caution of a man who had learned that moving carefully through spaces was smarter than moving aggressively, and had been practicing it long enough that the carefulness had become natural.

He set his list on the counter and waited for the trader.

She went back to her own transaction. The trader started to speak again.

Then his eyes moved to her.

She felt it before she looked up at him. The specific weight of being looked at by someone whose look had a quality to it she had encountered before in her life and had learned to be careful around. She looked back, briefly, then let her eyes drop. Holding his stare wasn't comfortable.

His eyes were flat. Not cold, cold would have been something, cold would have been a feeling, an investment. These were the eyes of a man reading terrain, taking in what was there rather than what he wanted it to be. They moved over her face and stayed.

She glanced back and held his gaze for a moment.

Her eyes dropped again.

She picked up her package from the counter.

She turned toward the door.

He was between her and it.

Not blocking it. There was room to go around him, but stepping towards the door meant stepping towards him, towards what felt like grief and danger. He was large and still. His eyes had not moved from her. The distance between where he stood and the door was not great, but it was the distance between her and the outside, and she found herself stopping rather than crossing it.

She was not afraid. She did not think of it as fear. She thought of it as an accurate assessment of a situation that had not yet declared itself.

The door opened.

Watches Twice came in out of the afternoon light.

* * *

He saw Declan first.

The recognition arrived complete, before the mind caught up to it. He stopped just inside the doorway. He had not seen this man in nine years. He had been fifteen years old, sitting on a rise watching a large, still man shoot nine buffalo from a hollow below him, and the man had turned and looked at him across a hundred and thirty yards with eyes that saw everything and were moved by nothing. He had told it to Old Hawk. Old Hawk had said, the Cheyenne call him Heávohe.

He was older. The hair at his temples had gone grey, and the face had taken on more of what the years had added to it. He was riding a mule now. Watches Twice had seen it at the rail outside, a good animal, patient, standing with the indifference mules brought to everything.

Then he saw Eméškeha'e's face.

He understood immediately.

The cheekbones. The stillness. Her presence in a space, there without filling it unnecessarily. Declan was looking at a Cheyenne woman in a trader's store in Ashland, Montana, and seeing a Crow woman named Ashkáale who had the same quality, the same bearing, the same competence that didn't announce itself, and who had been dead for three years.

He was not going to find her here.

But the look was the kind that didn't know how to stop.

The woman was waiting with accurate stillness for the eyes to move.

Watches Twice crossed the room.

He went to where Eméškeha'e was standing and said, in a voice that had the quality of continuation rather than beginning, the voice of a conversation already in progress, "Hartley said the ford is high this week. Did you come in on the north road?"

She looked at him.

A beat, brief, the space of a breath, in which he saw her understand what he was doing. Then she said, evenly, "The north road. Yes."

"Good." He set his own list on the counter beside hers as if this were the natural thing, as if they had arranged to meet here and were simply completing the arrangement. "He said he'd have the papers ready by Thursday."

"Thursday," she said. "All right."

He did not look at Declan. He did not need to. He felt the eyes move, the flat assessment shifting from Eméškeha'e to him, those eyes reading everything, taking in what was there and recalibrating.

The trader came back from the storeroom with a box of supplies.

The room was quiet for a moment.

Then Declan picked up his order from the counter, tucked it under one arm, and walked to the door. He did not hurry. He did not look back. He went out, and the door closed behind him. The quality of the room changed again. The pressure lifted, the air returning to what it had been before he arrived.

Watches Twice did not move for a moment.

Through the window, he watched Declan load the mule, methodical and unhurried, with the same precision he brought to everything. The mule stood with its ears back in mild objection and then forward again in resignation. Declan checked the load, checked the cinch, and mounted. He sat for a moment on the mule in the street outside the trader's store in Ashland, Montana, in the fall of 1884, a large, weathered man on a patient mule with a Cheyenne scabbard still on the saddle, the scabbard worn now, the pattern faded from years of weather and use.

Then he rode east.

He did not look back.

He never looked back.

* * *

Watches Twice watched him go until the bend in the river road took him.

Eméškeha'e was still standing beside him.

She was looking at the window too. Then she looked at Watches Twice.

He turned.

She studied his face for a moment, the specific quality of her looking, the assessment that was quick and complete.

"You knew him," she said. Not a question.

"I knew of him," Watches Twice said.

She considered the distinction. Then she said, "What was that?"

Not a question exactly. More the shape of a question, the sound of a woman who had accurate instincts and wanted them confirmed.

"A man who lost something," Watches Twice said. "A long time ago."

She looked at the window again. The street was empty now. The mule and its rider were gone around the bend, gone east, gone back into whatever story they belonged to.

"He was looking at me," she said.

"Yes."

"Not at me."

"No," Watches Twice said. "Not at you."

She was quiet for a moment. Then she said, "What's your name?"

"Bíalish Dúua."

She heard it and nodded. Then, "Eméškeha'e."

He received it as she had received his, completely, without making anything of it.

The trader finished tallying her order and read the total back to her. She paid. She picked up her package. She looked at Watches Twice once more, the same quick, complete assessment, and then she went out.

He stood at the counter and listened to her horse move away from the rail and down the street.

Then he gave the trader his own list.

* * *

She rode west in the afternoon light.

The river ran beside her, shallow and quick, the cottonwoods along the bank casting long shadows across the road. The sandstone bluffs above were red now in the low sun, the pines above them dark.

She thought about what he had said.

A man who lost something. A long time ago.

She knew what that looked like from the inside. She knew the specific quality of loss that had been carried so long it became part of how she moved through the world, not grief anymore, just weight. Permanent, structural, the load-bearing kind.

She thought about Watches Twice crossing the room. Not rushing. Not announcing himself. Just crossing the distance and being present and saying something ordinary as if the ordinary thing were all there was.

She had done that herself. Walked into situations and made herself present without making herself the reason. She knew how much that cost and how much practice it took.

She rode along the Tongue River in the afternoon light and thought about a man who had done a thing she recognized and had not asked for anything in return for doing it.

* * *

He rode north. By the time he reached the draw above the river, the light was almost gone. The sandstone bluffs had gone from red to grey. The pines were losing their shape against the dark. The river sounded the same as always, steady and indifferent, the country being what it was.

He tended his horse.

He went inside, built the fire, and sat with it for a while.

He thought about Declan riding east on the mule with the Cheyenne scabbard on the saddle. Nine years since the hollow and the nine buffalo and the eyes across a hundred and thirty yards. The boy on the rise had not known then what he understood now, that a man could lose something so completely that he carried the shape of it everywhere he went and kept finding it in places it wasn't.

He thought about Eméškeha'e saying not at me and meaning it accurately, her precision with words, her refusal to take more from his answer than it contained.

He thought about her name.

Eméškeha'e.

He did not say it aloud. He just held it where it was — filed, available, the information there when he needed it.

The fire moved.

The river moved outside.

He was still here.

14

St. Labre

St. Labre Indian School sat on the north side of Ashland, where the Tongue River made a broad bend, and the land flattened enough to build on. The buildings were new, raw lumber still pale from the mill, the smell of cut pine and fresh plaster not yet worn away by the seasons. A bell tower rose above the main building, visible from the river road a mile out. A fence ran the perimeter, not high, not the fence of a prison but the fence of an institution, the kind that said *here* and *there* and made the difference between them official.

The Ursuline nuns who ran it had come from the east with their habits, their mission, and their genuine belief that what they were doing was necessary and good. They were not cruel women. They were women who had been given a task by their church and their government and had organized themselves to accomplish it with the efficiency of people who believed in their work. The task was to take Cheyenne children and make them into something the government found acceptable. The belief was that this was salvation. The children did not always understand it as salvation. The children were learning.

In the fall of 1884, there were thirty-one children at St. Labre. Some had been brought willingly from families who had been told that education was survival, that the world had changed, and their children would need different tools to move through it, that this school was the tool. Some had been brought unwillingly. A few had been brought in the night, which was something that had happened elsewhere and would happen here too before long, though it had not happened yet.

They slept in dormitories on iron cots with wool blankets. They ate at long tables in a room that smelled of boiled food. They wore the clothes the school provided, grey for the boys, dark blue for the girls, the same for everyone, the sameness the point.

They were thirty-one Cheyenne children on the Tongue River in the country their people had walked five hundred miles to get back to, and they were learning to be something else.

* * *

Eméškeha'e arrived before the bell most mornings.

She came in through the side gate, tied her horse to the post the nuns had designated for her, and went to the room where the younger children spent their first hours of the day. She was the interpreter. She was the bridge. That was the word Sister Marguerite used: bridge, as if the distance between Cheyenne and English were a river to be crossed rather than something taken away. Eméškeha'e had not corrected her. Sister Marguerite meant well. Most of them meant well.

She hung her coat on the hook inside the door and looked at the room.

Fourteen children, ages five to ten, seated at desks arranged in rows. The desks were new, everything here was new, the wood still bright, the inkwells not yet stained. The children sat with the particular stillness of children who had learned that stillness was what was required of them here. Not the stillness of comfort. The stillness of caution.

Sister Anne was at the front of the room, writing words on the blackboard in her careful hand. The children watched the chalk move. Some of them were following the lesson. Others were watching the window, the Tongue River visible through it, the cottonwoods bare now, the water catching the morning light.

Eméškeha'e took her place at the side of the room where she could see both the children and the sister and be available when either needed her.

The lesson continued.

After a while, Sister Anne moved to the window to adjust the curtain against the glare, and for a moment her back was to the room.

In the corner, two boys leaned toward each other, and one of them said something in Cheyenne, something small and quick, the kind of thing children said to each other in the margins of adult attention. The sound of it moved through the room like water finding a low place. Three or four of the other children heard it, and something in their posture changed. Like a small loosening, the breath dropping, the particular ease that came from hearing the sounds that meant home.

Then Sister Anne turned back from the window.

The two boys straightened. The sound stopped. The loosening reversed itself, the children returning to their careful stillness, their eyes to the blackboard.

Sister Anne had not heard it. She picked up her chalk and continued the lesson.

Eméškeha'e stood at the side of the room and watched the children watching the blackboard and did not move.

She had not been asked to stop them from speaking Cheyenne to each other. That rule existed; it was in the document she had been given when she started, the list of the school's expectations, *English only in the classrooms and dormitories.* But no one had yet enforced it directly in front of her.

The children had enforced it themselves.

They knew what was required before anyone told them. They had learned this place and what it wanted, and they were already giving in. She stood at the side of the room and looked at fourteen children in rows. She could not name the thing she saw there, the beginning of the worst of it. She carried it out through the side gate at day's end and rode home with it down the river road.

* * *

Watches Twice had been to Ashland four times in six days.

The first time was legitimate. Hartley had papers to deliver to the agency office, and Watches Twice happened to be there when Hartley needed them moved. He delivered them. He went directly to the office, directly back to his horse, and directly home and did not go past the school.

He told himself this on the ride back. He had not gone past the school. He had done his work and left.

The second time, he checked the ford. The ford was the shallow crossing point a mile south of Ashland, where the river could be read for depth and current before wagons committed to it. Useful in spring when the snowmelt ran it high and fast, considerably less useful in October when the Tongue was running clear and ankle-deep and had been for two months. He checked it anyway. It was fine. He rode back through Ashland on his way home because it was on the way, and it would have been inefficient to go around it.

He did not see her.

He did not tell himself he had not been looking.

The third time, he had business at the trader's. Real business, salt, and a new lead rope, things he needed. He bought what he needed and came out and stood at the rail for longer than the tying and untying of a horse required.

He did not see her.

He rode home.

The fourth time, he did not invent a reason. He simply rode into Ashland in the late afternoon and tied his horse at the rail outside the trader's and stood there with the patient expression he brought to waiting and waited.

He had been there perhaps twenty minutes when she came out of the school gate.

She was moving at the pace of a woman who had somewhere to be. Her coat was on. Her hat was on. She had a bag over one shoulder, and she was walking with the particular efficiency he had noticed the first time he saw her. The competence that didn't announce itself, the movement of someone who knew exactly where they were going and how long it would take to get there.

She had seen him.

He could tell by the slight adjustment in her bearing as she came down the street, the set of her shoulders, the quality of her attention, going carefully neutral, the way attention went neutral when someone was working not to show they had noticed something. She was going to walk past him. She was going to walk past him and keep going, and he would have to decide whether to let her.

She reached him.

She passed him.

"Eméškeha'e," he said.

She stopped.

Not because she was surprised. She had known he was there. She stopped because he had used her name, her real name, the one she had given him in the trader's store eleven days ago, and that was a different thing from calling out to a stranger.

He crossed the distance between them.

She turned and looked at him with an assessment that was quick and complete, and this time it had something in it that had not been there before, something not quite amusement but in the neighborhood of it.

"You walk fast," he said.

"Yes," she said. "I walk fast because I am not lazy. I do not loiter outside of schools and shops."

He opened his mouth.

He closed it.

Something happened to his face that had not happened to his face in recent memory. The heat rising in it, the particular warmth of a man who has been seen doing exactly what he was doing and has no adequate response to the seeing of it. He was a man who had tracked 353 people through the Nebraska sandhills. He had stood on ridges above things that would have broken most men and reported what he saw without his voice changing. He had set silver on a counter and looked a man into compliance without saying anything at all.

He turned red.

"I..." he said. "I, umm..."

She laughed.

It came out of her the way things do when they've been held too long. Not polite. Not careful. Just there and real, a true laugh at a true thing. He had never heard her laugh before and did not know what it would sound like. It was lower than he expected, and it stayed with her longer. When it faded into a smile, he forgot what he meant to say.

She looked at him with the smile still present at the corners of her mouth.

"Walk me to Vóhkohe-méne," she said.

He looked at her.

"My horse," she said.

It was not a question. She was already moving.

He fell into step beside her.

They walked the short distance to the school gate, where her horse was tied at the post. She untied it and checked the cinch with the efficiency of someone who always checked the cinch and did not assume things were as she had left them.

"You have been to Ashland four times this week," she said. Not looking at him. Checking the cinch.

"Six days," he said.

She looked at him then.

"Six days," she said.

"Four times," he said.

Something moved across her face. Not the laugh again, something quieter than the laugh and more considered.

"The ford," she said.

"It was fine."

"I imagine it was."

She gathered the reins. She had not mounted yet. She stood at her horse's shoulder and looked at him with the assessment that had been quick and complete every time before and was now something slightly different, slower, or not slower exactly, but deeper. The same way the river was deeper in certain places where the current had been working the bottom long enough to make something permanent.

"I saw two boys today," she said. "In the classroom. They were speaking to each other in Cheyenne. Just a few words. Sister Anne's back was turned."

He waited.

"Before she turned around," Eméškeha'e said, "they stopped. On their own. No one told them to. They just stopped."

She looked at the river. The Tongue running shallow in the October light, the cottonwoods bare along the bank, the water moving south.

"They are five and six years old," she said. "And they already know."

He did not say anything. There was nothing to say that was adequate to what she had just told him. He stood beside her horse and listened and let what she had said be what it was.

After a moment, she mounted. She looked down at him with the expression he was beginning to know, the one that took what was there and asked nothing more of it. "Tomorrow," she said.

"Tomorrow," he said.

She rode west along the river road. He stood at the school gate and watched her go until the bend took her.

Then he went to his horse and rode north.

* * *

The fire was going by the time he reached the cabin. He had built it that morning before he left and banked it, and it had held. He added wood, sat with it, and listened to the river.

He thought about two boys in a classroom on the Tongue River who had stopped speaking their own language before anyone made them.

He thought about Emėškeha'e saying they already know with the specific quality of a woman who also already knew and had been knowing it for eleven days and had not had anyone to say it to until now.

He thought about her laugh.

The fire moved.

The river moved outside.

Tomorrow, he had said.

He was still here.

15

Vohkoohe

She left before first light.

This was her habit, and had been since she started at St. Labre, the early leaving giving her time on the river road before the day made its demands. She liked the road in the dark. Liked the specific quality of the country before the sun arrived. The sandstone bluffs were shapes rather than things. The river sounded louder in the dark because there was nothing else to listen to.

Vóhkohe-méne knew the road. She had ridden her enough times that she moved without being asked, the particular intelligence of a horse that had learned a route and taken some satisfaction in knowing it. She was a good horse. She had paid more than she should have for her and had not regretted it. She was strong and steady, and she had not given her any reason to question the transaction.

Until today.

She was perhaps two miles from home, the sky beginning to gray at the eastern edge, the cottonwoods along the river still dark against it, when Vóhkohe-méne stopped.

Not the gradual slowing of a horse that had found something interesting. A stop. Immediate, complete, the forward motion simply ending, her weight shifting back onto her haunches, her head coming up.

She felt it before she understood it, the specific quality of a horse that had decided something was wrong and was prepared to argue about it.

She looked ahead.

In the road, perhaps fifteen feet ahead, a cottontail rabbit sat.

It was not doing anything. It was simply sitting, back legs folded, front paws together, ears up, regarding the road with the calm, philosophical attention of something that had nowhere to be and no opinion about anything. It was perhaps the least threatening thing in the Tongue River country that morning.

Vóhkohe-méne did not see it that way.

Her ears went flat. Her head came up higher, turned toward the rabbit at the specific angle horses use when they have identified something as a credible threat and are monitoring it closely. A sound came out of her. It was not quite a whinny, lower than that, the vibrating protest horses made when the world had presented them with something unacceptable.

She squeezed with her legs.

She did not move forward. She moved sideways instead. One step, two steps, to the edge of the road where the bank dropped toward the river, and then she stopped again and reassessed the rabbit, which had not moved, which had not done anything, which was simply sitting there being a rabbit in a road.

"Vóhkohe-méne," she said. Firmly. The voice she used when she meant business.

The rabbit's nose twitched.

This was apparently enough. Vóhkohe-méne made her decision —the decision horses made when they had concluded that the situation required immediate unilateral action, and she executed it with great commitment. She went left, then right, then up, and Eméškeha'e, who had been a horsewoman her whole life and had ridden through things that would have unseated most riders, was not expecting the combination of left-right-up in that particular sequence and went off his right side with the specific gracelessness of someone who had been given no time to be graceful about it.

She hit the mud at the edge of the bank.

For a moment, she simply lay there and looked at the sky, which was getting lighter by degrees and was indifferent to what had just happened.

Then she sat up.

Vóhkohe-méne had relocated herself to the far side of the road. She stood with her ears pinned, her head high and angled toward the rabbit, taking small incremental steps backward. She was not running, just the steady retreat of an animal continuously revising its estimate of safe distance in the rabbit's favor.

The rabbit sat.

The horse stepped back.

The rabbit's nose twitched again.

The horse made the sound again and tossed his head with great conviction, as if this would help.

The rabbit regarded him briefly with one eye and then looked away.

Eméškeha'e looked at her horse. She looked at the rabbit. She looked at her coat, which was muddy, and her hands, which were muddy, and considered her situation.

"Hóo'o, néstse! Néhešéhe, mo'éhno'ha!"

The sound of her own voice in the gray morning, the specific precision of Cheyenne profanity delivered to a horse who had earned it, was slightly satisfying. She began trying to wipe the mud from her face with the back of her hand, which was also muddy, which was not improving things.

She did not hear the rider coming until the horse was nearly at the bend.

* * *

Watches Twice had been riding south.

This was his habit lately, South in the mornings, the river road, the specific quality of the Tongue in the early light. He was simply riding south, which happened to be the direction that eventually reached the school and the road Eméškeha'e used to get there, and the general vicinity of where she was at this hour of the morning.

He heard her before he saw her.

The words came from around the bend, a woman's voice, not frightened, not calling for help, just the precise sound of someone delivering a thorough assessment of a situation they found unacceptable. He caught *mo'éhno'ha* clearly. The rest he caught enough of to understand the direction.

He rode around the bend.

She was sitting in the mud at the edge of the road where the bank dropped toward the river. Not injured, he could see that immediately. The way she was sitting was that of someone angry rather than hurt, upright, hands pressed flat on the ground on either side of her, in the posture of someone who had arrived somewhere they had not intended to be. Her coat was muddy. Her hat was muddy. There was mud on her face and in her hair, and she was wiping it away with the back of her hand, which was not improving the situation.

Her horse stood on the far side of the road.

She was a good-looking animal. The dark bay with the white blaze that Watches Twice had seen tied at the school gate. She stood with her ears flat and her head high and turned toward the center of the road, where a cottontail rabbit sat with complete indifference to everything around it. Every few seconds, Vóhkohe-méne took another small step backward, not fleeing, just the steady incremental retreat of a horse that had made a decision about safe distance and was continuously revising it.

The rabbit sat.

The horse stepped back.

Watches Twice looked at the rabbit.

He looked at the horse.

He looked at Emėškeha'e sitting in the mud with her opinion of the morning.

He dismounted.

He went to Vóhkohe-méne first, speaking quietly, not reaching for the lead rope immediately, just being present and still. That worked with horses who had decided the world was dangerous. The horse's ears came forward cautiously. She allowed Watches Twice to take the reins. She came along but kept herself angled so that Watches Twice was between her and the rabbit, which she continued to monitor with one eye.

Watches Twice walked her to where Emėškeha'e was sitting.

She looked up.

She had mud on her nose. There was a streak of it across her left cheekbone. She had stopped trying to wipe it off, which suggested she had accepted that the wiping was not helping and was now simply sitting with it, along with her assessment of the morning.

He held out the reins.

She did not take them immediately. She looked at her horse with the expression of a woman reassessing a relationship she had considered settled.

"Vóhkohe-méne," she said.

The name came out with the weight of a name that no longer fit the animal it belonged to.

The horse nickered softly and dipped her head once in the gesture that could mean several things and, in this case, appeared to mean nothing useful.

"A rabbit," she said. She said it in English with great deliberateness, the way you said a thing you needed to be absolutely clear about. "A horse. A big, strong horse. Afraid of a rabbit."

Watches Twice said nothing.

He was being very careful.

She looked at him.

"Her name is Vohkoohe," she said. "From this day."

Something moved in Watches Twice's face. He could not prevent it entirely. He managed to prevent it from becoming what it wanted to become, which was a laugh, and converted it instead into something that was not quite a smile and not quite nothing.

"Do not," she said.

He did not.

The rabbit, apparently satisfied with its morning, hopped away in no particular direction and disappeared into the brush at its own pace. Not because of anything anyone did. Just because it was done.

The horse watched it go.

Her ears came forward.

She was not fully convinced it was over.

Watches Twice offered Eméškeha'e his hand.

She looked at it for a moment with a quick, complete assessment. Then she took it, and he helped her up, and she stood and looked at her coat and her boots and the general state of herself and made a sound that was not a word in any language but communicated clearly.

She took the reins from him. She looked at her horse, *Vohkoohe* now, apparently permanently, and she looked back at her with the expression of an animal that understood something had changed and was not sure it was good.

"She runs like a deer," Watches Twice said.

She looked at her.

"She used to," she said.

* * *

He rode with her to Ashland.

Not because she asked him to. Not because she needed him to. She was perfectly capable of riding to Ashland on her own and had been doing it every morning for weeks. But she had mud on her face, and her horse had apparently lost his name this morning. Watches Twice had nowhere else to be, and she did not tell him not to come.

So he rode along.

They rode south on the river road in the early light, the Tongue on their left running shallow and clear, the cottonwoods bare along the bank, the sandstone bluffs going orange as the sun cleared the ridge. The cold was sharp but not bitter. The kind of cold that felt clean rather than threatening, the kind that would be gone by midmorning.

She had cleaned her face as best she could at the river, crouching at the bank, the cold water doing what it could. The mud was mostly gone from her face. Her coat was a different matter.

They rode without talking for a while. This was comfortable in the specific way that silence was comfortable between people who had established it was not a problem between them.

After a while, she said, "How much Cheyenne do you understand?"

"Some," he said. "Enough to know what you were saying to your horse."

She looked at him.

"Not all of it," he said. "But enough."

Something moved at the corners of her mouth.

"Years near the camps," he said. "The march south. Words come in whether you want them or not."

She considered this. They rode on.

"You did not say anything," she said. "When I was, when you came around the bend."

"You were not finished," he said.

She looked at him. Then she looked at the river.

"No," she said. "I was not."

The horse, Vohkoohe, he was going to need to remember that, walked with the slightly chastened quality of an animal that had disgraced itself and knew it. His ears were forward now, scanning the road ahead with more attention than usual, as if he had decided that vigilance was the appropriate response to having failed so completely at vigilance.

A ground squirrel crossed the road ahead of them.

Vohkoohe stopped dead.

"Vohkoohe," Eméškeha'e said. The name was delivered with the specific tone of someone who had expected this and was not pleased to have been right.

The horse collected himself and moved forward.

Watches Twice said nothing.

He was being very careful.

"Do not," she said, without looking at him.

He did not.

But she was smiling when she said it. She did not try to hide it, and he rode beside her into Ashland in the morning light.

* * *

At the school gate, she dismounted, tied Vohkoohe to the post, and checked the cinch as she always checked everything, not trusting, just verifying. She looked at the school buildings, pale in the morning light, the bell tower against the sky. The specific quality of her look when she looked at the school was different from how she looked at everything else. Not dread exactly. Just the gathering of something. The way you gathered yourself before you went into a place that was going to require all of you.

He had noticed this before. He noticed it now.

"Tomorrow," he said.

She looked at him.

"The ford needs checking," he said.

She looked at him for a long moment, her assessment quick and complete, and it had been getting slower and deeper every time.

"The ford," she said.

"It has been a week," he said.

"Has it," she said.

She went through the gate.

He sat on his horse outside the school in Ashland, Montana, in the morning light, and watched the gate close behind her, and there was something at the corners of his mouth that had been there most of the morning and showed no signs of leaving.

He turned his horse north.

He rode home.

The river moved beside him. The cottonwoods bare. The sandstone bluffs, red in the morning light. The cold air is sharp and clean.

He thought about a ground squirrel crossing the road.

He thought about *do not,* said without looking at him, and the smile she had not hidden.

He thought about the ford.

It had been a week. He would need to check it tomorrow.

The river moved.

He rode.

16

Fenced

She smelled of mud and horse when she came through the side gate.

This was not how she arrived at St. Labre. She arrived before the bell, coat straight, hat straight, ready for whatever the day required of her. She was the interpreter. She was the bridge. She represented something to these children, and she was careful about what she represented.

This morning, she was muddy from the collar down. Her hat had a dent in the left side where it had met the road. She smelled of the Tongue River bank, and she needed to clean her face before Sister Marguerite saw her and asked questions she did not have time to answer.

The washing room was off the main dormitory. It was a narrow room with a long zinc trough, a pump at one end, and a row of hooks on the wall where towels hung in a line. The girls used it in the mornings before breakfast. At this hour, it should have been empty.

She pushed open the door.

Sister Anne was there, her back to the door, speaking quietly in English. And there was a girl, one of the older girls, twelve or perhaps thirteen, Eméškeha'e did not know her well; she had been at the school only a few weeks, sitting on the bench along the wall with her hands in her lap and her eyes down and her face doing the specific work of a face that was trying very hard to show nothing at all.

Sister Anne had clean rags folded over her arm. She was explaining something. Her voice was kind and matter-of-fact, the voice of a woman who dealt with practical things practically and saw no reason to make more of this than it was.

The girl was not looking at her.

Eméškeha'e understood immediately.

She stood in the doorway and understood what she was seeing and what she was not seeing.

She was not seeing the women of the girls' lodge. She was not seeing the older female relatives who should have been the ones in this room, who should have been the first faces the girl saw this morning, the voices she heard, the hands that guided her through what this day should have been. They were not here because the school had taken this girl from them and put a fence between them. The school had looked at a Cheyenne girl and seen a practical problem to be managed and had organized itself to manage it and had never once asked what the girl's mother would have done, what the older women of her family would have said, what knowledge should have been passing from one generation to the next in a room like this on a morning like this.

The girl's mother was perhaps three miles away on the reservation.

She might as well have been in another country.

She was not seeing the quiet, deliberate passing of knowledge from women who knew what they were passing on, and to whom they were passing it. The behavioral restrictions that would have marked this time as different from ordinary times. The girl's own utensils, set apart. Perhaps a small meal, a gift, the specific acknowledgment that what was happening to her was significant and she was significant. The women of her family were here to say so.

She was seeing a nun with clean rags explaining something in English to a girl who barely spoke English, in a narrow room that smelled of soap and cold water, with no one the girl loved anywhere nearby. Not because they did not love her. Because they were on the other side of a fence that did not open for this.

Sister Anne heard the door and turned.

"Oh, good morning." A brief assessing look at Emėškeha'e's coat. "There's a pump outside if you need it."

"Yes," Emėškeha'e said. "Thank you. I'm sorry to interrupt."

She stepped back and let the door close.

She stood outside in the cold morning air and listened to the river for a moment. Then she went to the pump at the side of the building, worked the handle until the water ran, and bent to clean her face in cold water, the mud coming away in gray water that ran off into the ground.

She straightened, brushed her clothes off the best she could, and put her hat back on.

She went inside.

* * *

She moved between the classrooms, the younger children's room first, where Sister Anne was back at the blackboard by the time Emėškeha'e arrived, the lesson continuing as if nothing had interrupted it.

A boy in the third row had not slept. She could see it in the specific way he was sitting upright, with effort, his eyes working harder than they should have had to work to track the chalk on the board. He had been crying in the night, or had lain awake listening to the other boys breathe in the dark of the dormitory, or had spent the hours between midnight and dawn doing whatever it was children did in the dark of a place they had not chosen to be. She noted it. There was nothing to do about it. She noted it and moved on.

Sister Marguerite needed a letter translated. It was a family's response to the school's last communication, written in Cheyenne by someone whose hand was not practiced, the words carefully formed. She translated it into English and wrote it out in the school's ledger in the clean script Sister Marguerite required.

Between tasks, she thought about the girl on the bench.

She thought about what the morning should have been. The women of the girls' lodge gathered close. Older female relatives whose voices the girl had heard her whole life. The specific quiet of women passing knowledge deliberately to someone who needed it, not as a practical problem to be managed but as a moment to be honored. The girl's own utensils set apart. The behavioral restrictions that marked this time as different from ordinary time, that said, what is happening to you is significant, you are significant, you are becoming something, and we are here to witness it and teach you what it means.

None of that existed in this building. The school did not know it had taken something this morning. It did not know because it had never known.

She translated another letter. She explained something to a boy who did not understand his assignment. She was present and useful, and did her work.

* * *

She found the girl in the yard after the midday meal.

The other children had gone back inside. The girl was standing near the fence at the edge of the yard, not doing anything, just standing the way children stood when they were waiting for something to be over. She had her arms crossed and her chin down. She was looking at the ground with the specific look of someone who had been carrying something heavy since morning and had not yet found anywhere to set it down.

Emėškeha'e crossed the yard.

She did not approach directly or quickly, not with a purpose that announced itself. Just a woman moving across a yard, not to require anything of you.

She stopped beside the girl.

They stood together for a moment, looking at the fence and the country beyond it, the bare cottonwoods, the river, the sandstone bluffs going red in the midday light.

Then Emėškeha'e said, quietly, in Cheyenne, *"I know what this morning should have been. The women of your family should have been the ones in that room. Your mother. Your aunts. The older women who know what to pass on and how to pass it. They were not here because there is a fence, and the fence does not open for this. That is not your failure, and it is not theirs. It is what this place is."*

The girl did not move. But something in her changed, a small shift, barely visible, the specific change in a person who has been listening with their whole body.

"What happened to you this morning was not wrong because of what it was," Emėškeha'e said. *"It was wrong because of what it was not. You understand the difference."*

A pause. The river moving beyond the fence. The cottonwoods bare and still.

"You are becoming a woman in a hard place," she said. *"That is hard. But you are not less than what you should be because of it. The women of your family will tell you what they should have told you this morning. When you go home. They will tell you."*

She did not say if. She said when.

The girl looked up.

Her face was the face of someone who had been seen, not managed, not processed, not explained in a language she barely understood, but seen. The specific look of a person who had been carrying something alone all morning and had just had someone stand beside them and say, *I see what you are carrying.*

She did not say anything.

Eméškeha'e did not require her to.

She stood with her for a moment longer, and then she said, *"Go inside now. Do your work. You are strong enough for this day."*

The girl went inside.

Eméškeha'e stood in the yard for a moment. The river beyond the fence. The bluffs red in the early afternoon light. The cold air, sharp and clean.

Then she went inside, too.

* * *

The afternoon brought its own work.

Sister Marguerite needed three things translated. Two younger children had a dispute about something small, the way children's disputes were always about something small, a pencil, a seat, a look, and she was asked to mediate, which she did in Cheyenne, quickly, both children satisfied and returned to their desks before Sister Marguerite had finished watching. A boy needed a message carried to the dormitory matron. A girl who had been sick for three days was well enough to return to class and needed to be shown what she had missed.

She did all of it.

At one point, she passed through the room where the older girls were learning to sew. The girl was at the end of the second row, bent over her work with the careful attention of someone concentrating hard on something small. Her needle moved. Her thread caught the

151

light.

She looked up.

Their eyes met across the room, a brief exchange, a second or less, the specific quality of two people who share something no one else in the room knows they share.

The girl smiled.

Not a large smile. Not happiness exactly. Just the small specific expression of a person who had been carrying something heavy since morning and had found, not a way to put it down, but someone to carry it with her for a moment. The acknowledgment that she had been seen and spoken to and was not alone in this place.

Eméškeha'e held her gaze for a moment.

Then she went on about her work.

* * *

She rode home in the early dark.

The Tongue River on her right, running shallow and cold, the sound of it carrying in the still air. Vohkoohe moved at the pace she asked of him and no faster, his ears forward, scanning the road ahead with the vigilance of a horse who had learned something about himself that morning and was not prepared to learn it again.

The cold was coming in from the north now. Not bitter yet, but present, the specific cold that arrived in the Tongue River country in late October and stayed until April. Her breath showed. Vohkoohe's did too.

She rode and let the day settle into itself.

Her place was dark when she arrived. The small cabin on the Tongue River, two miles outside Ashland, the cottonwoods along the bank bare now, the river audible through the walls. She tied Vohkoohe at the picket, unsaddled him, gave him water and grain, and checked his feet the way she checked everything, not trusting, just verifying.

She went inside.

She built the fire from the banked coals and sat with it while the cabin warmed and listened to the river and held what the day had given her, both things, the weight of what was wrong and the small thing that had been right inside it, and did not try to make either of them into something they weren't.

The fire moved.

The river moved outside.

She was still here.

17

What Counts

She saw him the second time just after midday.

She was at the window with the last of her tea when he came around the bend in the river road. His horse moving at the particular unhurried pace of an animal that had made this trip recently and expected to make it again shortly. He did not look at her gate as he passed it. He looked at the river road and the country ahead of him with the careful attention of a man who was absolutely not looking at her gate.

She laughed.

Quietly. There was no one to hear it either way.

She set her cup down, looked at what remained of her lunch, and began to tidy it away. She was not hurrying. She knew his route. She knew approximately how long it took to ride from here to the ford, assess the depth of a river that had not changed its character since September, and ride back. She had been making this calculation for some time now without examining why.

She washed the cup.

She straightened the things on the shelf that did not need straightening.

She put on her coat.

She went out to the gate.

She waited.

The river moved on her left. The cottonwoods, bare along the bank. The sandstone bluffs catching the afternoon light. Vohkoohe watched her from the corral with the expression of a mare who found human behavior consistently baffling but had learned to observe it without comment.

Then hoofbeats. Around the bend.

Here he came.

He saw her standing at the gate when he cleared the bend, and his horse slowed without being asked.

She did not help him.

She let him sit there.

Then she said it.

"You have ridden past this gate three times today," she said. "The ford has not changed since the last time you checked it, or the time before that, or any of the times before those. You are going to kill your horse with the saddling and unsaddling." She paused. "Save the poor beast. Go get your things and bring them here."

He opened his mouth.

He closed it.

He opened it again.

The sound that came out was not quite a word.

She was already walking back toward the cabin.

"Well," she said over her shoulder. "Go."

* * *

He came back an hour later.

She heard him before she saw him, the specific sound of a horse moving slowly. A horse moves differently when their rider is not in a hurry because the rider is thinking rather than riding. She was by the window again, not watching for him, just near the window.

He came through the gate on foot, leading his horse, his belongings tied behind the saddle and in a roll over one arm. She went to the door.

He had almost nothing. She had known this, had understood it from the quality of how he moved through the world, the man who checked the ford three times a day rather than knock on a door, the man who had been living alone on the Tongue River for a year and had organized his life around the minimum required. Still, seeing it. The bedroll. The rifle. A kit worn to the shape of his hands. Some tools. Dried food. An extra shirt. A cast-iron pan he was carrying separately from everything else with the particular care of a man who considered it a significant possession.

And one other thing, small, wrapped in worn leather, carried in his left hand apart from everything else. She did not know what it was. She did not ask.

He stood in the doorway and looked around the cabin.

She watched him look. Watched him take in the space. The fire, the shelf, the table, the two chairs, the way she had arranged things over the months she had been here. The specific quality of a space that had been lived in carefully by someone who knew what they needed.

Then he looked at the sleeping area.

She watched him understand.

The understanding moved across his face in stages. Arrival, recognition, the full arrival of what recognition meant, and when it was complete, he looked at the sleeping area for another moment, and then he said, with great seriousness, "I could put up a shelter. In the back, by the corral. A temporary..." He didn't finish the thought.

She made a sound. Not quite a laugh. The sound of a woman

who found something both funny and mildly exasperating in equal measure. She shook her head once, the slow, deliberate shake of someone confronted with a particular variety of foolishness they had not quite anticipated.

She crossed to him.

She took the bedroll from under his arm. She took the kit. She took the extra shirt, the tools, and the worn leather bundle, carefully, the way you took something you understood mattered without knowing why. She left him holding the pan.

She carried everything into the sleeping area.

He heard the sounds of his things finding their places alongside hers. The soft weight of the bedroll. The small sounds of a life being placed next to another life.

She came back out.

She looked at the pan.

He was still holding it.

"I have a pan," she said.

"I know," he said.

She took it from him anyway. She looked at it for a moment, a woman assessing a redundancy, weighing its qualities against the pan she already had, and then she set it on the shelf next to hers.

Two pans. One shelf.

"Sit down," she said. "I'll make something."

He sat down.

She made him something to eat.

Neither of them said anything for a while.

The specific quality of a silence that did not need to be filled.

* * *

He went out to put his horse in the corral.

Vohkoohe was at the far end, watching him come with her ears forward and her head up, the posture of a mare who had organized her space carefully over several months and was now being informed that the organization was subject to revision. She was a dark bay with a white blaze and opinions. She expressed her opinions through the precise positioning of her body in relation to the gate and the water and the best corner of the corral, all of which she had claimed and was not prepared to renegotiate.

His horse, who had been called the Crow word for horse for two years because that was sufficient, and Watches Twice had never needed more than sufficient, stood at the gate and read the situation with the patient wariness of an animal that had been in enough situations to know when to wait.

Eméškeha'e came out and stood at the corral fence.

They watched the horses for a moment. Vohkoohe moved two steps to the left, maintaining her claim on the best corner. His horse stayed where it was and watched her with one eye.

"What is his name?" she said.

Watches Twice told her the Crow word for horse.

She looked at him.

He had seen that look before. It was the look she reserved for things that did not meet her minimum standard.

"That is not a name," she said. "That is what he is."

"Yes, that is what he is."

"It is not a name." She looked at the horse. The horse looked back at her with the patient expression of an animal that had been called the Crow word for horse for two years and had no strong feelings about it either way. "Everything needs a name."

She looked at him for a moment. Then at the horse. Then somewhere in the middle distance, deciding.

"Néše'še-méšéne," she said.

It came out with the quality of a name being recognized rather than invented, three syllables that sounded like something earned, something that spoke to a horse's character, purpose, and place in the world.

Watches Twice looked at his horse.

"What does it mean?" he said.

She was already walking back toward the cabin.

"It suits him," she said.

He looked at the horse. The horse looked back at him, the specific patient expression of an animal waiting for something to be resolved.

Watches Twice said the name softly. Testing it. *Néše'še-méšéne.*

The horse whickered.

One short sound. A sound that seemed to admit defeat.

Watches Twice looked at the horse for a moment longer.

"Yes," he said quietly. "I know."

* * *

He rode out the next morning before she left for the school.

He had work, a paper from Hartley that needed to be delivered to a Cheyenne settlement six miles east. He collected it at the agency office and read it on the road.

Three weeks ago, a man at the settlement had beaten another man badly enough to break bones. The community had handled it in the traditional manner. The headmen, the council, the specific reckoning of people who knew both men and the history between them. The offender had made restitution. The injured man had accepted it. The matter was resolved.

The paper said the matter was not resolved. The paper said that under the Major Crimes Act of 1885, crimes of this nature on reservation land fell under federal jurisdiction. The paper said a federal marshal would be coming. The paper said what the community had decided did not count.

He rode into the settlement and found the headman outside his lodge in the thin winter sun.

The headman was an older man. Watches Twice had delivered things to him before. He waited while a younger man with enough English read the paper aloud in Cheyenne.

The headman listened without looking up. When the reading was done, he was quiet for a moment. Then he said something to the younger man, quietly, not to Watches Twice, and the younger man nodded.

Watches Twice did not ask what had been said. He already knew.

He rode away.

The settlement behind him. The river road ahead. The country reading itself to him. The sandstone bluffs, the bare cottonwoods, the shallow Tongue running clear in the winter light.

He rode home.

* * *

She was back from school when he came through the gate.

He could tell from the specific quality of her stillness when he came in that her day had been long. He did not ask directly. He had learned that asking directly was not the right approach. He tended his horse, came inside, sat, and let the evening find its shape.

After a while, she said, "The girl smiled at me today. Across the room."

He waited.

"Not the girl from before," she said. "A different girl. A small one. She had been watching me for weeks. Today she smiled."

She looked at the fire.

"That was something," she said.

He thought about the headman looking at the ground. About the paper and the community's resolution, which didn't count anymore.

"Yes," he said.

They sat with both things, his and hers, and let them be what they were.

Outside, in the small corral, Vohkoohe and Néše'še-méšéne had reached the specific negotiated peace of animals who had decided that coexistence was more practical than conflict. Not friendship. Just tolerance. Vohkoohe had conceded the gate end of the corral. Néše'še-méšéne had conceded the best corner. Both of them stood in the thin winter dark with their heads down and their breath showing in the cold air.

The fire moved.

The river moved outside.

They were still here.

Both of them.

In the same place.

18

Éstávé-vóhe

The winter came in from the northwest, not gradually but all at once, the temperature dropping overnight in the first week of November and the sandstone bluffs going from red to grey and staying grey, the Tongue narrowing as the shallows froze at the edges and the deeper channel ran dark between them.

They learned about each other in the cold.

This was different from learning each other in the fall, different from the river road and the school gate and the trader's store and the careful distance of two people who were not yet sure what they were to each other. That distance was gone. In its place was something more complicated and more ordinary, the specific negotiation of two solitary people who had organized their lives carefully around their own habits and were now discovering that the other person also had habits and that some of those habits were not compatible.

She stacked wood in alternating rows, cross-hatched, as her mother had taught her. He stacked it in parallel rows, which he maintained was faster to build and faster to access.

She looked at his stack.

He looked at hers.

Neither of them said anything for a moment.

"Cross-hatched does not fall," she said.

"Parallel does not require thinking about," he said.

She looked at him with an assessment that was quick and complete.

"That," she said, "is exactly the problem."

She restacked his wood. He watched her do it without comment, which she noted and which he noted that she noted, and they went inside, and neither of them mentioned it again, which was its own kind of negotiation.

The two pans had also required negotiation. Hers was seasoned. His ran hot. She used hers for everything that required even heat, like the flatbread, the beans, and the occasional egg when the trader had them. She used his for things that benefited from a hot side. Things like meat seared quickly, the occasional fish when the Tongue was not yet fully frozen, and he came home in the morning with something from the river. He had not known there was a difference between the pans until she explained it. She had not known he would accept the explanation without argument.

"Most men," she said one morning, watching him transfer the fish to her pan to finish, "do not listen."

"I listen," he said.

"You do," she said. The specific quality of a woman revising an assumption she had held for a long time.

The cabin was small. Two people in a small cabin in winter learned each other faster than two people in the open country. He learned that she was awake before he was, always, and had the fire built and the water heated before he had fully surfaced from sleep. He learned that she had a specific quality of being in the morning. Quiet, contained, not available for conversation until she had been awake long enough to have her tea and had looked out at the draw above the cabin for whatever she looked for there in the early light.

She learned that he was awake before he appeared to be, that the stillness he brought to early mornings was not sleep but something else, a quality of being present without announcing it that she recognized because she had it too. She learned that he had specific, technical opinions about leather maintenance in cold weather, and that his opinions were correct, which she found mildly irritating and did not tell him.

The draw above the cabin she had named Méanôhtse, which meant the quiet draw, the still place. He heard it and used it without asking what it meant, which she found correct.

* * *

He was not thinking about the tree.

He was outside in the thin December sun, splitting wood. When he was done splitting the day's supply, he stood the axe against the pile and looked at the cottonwood at the bank's edge. He took out his knife and walked to it. He walked to it because his hands were idle, and he was happy in a place and wanted to put some mark of his happiness on it.

It was a large tree. Split at the trunk eight feet up into two leaders, both still living, the bark pale and deeply furrowed. He had been looking at it every morning since he arrived. It was the first thing visible from the door in the early light. The pale trunk against the darker country behind it, the two leaders against the winter sky.

He set the knife against the bark.

"Bíalish Dúua."

The full name, the Crow name, the way she said it when something required his complete attention.

He turned.

She was in the doorway. Not alarmed. Not angry. The expression of someone who had just seen something about to happen that she needed to stop before it happened.

"What are you doing to him?"

He looked at the knife in his hand. At the small mark he had begun in the bark, barely a scratch.

"I was just —"

"He has not harmed you," she said. She came out of the doorway and crossed the yard toward him. "He watches the morning while you are still sleeping. He lets the woodpecker live in his branches in peace." She stopped beside him and looked up into the bare winter branches, the two pale leaders against the grey sky. "He holds stars, Bíalish Dúua."

He looked at her.

"My people know this," she said. "The stars travel from deep in the earth, up through the roots and the trunk, up into the highest branches. They wait in the tips of the branches for the wind to release them into the sky. Every star you see on a winter night has come through a cottonwood tree."

She said it plainly. Not as a legend. Not as instruction. As something true that he needed to know because he had been about to do something to a tree that held stars.

"This tree," she said as she put a hand on its bark. "This specific tree. He has been holding stars since before your grandfather's grandfather was born."

He looked at the cottonwood. He looked at the small scratch in the bark, barely anything, barely a mark. He closed the knife and put it in his pocket.

"I did not know," he said.

"Now you know," she said. "His name is Éstávé-vóhe."

She went back inside.

He stood at the base of the cottonwood for a moment. He looked up into the bare branches, the woodpecker's cavity visible in the left fork, the pale bark going silver in the winter light. He put his hand flat against the trunk. He was not Cheyenne. The stars in the cottonwood were not his stars. But she had told him, and now he knew, and the tree had a name.

He went inside.

"I am sorry," he said. "About the tree."

She was at the fire. She looked at him over her shoulder.

"You could not have known," she said. "Now you do."

He sat down. He thought that was perhaps the most complete form of forgiveness available in this world; *you could not have known, now you do.* That she had given it to him about a cottonwood tree without knowing or perhaps knowing entirely that she was giving it to him about everything else as well.

He did not examine this. He just sat with the fire between them and listened to the woodpecker working the left fork of Éstávé-vóhe outside.

* * *

He came home in the second week of December with coins from a courier run to Miles City and back, four days of riding in the cold, the agency papers delivered, the return papers collected. Not much. Enough.

He set them on the table.

She looked at them. Then at him.

"There is a family," she said. Not a question.

"Yellow Hawk's family," he said. "The trader has been running their account forward since October. By spring, it will be more than the horses."

She was quiet for a moment.

166

"Yellow Hawk's daughter is in my classroom," she said.

"I know."

She looked at the coins on the table. She looked at the fire.

"Go in the morning," she said. "Before the school."

He went in the morning before school. He set the coins on the trader's counter and said which account. The trader looked at him with the specific calculation of a man assessing whether this was a transaction he wanted to complete.

Watches Twice waited.

The trader made the adjustment in his ledger.

He rode home. She was already gone, Vohkoohe's tracks fresh in the thin snow on the river road. He went inside, built up the fire, and did not think about the ledger or the coins. The thing was done. The coins were gone. Yellow Hawk's daughter had a name he did not know. She was one of thirty-one children in a school on the Tongue River. Her father's debt was settled. That was what was available. He had done what was available.

He went out and stacked the day's wood cross-hatched.

* * *

She came home in the early dark of a December afternoon, and he was in the yard.

He saw her face before she dismounted.

He finished the round he had started. He set the axe down. He went inside and put more wood on the fire.

She came in. She hung her coat. She sat.

He made tea the way she made it, the proportions and the time learned without being taught, watching until he knew.

He set it in front of her.

She held the cup.

After a while, she said, "They cut the children's hair today."

He waited.

"New children arrived yesterday. Three of them. This morning Sister Anne cut their hair."

She looked at the fire.

"The oldest was a boy, perhaps ten. He had worn his hair in two braids since he was small, you could see it in how he held his head, the weight he expected that wasn't there anymore. He kept reaching up for it. All morning. Reaching for something that was gone."

Watches Twice said nothing.

"Among my people, you cut your hair when someone dies."

She said it plainly. Not for effect. The fact of it, placed on the table.

"Sister Anne does not know this. She is cutting their hair because short hair is clean and practical. She has no idea what she is making them look like. What she is making them feel. Like they are mourning a death."

She looked at the cup in her hands.

"The boy kept reaching up," she said again. "All morning."

Watches Twice looked at the fire. He thought about a boy reaching for the weight of something that was gone.

After a while, he said, "When did you go north?"

She looked at him.

"September 1878," she said. "We left Darlington on the ninth."

He nodded slowly. He was quiet for a moment.

"When Vávàhke died," he said.

She was very still.

"When was that," he said. Not a question exactly. Something else.

"November," she said. "1877."

He looked at the fire. Something was moving in him. He was going to say it. He had been carrying it since she said the name, and now he was going to say it.

"I was on that march south," he said. "In the summer of 1877. I was on the flank of the column."

She looked at him.

"I escorted them south. From Red Cloud Agency to Darlington. Seventy days. I rode the flank and watched the column."

She was very still.

"Forty days into the march, we were in Kansas. The heat was wrong for them, you could see it. The elders moved more slowly, and the women shaded the youngest children. I was on the flank, reading the country."

He stopped. He was staring at the fire without seeing it.

"There was a girl," he said. "Perhaps three years old. Walking at the edge of the column, near her mother. She stopped."

Eméškeha'e did not move.

"She stopped in the middle of the moving column and looked at something in the grass. A yellow butterfly. The column moved around her, and she stood still and watched it. As if nothing else existed."

He said it plainly. Each word chosen.

"Her mother came back for her without breaking stride. One arm swinging out, scooping the girl up against her side. The girl looked back at the butterfly as they moved forward."

The fire moved between them.

"I sat my horse and watched this and did not move for a long time."

He looked at her.

"At Darlington, when the column arrived, I turned from the payment table with the coins still in my hand. And I saw her again. The same girl. Standing at the edge of where the Cheyenne were making their camp. Not looking at the grass this time. Looking at the Agency. At the flat ground and the wrong sky. Standing still with her hands at her sides."

He stopped.

"Her mother came and took her hand. Did not scoop her up this time. Took her hand and walked her forward into it."

The silence in the cabin was complete. Outside, the river moved. Éstávé-vóhe stood at the bank in the dark.

"When you said Vávàhke's name," he said. "When you told me about the moccasins."

He looked at the fire.

"I knew who she was."

Eméškeha'e was very still. The quality of her stillness had changed. It was not the stillness of someone receiving information. It was the stillness of someone who had already understood something and was now hearing it confirmed.

"She always stopped for butterflies," she said. Very quiet.

"Yes," he said.

"Every time. She could not help it. She would just stop. And look. As if the butterfly was the most important thing that had ever existed."

Her hands were in her lap. Still.

"She was like that with everything small," she said. "Beetles. Flowers. A piece of mica in the dirt. She would crouch down and study it with her whole self. She never just looked. She always looked completely."

He listened.

"I used to tell her, *Vávàhke, we have to keep moving, the column is moving*. And she would look up at me with that face. Like I was the one who had missed something important."

Something moved in his face. He let it.

"You were the man on the flank," she said.

"Yes."

"I knew there was a Crow scout. I did not look at you directly. I had enough to carry."

"Yes."

She was quiet for a long time.

Then she said, "There is more."

It was not a question.

"Yes," he said. "I was on a ridge above the Niobrara in October of 1878. I had been following Dull Knife's band through the Pine Ridge country for three days. Trying to understand what they were doing, whether they were going to fight or surrender."

She looked at him.

"On the third day, I came up on a rise above a valley where they had camped. It was evening. The fires were burning at the right height. Campfires. The kind you built when you were staying."

He looked at the fire between them.

"I watched for a long time. And I understood. They were not running away. They were running to something. Fort Robinson. They wanted to surrender and come home."

She said nothing.

"I reported what I saw. Their location. Their direction. Their intention. Not hostile, moving to surrender. I reported it plainly because that was what I did."

She looked at him.

"You were twenty-three," she said.

"Yes."

"You were doing your job."

"Yes."

She said it without absolution or accusation. She said it the way she said things that were true and needed to be said, and did not need anything added to them.

"I know what the job was," she said. "I know what the Army needed from men who could read country." She looked at the fire. "I know all of this."

He waited.

"And I know," she said, "that you were on the flank of that column for seventy days. That you watched us walk into Darlington. That you stood there with coins in your hand and watched my daughter be walked into that place."

Her voice did not change. It carried what it carried without breaking.

"And I know that you found us in the Pine Ridge country and reported honestly what you saw. And the Army came anyway."

"Yes."

"And I climbed those cliffs in January," she said. "In the dark. With children passed up hand to hand."

"Yes."

"And I came north," she said. "And I ended up on this river. In this cabin."

She looked at him.

"With you."

He looked back at her. He did not try to make it easier than it was.

"Yes," he said. "With me."

The fire moved.

After a long time, she said, "I cannot tell you that none of it was your fault. Some of it was. Just as some of it was Dull Knife's fault for trusting the Army's decency. As some of it was my fault for believing that if I worked at that school, I could make the fence mean something different than it meant."

She was quiet.

"We were all part of it," she said. "Some of us built it. Some of us ran it. Some of us just walked through it. Tried to keep our children alive inside it."

She looked at him.

"Vávàhke stopped for the butterfly," she said. "In Kansas. In the middle of all of it. She stopped and looked at the butterfly with her whole self."

"Yes," he said.

"You saw that."

"Yes."

"Then you know," she said, "who she was."

He did not trust himself to speak. He nodded.

She looked at the fire.

"That is not nothing," she said. "That someone saw her. That someone remembers her stopping. I am happy that you saw her."

"I'm sorry," he said to her.

"You could not have known," she said. "Now you do."

The fire moved between them. Outside, the woodpecker slept in the left fork of Éstávé-vóhe. The draw above the cabin was dark and still.

She reached across and put her hand over his.

She left it there.

The fire burned down.

Neither of them moved.

Outside, Néše'še-méšéne and Vohkoohe stood in the small corral with their breath showing in the cold. The river moved between its frozen edges. Éstávé-vóhe held its stars.

They were still here.

Both of them.

In the same place.

19

The Coot

Spring came to the Tongue River. Not gently but with intention, the snowmelt running hard off the bluffs, the river rising dark and fast between its banks, and the ground going from frozen to mud to something that might eventually be workable if you were patient with it.

He was in the corral tending Néše'še-méšéne's left foreleg when Vohkoohe came back.

He heard her before he saw her. The particular sound of the gate latch lifting from the outside, which should not have been possible given that he had rebuilt the latch in January specifically to prevent this, and yet here was the sound of it, the gate swinging open, and Vohkoohe walking through it with the unhurried confidence of a horse returning from somewhere she had every right to have been.

She was not alone.

The foal was already on his feet, which meant she had foaled somewhere out in the country above the river and walked him home at whatever pace suited her. His legs had the look of something that had been practicing. He was perhaps a day old. Dark like his mother across the back and hindquarters, but his chest and belly and the left side of

174

his face were white, broad irregular patches that had no symmetry and no apology, the paint pattern of some unknown father who had found Vohkoohe on one of her unsanctioned excursions above the river and left his mark on the result. He was the most conspicuous horse Watches Twice had ever seen. He walked beside his mother into the corral and looked at Néše'še-méšéne with the complete fearlessness of a creature that had not yet learned what things were worth fearing.

Néše'še-méšéne looked back at him with an expression that suggested this was not a development he had been consulted about.

Watches Twice set down Néše'še-méšéne's leg and looked at Vohkoohe. She looked back at him with the expression she used when she had done something entirely reasonable and was prepared to wait for the rest of the world to arrive at the same conclusion.

He went inside.

"Vohkoohe is back," he said.

Eméškeha'e looked up from the fire.

"She brought something with her," he said.

She was outside before he finished the sentence.

She stood at the corral fence and looked at the foal for a long time. The foal looked back at her with his mother's directness and his father's unknown qualities, dark like Vohkoohe, a splash of white on his chest that neither of them could account for, legs that were still deciding whether they trusted the ground.

She looked at Vohkoohe.

Vohkoohe looked at the middle distance.

"You fixed the latch," Eméškeha'e said.

"In January," he said.

"Too late," she said.

"Yes."

She watched the foal take three steps toward the fence, stop, and consider her with great seriousness.

"Náhko'e-vó'kóhéva," she said. Half a laugh in it. She was looking at the paint patches, the bold, irregular white against the dark, the left side of his face white from ear to nostril as if he had been dipped. There was nothing subtle about this horse. He had arrived without warning, and he intended to be seen. The name arriving as her names always arrived, not decided so much as recognized.

He said it quietly to himself. It sat right.

"Náhko," she said, shorter, affectionate, looking at the foal. "Come here then."

The foal considered this invitation with the same seriousness he had considered everything so far, then walked to the fence and put his nose against her hand.

Néše'še-méséne moved to the far end of the corral and stood with his back to all of it.

* * *

The garden was her idea, and the fence was his.

She had pointed to the draw above the cabin, Méanôhtse, the still place, in the first week of March, when the ground was still hard. The light had changed enough to think about what it would become. She had described what she wanted. Small. Practical. The things that kept well through winter and could be dried or stored.

He built the fence without being asked. Four days of work in the cold, the posts set deep enough to hold, the rails tight enough to keep the horses out. When it was done, he said nothing about it. She said nothing about it either, which he took to be the correct response.

She started the garden in the second week of April. He watched her work from the doorway in the early mornings before the day's business began. She moved through the turned earth with the specific attention of someone who knew what she was doing, who had done this before in some other life, in some other ground.

The ground here was hers, or she was its, or both. He could not have said exactly which. He just watched her work in the early light and felt the particular quality of a man who understands that he is watching something important and has the good sense not to interrupt it.

Náhko watched from the corral fence every morning with his chin on the top rail.

The agency sent word in the third week of April.

* * *

Two government surveyors needed a guide. Someone who knew the reservation ground, the draws, the drainages, the ridge lines, the creek crossings. Three days, maybe four. Standard wages.

He said yes because it was work and because the agency did not phrase these requests in ways that left much room for no.

The surveyors were waiting at the agency the next morning. Two men, both from the east by their boots and their instruments and the way they looked at the country around them without reading it, just looking at it. One was older, heavyset, with the bearing of a man accustomed to being the authority in any room he entered. The other was younger, deferential to the first, carrying the notebook.

They looked at Watches Twice. The assessment was brief and complete, and arrived at its conclusion without visible effort. He was the guide. He knew the ground. That was the extent of what they needed from him and what they believed he was capable of providing.

He looked back at them without expression.

"You know the reservation boundaries?" the older one said. Slowly, with the particular enunciation of a man addressing someone he believes may not fully understand him.

"Yes," Watches Twice said.

"All of it? The draws, the creek drainages, the high ground?"

"Yes."

The older man looked at him for a moment, then at his colleague, then back at Watches Twice with the satisfied expression of a man who has confirmed his prior assessment.

"Good," he said. "We'll start at the northern boundary and work south."

They rode out.

He had been reading country since he was seven years old. He had read it in Montana and Wyoming and Nebraska and Kansas and Oklahoma, grassland and canyon and sandhill and river bottom, in every season and every weather. He knew how to look at a piece of ground and understand its water, its shelter, its approaches, its vulnerabilities. He knew how to read what the land said about itself if you were patient enough to listen.

The surveyors had instruments for reading the country. A theodolite on a tripod. A measuring chain. Notebooks filled with columns of numbers. They took readings, recorded them, and discussed the results in the specific technical language of their profession, which they used freely in front of him because it did not occur to them that he might follow it.

He followed all of it.

He had seen surveying before, the early work on the reservation boundaries, the agency lots, the mission land. He understood what the instruments measured and what the numbers in the notebooks represented. He understood that a survey line was an argument, a claim made against the ground that the ground itself did not recognize, but that governments and courts and land offices treated as more real than the ground.

On the first day, they ran lines along the northern boundary, and he listened to them talk.

"The allotment schedule gives each head of household a hundred and sixty acres," the younger one said, copying numbers into the notebook. "Individual parcels. Deeded in trust."

"And the surplus?" the older one said. He was looking through the theodolite, not at his colleague.

"Opens for settlement. After the allotments are assigned."

"How much surplus are we looking at?"

The younger one consulted his papers. He gave a number.

The older one straightened up from the theodolite and looked at the country around him, the river bottom and the bluffs and the draws running up into the high ground, with the expression of a man calculating something pleasant.

"Good country," he said. "Once it's properly developed."

Watches Twice held his horse still and looked at the survey stake in the ground. He said nothing.

On the second day, they worked the eastern boundary, and he listened to them talk about the men in Washington who had designed the allotment system. They talked of the policy goals and what they were meant to achieve. About the civilizing effect of individual land ownership on communal peoples. They used the word *civilizing* without self-consciousness, a word they'd never examined. They discussed the surplus land, settlement opportunities, and development potential of the river bottom.

They did not talk to him. They talked in front of him, which was different.

On the third day, they worked the ground above the river, the ridges and draws south of Ashland, the country he could read in his sleep, the ground he had been crossing since he came to live on the Tongue. He watched them set their stakes and run their lines through country he knew like his own hands.

The lines did not care what he knew.

At the end of the third day, the older surveyor paid him his wages without looking at him, the coins counted into his hand with the mechanical efficiency of a transaction completed, and rode back toward the agency with his colleague, and Watches Twice sat his horse on the ridge above the river and watched them go.

Below him, the Tongue moved fast with the last of the snowmelt. The reservation spread out in every direction. The bluffs and the draws and the river bottom and the high grass country to the south. His home was down there somewhere, the smoke from the cabin's chimney visible in the evening air.

The survey stakes were in the ground.

He checked the ford as he rode home. He hadn't checked it in weeks.

* * *

"In the beginning," she said, "there was only Maheo and the water."

The younger children had gathered around her in the corner of the room during the midday break. Six of them, the ones who still had Cheyenne, who still dreamed in it. They sat close, the particular closeness of children who understood that what was coming was for them specifically.

"The water went on forever in every direction. No land. No sky. Only the water and Maheo moving through it, and the waterbirds swimming on the surface, the geese and the loons and the ducks and the coots, because the waterbirds existed before the land did."

She told it as she had heard it told. Her mother's voice in it, and her mother's mother's voice before that. Not performing it. Just saying it, in Cheyenne, in the voice for true things.

"Maheo looked at the water and thought, *this is not enough*. There should be land. There should be a place for things to stand. So he asked the birds to help him. He asked them one by one to dive down through the water to the bottom and bring up earth."

The children were very still. They knew this story. That was not the point. The point was hearing it here, in this room, in this language, on this particular day.

"The big birds went first. The goose dove. The loon dove. They swam down as far as they could go and came back up with nothing. The water was too deep, the bottom too far. One after another they tried and one after another they failed."

She paused. Not for effect. Because the pause belonged there.

"Then the coot offered. The small one. The plain one. The one nobody had been waiting for."

One of the younger boys, five years old, round-faced, the one who still talked to his grandmother in Cheyenne, leaned forward slightly. He knew what was coming and he wanted it anyway.

"The coot dove. Down through the dark water, deeper than the goose, deeper than the loon, deeper than anyone had gone. Down until the water was cold and dark and the surface was gone. And at the very bottom, where nobody else had reached, the coot found it, a small ball of mud. He took it in his bill and swam back up."

She could feel the room behind her without looking. Sister Anne had been at the front working at her desk. The lesson was finished. The children were supposed to be at their midday break. What she was doing was not the lesson.

She did not stop.

"The coot brought the mud to Maheo. Maheo took it in his hands and worked it with his fingers, turning it, shaping it, drying it, until it became something. Then Grandmother Turtle came forward and said, *put it on my back. I will carry it.* And Maheo placed the mud on Grandmother Turtle's back and it began to grow."

The five-year-old boy's lips were moving slightly. Following the words.

"It grew and spread and flattened and rose and spread further, until there was land as far as anyone could see. Solid ground. A place for things to stand. And that is why," she said, "the turtle moves slowly. She is carrying the world. She has always been carrying the world. She does not put it down."

She stopped.

The children sat with it for a moment. The stillness of children who have heard something meant for them.

Then she heard the sound of Sister Anne's chair.

She did not turn immediately. She let the story finish settling. Then she looked up.

Sister Anne was standing at the front of the room. She had turned from her desk at some point, Emėškeha'e did not know exactly when. Her expression was that of a woman who has heard something she was not supposed to hear, deciding what to do with it. Not angry. Not yet. Something more careful than anger. An institution feeling the edge of something it would need to address.

She looked at Emėškeha'e. She looked at the children. She looked at Emėškeha'e again.

She did not speak.

She turned back to her desk.

The children dispersed quietly for their break. The five-year-old boy looked back at Emėškeha'e once before he went out the door. She looked back at him.

She knew what Sister Anne's silence meant. She had known before she opened her mouth.

She had told it anyway.

* * *

She was already home when he arrived. Later than usual, something

182

had kept her at the school. He could see it in her face before she spoke, not grief and not anger, the particular tension of a person who has done something they knew might cost them and is waiting to find out the price.

He tended the horses. Náhko pressed his nose against his arm while he worked, apparently having decided this was acceptable behavior. Néše'še-mééséne observed from a distance with the resigned expression of a horse that has accepted a situation it did not choose.

He went inside.

She had made the tea. She handed him his cup and sat.

He waited.

"Sister Anne taught Genesis today," she said. "Six days. The children listened."

She held her cup.

"During the break I gathered the younger ones. The ones who still had Cheyenne." She looked at the fire. "I told them how the world was made."

He looked at her.

"She heard the language. She turned."

She stopped there.

"What did she say?"

"Nothing. She did not have to."

She drank her tea.

"I knew when I was telling it that it would cost something. I told it anyway."

He looked at his cup. He thought about a man standing on a ridge, watching survey stakes go into the ground, saying nothing, showing the surveyors where to go, and coming home with their wages in his pocket.

"I rode with the surveyors for three days," he said.

She looked at him.

"They are dividing the reservation into individual parcels. A hundred and sixty acres for each head of household. The land that is left after the allotments, they call it surplus. It will be opened for white settlement."

She was very still.

"They talked about this in front of you," she said.

"They did not think I could follow what they were saying."

She looked at the fire. Something moved through her face that was not quite anger and not quite grief. Something older than both.

"How much of it?" she said. "How much surplus?"

He told her the number the younger surveyor had given.

She sat with it.

Outside, Náhko moved in the corral, his hooves quiet in the mud. The river ran fast below the bank. In Méanôhtse, the garden fence stood in the last of the evening light, the posts he had set deep, the rails tight, the small enclosed space of turned earth she had been working since the ground thawed.

"We knew this was coming," she said finally. It was not resignation. It was the statement of a woman who has been reading the machinery long enough to recognize its next movement before it arrives.

"Yes," he said.

"We knew, and it is still coming."

"Yes."

She looked at her hands.

He looked at the fire.

Outside the fence, the garden held in the fading light. The survey stakes held the reservation's new geometry in the ground above the river. The same gesture at different scales, for different purposes, with different consequences.

Neither of them said this.

They sat with the fire between them and the spring evening settling around the cabin and Náhko moving quietly in the corral outside and the river running fast below Éstávé-vóhe's roots, carrying the last of the winter away.

20

Tobias

She came in from the yard to find them already in their seats.

Six children. The ones she had gathered around her in the corner of the room during the midday break on that April afternoon when Sister Anne had taught Genesis, and she had told them how the world was really made.

They were sitting with their hands in their laps and their eyes forward, signs around their necks.

Thin pasteboard. Ink. A nun's careful hand.

I Will Not Speak Cheyenne.

The five-year-old boy, the round-faced one, the one who still talked to his grandmother, whose lips had moved following her words while the coot dove down through the dark water, had his hands folded in his lap and his eyes on the desk in front of him. The sign was too large for his small chest. The twine cut into the back of his neck where it had been sitting.

She stood in the doorway and looked at what she had done.

Sister Anne was at the front of the room. She turned when Eméškeha'e entered. Her expression was the expression she used for institutional matters, composed, deliberate, the face of a woman

186

who has made a considered decision and is prepared to explain it.

"The children were speaking Cheyenne among themselves," she said. "This cannot continue. The directive is clear. English only. They need to understand that their language has no place here."

Eméškeha'e looked at the six children. At the signs around their necks. The five-year-old boy's hands were folded in his lap.

She said nothing.

"There is something else," Sister Anne said.

She waited.

"The children have been given an incorrect account of creation. They need to hear the correct one. In English." Sister Anne looked at her steadily. "From you. They will listen to you."

The other children, the ones without signs, the ones who had learned already to keep their Cheyenne invisible, sat at their desks and looked at nothing in particular with the careful attention of children who understand that something is happening that they should not appear to notice.

Eméškeha'e looked at Sister Anne for a moment.

Then she walked to the front of the room.

* * *

She stood before them. The six children with the signs around their necks and the twenty others behind them. The five-year-old boy had his hands folded and his eyes now on her face.

She began.

"In the beginning," she said, "God created the heavens and the earth."

Her voice was level. She did not rush. She had done difficult things in front of people before. Climbed cliffs in the dark with children passed up hand to hand, walked into Fort Robinson on an October morning knowing what it was, stood at the edge of Darlington Agency,

187

and understood where she was. She knew how to keep her voice level when the task required it.

"The earth was without form and void, and darkness was over the face of the deep."

The words in English. The language of the signs around their necks. The language the institution required. She said each word completely, with full attention, as if the thing she was doing deserved to be done well.

"And God said, let there be light. And there was light."

Somewhere in the second day, God dividing the waters, God gathering the seas, God making the dry land appear, the tears came.

Not a sound. Not a trembling in her voice. Just tears running down her face as she continued, not stopping or wiping them away. Her voice stayed level. Her eyes stayed on the children. She kept teaching.

The five-year-old boy watched her face. He did not look away.

The other children watched her too, all of them, the ones with signs and the ones without, watching the adult at the front of the room who was crying without stopping, whose voice did not break, who was telling them this story with her face completely open and wet and her voice completely steady, as if both things could be true at once and she was going to let them see that they were.

Sister Anne saw the tears.

She looked at Eméškeha'e from the side of the room with something that was not quite sympathy and not quite satisfaction. Something more complicated than either. The expression of a woman who believes what she is doing is necessary and is willing to acknowledge that necessary things sometimes cause pain, and who has made her peace with that acknowledgment long ago. She nodded once, very slightly.

She did not stop it.

Eméškeha'e taught to the end.

The sixth day. God made man from the dust of the ground. God breathed life into him. God saw that it was not good for man to be alone and made a woman. God looked at everything he had made and saw that it was very good.

She stopped.

The room was quiet.

"You may go for your break," Sister Anne said.

The children rose. Filed out. The ones with signs last, moving carefully with the pasteboard against their chests, the twine around their necks.

The five-year-old boy was last of all.

He stopped beside her on his way to the door. He was small enough that he had to look up at her. He looked at her face, still wet, though she had finally pressed her sleeve against it, and then he reached up with both hands and lifted the sign from around his neck.

He held it out to her.

She took it.

He went outside.

She stood in the empty room. The fire in the small stove. The desks in their rows. The slates on their hooks. The smell of chalk and woodsmoke and the particular smell of many small children in a closed room.

She looked at the sign in her hands.

I Will Not Speak Cheyenne.

The ink permanent. The nun's hand, careful and even. The pasteboard was slightly damp from where it had rested against the boy's chest all morning.

She folded it once. She put it in her coat pocket. She put on her coat and went out to where Vohkoohe was waiting.

* * *

She rode home along the river road.

Vohkoohe moved steadily beneath her, unhurried, reading the road with complete attention and no particular urgency. The Tongue ran high and fast on the left. The bluffs held the last of the afternoon light on their faces. Somewhere ahead, the cabin smoke would be visible above the draw.

Eméškeha'e did not think about what had happened. She had thought about it enough. She let Vohkoohe carry her, watched the river, felt the folded pasteboard in her coat pocket, and rode home.

He was in the corral when she arrived. He looked up when he heard Vohkoohe on the river road, and he saw her face before she dismounted, and he did not say anything.

He took Vohkoohe's reins. He tended the horses while she went inside. Náhko pressed against his arm while he worked. Néše'šeméšéne stood at the far end of the corral in his customary position of dignified disapproval.

When he came inside, she was sitting at the table. The fire was not yet built up. He built it. He made the tea. He set it in front of her and sat.

She held the cup.

After a while, she said, "They punished the children."

He waited.

"The ones I told the story to. In April." She looked at the fire. "Signs around their necks. A ruler across their palms. Because they were speaking Cheyenne."

He said nothing.

"Because I spoke it to them there. In that room. On that day."

She held her cup with both hands.

"Sister Anne told me I had to teach them Genesis. In English. From me." She stopped. "So they would hear it from someone they trusted."

He looked at her.

"I taught it," she said.

He waited.

"I cried," she said. "I did not mean to. I could not stop it. I kept teaching, and I could not stop the tears. The children saw, Sister Anne saw."

She was quiet for a moment.

"Tobias gave me his sign."

"Tobias," he said.

"The small one. The round-faced one." She looked at the fire. "They named him Tobias. He gave me his sign and went outside."

She reached into her coat pocket, took out the folded pasteboard, and set it on the table between them.

He looked at it. He did not touch it.

She unfolded it so he could read it.

I Will Not Speak Cheyenne.

The ink, even and permanent in the firelight. The careful hand of a woman who believed she was doing necessary work.

He looked at it for a long time.

Outside, Náhko moved in the corral. The river ran fast in the dark. Éstávé-vóhe stood at the bank holding the stars in its highest branches.

She folded the sign again.

She did not put it back in her pocket. She left it on the table between them.

They sat with the fire and the sign and the spring dark coming down around the cabin, and neither of them said what they were both thinking because some things did not need to be said to be completely understood by both people in the room.

She was still here.

But something had changed.

Both of them felt it.

21

Still Here

The second winter was different from the first.

The first winter had been a negotiation. The wood stacking, the two pans, the specific geography of two solitary people learning where the edges were. This winter had no edges left to find. They knew each other now in the deep knowledge that lived in the body rather than the mind, arriving without announcement and staying without effort.

The cabin was warm. The stores were laid in. The wood was stacked cross-hatched in the lean-to beside the door, enough for the season and past it. The Tongue had frozen solid in November and lay under a foot of snow, visible from the window as a slight depression in the white, a seam in the landscape where the river was, patient beneath it all, waiting for March.

He was reading by the stove.

She had taught him. Not as instruction, nothing so formal as that, but practically and without ceremony. He had wanted to read English better. She had books from the school, borrowed and returned. Over the course of a year, he had gone from laboring over individual words to reading with the steady, complete attention he brought to everything. Taking in the whole of it, understanding what it said, not missing things.

The book was by Cooper. *The Last of the Mohicans*, borrowed from the mission library, the spine worn from other hands. He had been reading it for three days.

She was at the table by the window where the light came in best, even in winter, even when it was grey. The scabbard was in her hands. Weeks of work already in it, the beading specific and deliberate, a pattern he had seen developing without asking what it was for. Her needle moved through the leather with the particular rhythm of someone doing something they knew how to do completely.

The stove ticked in the corner. Outside, Náhko stood at the corral fence with his chin on the top rail, his paint patches stark against the white. The dark of his hindquarters and the broad irregular white of his chest and the left side of his face, the most conspicuous horse on the Tongue River. He was apparently content with this.

Watches Twice turned a page.

"He wrote Indians the way a man writes about the dark," she said, without looking up from her work. "Guessing at shapes he never learned to see."

He looked at her. Then at the book in his hands. Then back to the page.

He read it differently after that.

* * *

By midmorning, the cabin was warm enough that he had moved his chair back from the stove by several inches. She noticed this and said nothing. After a while, she set her beading on the table, rose, opened the stove door, and put a stick of wood in.

He looked at her over the top of the book.

She put in another stick.

"It is warm enough," he said.

She looked at him for a moment longer. Then she closed the stove door, sat back down, and picked up her beading.

He moved his chair back another inch.

She got up and put in another stick. Her eyes on his. Not smiling. Completely serious, as if daring him to comment. The eyes of a woman who had decided on a temperature and was prepared to maintain it.

He put the book down without a word.

She closed the stove, turned, and sat down.

He picked the book back up.

The cabin was definitively her temperature.

* * *

Vó'kêséhe arrived in the mid-afternoon, when the snow had been coming down steadily since morning and showed no particular intention of stopping.

His knock was the knock of a man who knew he was welcome but respected the form of it. He came in with the cold still on him, shaking snow from his coat, and Eméškeha'e was already moving toward the stove before he had his coat off. She fed him without discussion. This was established practice, the understanding of a place that was on the road to Ashland, warm, and belonging to his cousin.

He sat at the table and ate and looked around the cabin with the easy assessment of a man who had been coming here long enough to notice when things changed and had stopped remarking on most of them.

He was perhaps forty, Vó'kêséhe, with the particular quality of a man who had survived things by staying light on his feet and had made a philosophy of it. His face had humor in it, the way certain faces permanently held weather, not performed, just present, a condition of being him.

He spoke English easily, the English of a man who had been navigating white institutions for years, and shifted into Cheyenne without announcement, as ground shifts underfoot when the terrain changes. Not for Watches Twice's benefit. Not against it either. Just the natural movement between two languages that had always lived in him at different depths.

"Cold," he said, which covered the weather and the ride and possibly several other things.

"Yes," Watches Twice said.

Vó'kêséhe looked around the cabin with the ease of a man arriving somewhere he had been many times. He looked at the stove. He looked at the scabbard on the table. He looked at Watches Twice.

"Still here," he said. Not a question.

"Still here," Watches Twice said.

The scabbard was on the table where she had set it when she got up to feed him. He picked it up. Turned it over. His eyes moved across the beadwork with the attention of a man reading something he was taking seriously, the pattern, the colors, the specific quality of the work. He looked at Watches Twice. He looked at Emėškeha'e. She didn't look up from the food she was wrapping for him to take.

He set the scabbard down.

He said nothing about it.

They talked, English mostly, with Cheyenne threading through naturally, a word arriving in one language because it was faster or more precise than its translation, the two of them shifting without announcement while Watches Twice followed what he could and let the rest go. He had learned that some conversations in this cabin would happen around him rather than to him, and that this was not exclusion. Simply the shape of a life that contained two languages, and he was still working his way into the second one.

He followed more than they thought he did.

* * *

Vó'kêséhe went out before leaving to check his horse, and Watches Twice went with him.

The cold hit hard after the warmth of the cabin, the particular cold of a Montana afternoon in deep winter, arriving in the lungs before it arrived anywhere else. The snow was still coming down, steady and without urgency, settling in for the long work of it.

Vó'kêséhe's horse was at the fence, a dark sorrel with two white stockings, patient in the cold. He checked the cinch and ran a hand along the horse's neck.

Then he saw Néše'še-méšéne.

The bay roan stood at the far end of the corral. The red-brown base coat thick with winter, the roaning heavy through it, lighter across the barrel and darker on the legs and face, the grey-white of the roan hairs giving him a quality of light particular to that color and no other. He stood watching Vó'kêséhe with his customary expression, contained, not committing to an opinion yet.

Vó'kêséhe looked at the horse for a moment.

"That one," he said. "What's his name?"

"Néše'še-méšéne," Watches Twice said.

Vó'kêséhe was quiet. He looked at the horse. He looked at Watches Twice. Something moved through his face that was not quite a smile and not quite a question.

"River Crossing Watcher," Watches Twice said.

"Yes," Vó'kêséhe said. "I know what it means."

He looked at the horse for another moment. Then he turned and went back inside. Watches Twice followed him.

* * *

Emėškeha'e was at the table with her beading when they came back in. She looked up when they entered, reading both their faces in one glance with the efficiency she brought to everything.

Vó'kêséhe sat down. He looked at her. He said it in Cheyenne, brief and pointed, the tone of a man who has understood something and is enjoying the understanding.

"Néstahe Náhko'e vó'kȯhéva néháahtse tsé-háe'ėstse."

She looked up from her beading.

One beat.

She laughed. The real laugh, not the controlled amusement she usually allowed herself, not the half-laugh that came with a name arrived at correctly, but the full laugh, sudden and complete, the laugh of a woman caught by something genuinely funny and without defense against it.

"He told you?" she said through her smile.

Vó'kêséhe laughed too.

Watches Twice looked up from his book. He had caught Náhko'e vó'kȯhéva, the Crow's horse, his horse, and the tone of it, and her laughing, and he understood with complete certainty that he was the subject of what had just been said. He did not understand the rest. He looked at Vó'kêséhe. He looked at Emėškeha'e, her eyes still smiling, not looking at him, her hand trying to hide the smile on her mouth now.

He looked back at his book.

He was a man who had accepted that some things in this life would not be explained to him. He had decided some time ago that this was correct and that the correct response was dignity.

He turned a page.

Vó'kêséhe looked at Emėškeha'e. Something passed between them, brief, warm, without ceremony. The acknowledgment of a man who had watched his cousin survive things he couldn't name and had arrived at a judgment about the man she had chosen to survive them with. He didn't say it. He didn't have to. She received it with a slight inclination of her head and went back to her beading.

The moment closed.

* * *

Vó'kêséhe left before dark. He had to make it to Ashland before full night, and the snow was still coming down. Watches Twice stood and shook his hand. Vó'kêséhe put a hand on his shoulder and said, "Néheše, ného'évoomáhe." He took his food and his horse and went with the ease of a man who had somewhere to be and was not troubled by the weather.

They stood in the doorway and watched him go. His sorrel moving steadily into the white, his shape diminishing, and then the snow taking him entirely.

She closed the door.

Watches Twice looked at Eméškeha'e.

"He said you are a good man," she said.

The cabin settled back into its winter quiet. The stove. The window going dark outside. The particular quality of an evening when the snow was still falling, and the world had contracted to what the lantern light reached.

He went back to his chair. He picked up the book. He read for a while, or appeared to. She noticed that he turned fewer pages than usual, and his eyes were not moving with their usual tracking across the page.

After a while, she set down her beading.

She picked up the scabbard. She carried it to his chair and set it on the arm beside his book.

He looked at it.

He looked at her.

She had already gone back to the table. She sat down, picked up her beading, and did not look at him.

He set the book down.

He picked up the scabbard. Turned it in his hands. The beadwork was specific. It was not trade work, not generic, something designed. The colors moved in a pattern he couldn't name but recognized. The recognition that lived in the body, not the mind, arrived from somewhere he couldn't account for and settled there. It was made for his rifle. It was made for him. Weeks of her hands in it. Weeks of the specific attention she brought to things that deserved it.

He held it for a long time.

Then he set it carefully on the table beside his book. It would be there when he needed it.

He did not say anything.

She did not say anything.

The stove ticked in the corner. Outside, the snow fell on Éstávé-vóhe, on the garden fence in Méanôhtse, on the corral where Náhko stood with his chin on the top rail, looking at the white world with his characteristic seriousness. The Tongue lay frozen and patient beneath its snow, waiting for March.

The scabbard on the table.

The book beside it.

Her needle, moving through the leather.

His eyes on the page, or on the fire, or on her. She didn't look up to check, and he didn't announce it.

Both of them, still here.

Both of them, exactly where they were.

22

Mótséhe-he'e

The cough had been in the dormitory for two weeks before Mótséhe-he'e stopped getting up in the morning.

Eméškeha'e had heard it, everyone had heard it, the sound moving through the sleeping room at night, one child and then another, the particular cough of cold air and thin blankets and bodies that had been given less than they needed for long enough that they had stopped being able to resist what came through the door. She had mentioned it to Sister Anne. Sister Anne had nodded and said they would monitor it and had not separated the sick children from the well ones because she did not understand that this was necessary, because no one had told her, because the school had been built on the assumption that prayer and discipline and the correct attitude toward suffering would manage what medicine and ventilation and adequate food might have managed better.

Mótséhe-he'e had been watching Eméškeha'e since the second week of school.

Not intrusively, the girl was not intrusive. She watched the way her name was said, quietly, completely, from a careful distance, how a person watched something they were trying to understand before they committed to understanding it. She had smiled at Emėškeha'e across the sewing room on a morning in October, a smile that arrived and departed quickly, the smile of a child who had decided something and was acknowledging the decision. Emėškeha'e had smiled back. That was all. But the thread between them had been there since then, present and unspoken, the specific thread that formed between two people who recognized something in each other without naming it.

She was nine years old. Her hair had been cut when she arrived. It was growing back.

* * *

On the third day after Mótséhe-he'e stopped getting up, the fever arrived.

Emėškeha'e was in the dormitory when it came. The small body going hot between one moment and the next, the forehead burning under her hand, the girl's eyes too bright and her breathing too quick. She had seen this before. She knew what this kind of fever asked of the person sitting beside it.

She sent word to Sister Anne.

Sister Anne came, looked at the girl, and said she would send for the doctor from Miles City if it did not improve by morning. She said it with the confidence of a woman who believed that sending for the doctor from Miles City was an adequate response to what was happening in the bed in front of her.

Emėškeha'e did not say what she was thinking.

She stayed.

The other children were moved to the far end of the dormitory, not separated, not taken to another room, just shifted to the other side of the same space, their cots pushed toward the far wall. Sister Anne did not understand what the cough meant or how it moved. She understood that the girl was sick, that prayer was appropriate, and that the doctor would come if things did not improve.

Things did not improve.

The night was long. Eméškeha'e sat beside the cot and did what she could. A damp cloth, the blanket adjusted, the small adjustments that could not fix anything, but were the only thing available. The fire in the stove at the end of the room was not enough to counter the cold coming through the walls. She could feel it on her back while the fever burned in front of her.

At some point in the night, Mótséhe-he'e spoke.

Not in English. English left first when the fever came. It was the learned language, the school language, the language that lived in the front of the mind where the fever reached first. What came back was Cheyenne, the language of her grandmother's lodge, the language her body had been built in.

She said something about her mother.

Eméškeha'e leaned close and answered in Cheyenne, quietly, the voice for true things, and the girl's face changed. Something in it settling, the specific settling of a person who has heard something they recognize in a place where recognition had stopped being available.

She answered back. Her mother's name. A place. Something about horses.

Eméškeha'e held her hand and answered what she could and did not look away.

Sister Anne came in twice during the night. She saw Eméškeha'e speaking Cheyenne to the girl and said nothing. This was not the moment for the English-only rule. Even Sister Anne understood that this was not the right moment.

* * *

The doctor came from Miles City on the second day.

He examined the girl with the efficiency of a man who had made this ride before and knew what he was going to find before he arrived. He spoke to Sister Anne in a low voice in the hallway. Eméškeha'e heard the word tuberculosis. She had heard it before, on the reservation, in the camps, the coughing sickness that had followed the Cheyenne north from Darlington and had not left.

She went back into the dormitory and sat beside Mótséhe-he'e.

The girl's eyes were open. She looked at Eméškeha'e. The watchfulness still present, dimmed but present, the girl she had always been still behind the fever.

Eméškeha'e thought about her family. Three miles away. Perhaps four. Her mother. Her grandmother. The women who should have been in this room, who would have known what to do, what to say, what ceremonies belonged to this moment, what Cheyenne words existed for the specific passage this child was making.

They were not here.

No one had sent for them.

She looked at Sister Anne in the hallway, still speaking with the doctor, and realized it had not occurred to her to send for them. Not from cruelty, Sister Anne was not cruel. From the deep and absolute conviction that what the Church offered was sufficient for every human passage, that the family's ceremonies were at best irrelevant and at worst an obstacle to the child's proper departure from this world. The family was three miles away and had not been sent for because the school had decided it knew what this moment required, and the family's knowledge did not enter into that calculation.

Eméškeha'e did not leave.

She sat beside Mótséhe-he'e, held her hand, and spoke to her in Cheyenne, the language her body knew, and did what she could with what she had, which was not enough and was everything available.

* * *

She came home in the dark.

Later than she had ever come home. Vohkoohe moved steadily on the river road, unhurried, reading the dark completely and without urgency. The Tongue was frozen beside them, visible as a pale depression in the darker ground, patient beneath its ice.

There was a light in the cabin.

He was there when she arrived. He came out when he heard Vohkoohe on the road. He took the reins without speaking, and he looked at her face once, then looked at the horse and began to tend her.

She went inside.

She sat at the table.

She did not take off her coat.

He came in after a while. He built the fire up. He made the tea. He set it in front of her, sat across from her, and did not speak or look at her with the particular quality of someone waiting for something. He just sat.

The fire ticked in the stove.

Outside, the river was quiet under its ice.

She held the cup with both hands and looked at the fire, and did not speak for a long time. The tea cooled. She did not drink it.

After a while, she said, "Mótséhe-he'e."

Once. Just the name. Placed on the table between them as something that was true and needed to be said, and did not need anything added to it.

He received it.

He did not ask what had happened. He did not ask about the school, the doctor, or the family that had not been sent for. He looked at the fire, received the name, sat with what it meant, and did not try to make it smaller than it was.

After some time, he reached across the table.

He took her hand.

It was not a thing either of them did easily, not a gesture that belonged to the ordinary texture of their life together, the pans and the wood and the tea and the specific negotiation of two solitary people who had found each other late and carefully. But he reached across and took her hand and held it on the table between them, and neither of them moved.

The fire burned down.

She did not speak again.

He did not speak.

They sat together with the fire and the name between them until she rose and went outside.

* * *

The night was very cold.

She stood in the yard and looked up.

Éstávé-vóhe stood at the bank of the frozen river, his two pale leaders against the winter sky, the bark silver in the starlight. She looked up through his bare branches, the two leaders spreading against the dark, the smaller branches spreading from those, and at the tips of everything the stars.

She had told him this. The stars traveled up from deep in the earth, through the roots, up through the trunk, and into the highest branches, and waited there for the wind to release them into the sky. She had told him this about a cottonwood tree on an afternoon in December. He had put his knife away. She had given him the tree's name.

She looked up through Éstávé-vóhe's branches at the stars sitting in his highest tips.

She stood very still.

Then one moved.

A streak of light releasing itself from the tip of the highest branch, there and then gone, traveling across the winter sky, the specific brief brightness of a thing set free. She watched it go until there was nothing left to watch.

She stood in the cold for a while longer.

Then she went back inside.

* * *

He was still at the table. He looked up when she came in. She took off her coat, hung it, sat back down, picked up the cold tea, and drank it.

He watched her face.

She looked at the fire.

After a while, she said, "Her family was three miles away."

He waited.

"No one sent for them." She held the cup. "They buried her in the school's ground."

He looked at the fire.

Neither of them said anything else.

The stove ticked in the corner. Outside Éstávé-vóhe stood at the bank holding his stars, the ones that remained, the ones not yet ready to go. The frozen Tongue lay patient beneath its ice. Náhko moved once in the corral, his hooves quiet, and then was still.

Both of them, still here.

Both of them exactly, where they were.

23

Passed Along

The paper sat on the table between them.

Vó'kêséhe had brought it from Two Moons, Éše'he Ohnéšesėstse, folded once, the writing inside in English, the words careful and measured, the specific English of a man who had learned that careful and measured was what the agency required if you wanted to be taken seriously, and who had decided to give them what they required while understanding it would change nothing.

Watches Twice looked at the paper without picking it up.

"The lines run through Joseph Limpy's corral," Vó'kêséhe said. "Through Martha Whitedirt's garden. Through the ground where Standing Cloud's family has been since they came north." He paused. "Two Moons wants it carried by someone who has the agent's ear."

"The agent will receive it," Watches Twice said. "He will thank me for bringing it. He will say it will be passed along."

"Yes," Vó'kêséhe said.

"I'll carry it."

Vó'kêséhe nodded once. He drank his tea. He looked around the cabin, the scabbard on the wall, the two pans on the shelf, the garden visible through the window, the first green of it in the morning light.

Eméškeha'e looked at the window. At the draw above the cabin, Méanôhtse, the still place, the fence he had built in the cold, catching the morning light. She looked at it for a moment. Then she looked back at the table.

Vó'kêséhe stood. He put on his coat. At the door, he stopped.

"The boy," he said. In Cheyenne. To her. "The small, round-faced one."

She looked at him.

"He ran," Vó'kêséhe said.

He went out.

She rode to the school.

* * *

The morning was clear, the Tongue running fast with the last of the snowmelt, the cottonwoods along the bank in their first leaf, pale green, the particular green of things just beginning. Vohkoohe moved steadily on the river road, and Eméškeha'e let her find her own pace and thought about Tobias.

He had been at the school since September. Seven months. She had watched him arrive, the round-faced boy who still talked to his grandmother in Cheyenne, who had leaned forward when she told the story of the coot, whose lips had moved following the words. She had watched Mótséhe-he'e find him in the first week and quietly make herself his person in the building, sitting beside him at meals, walking with him between lessons, the specific watchfulness of a girl who had decided this one needed someone watching over him and had appointed herself to the task without announcement.

She had watched him after Mótséhe-he'e died. The stillness that had changed in him, not his ordinary stillness, which was the stillness of a child who observed carefully before committing to anything. This

208

was the stillness of a child who had lost the one person in the building who was specifically his.

She tied Vohkoohe at the gate and went inside.

Sister Anne met her in the hallway. Her expression was the expression she kept for institutional matters, composed, deliberate, the face of a woman who has made a considered decision and is prepared to explain it.

"Tobias ran yesterday afternoon," she said. "During the afternoon break. He was found on the reservation road and returned by the agency policeman this morning." She paused. "He needs to understand that this cannot happen. That there are consequences." She looked at Eméškeha'e steadily. "He will hear it better from you."

Eméškeha'e looked at her.

She thought about Tobias on the reservation road. Four miles north. His grandmother's place was perhaps four miles away. She thought about him running, not in panic, not blindly, but with direction, a six-year-old boy who knew exactly where he was going. Who had decided to go there because Mótséhe-he'e was dead, and he had nothing left in this building that was specifically his.

She thought about how close he had been. Whether he had been close enough to see his grandmother's place from where the agency policeman stopped him.

She reached up and untied her apron.

She folded it and set it on the table beside her, carefully, with the same attention she brought to things that deserved to be done well, even when they were hard. She picked up her coat.

Sister Anne watched her.

Neither of them said what had just happened. They did not need to. The apron on the table said it. The coat in her hands said it.

She went out to where Vohkoohe was waiting.

She did not go after Tobias.

She rode home.

* * *

Watches Twice delivered the message to the agency that afternoon.

He rode into town, tied his horse at the rail, and went in. The agent received him with the practiced patience of a man who had been doing this long enough to have developed a specific way of acknowledging what was brought to him without being moved by it. He read the paper. He looked up. He thanked Watches Twice for bringing it. He said it would be passed along to the relevant office in Washington.

Watches Twice looked at him for a moment.

Then he went out.

He mounted and rode north. When he reached the ridge above the river, he stopped.

From the ridge, he could see the reservation spread below him. The river bottom and the bluffs and the draws running up into the high ground. He could see the survey stakes in the ground, their lines cutting across the landscape in a geometry the landscape did not recognize. He could see where the lines ran through Joseph Limpy's corral. Through Martha Whitedirt's garden.

He could see Méanôhtse.

The draw above the cabin. The still place. The garden fence he had built in the cold. The first green of her garden visible even from here, the careful rows of it, the work of her hands in it since the ground thawed.

He could see where the survey line ran.

He sat his horse on the ridge for a long time.

Then he rode down.

* * *

She was in the yard when he arrived. Not doing anything, just standing with her arms at her sides, looking at Méanôhtse. The afternoon light was on the draw, its green bright in the low sun, the fence rails casting long shadows across the turned earth.

He tended his horse. He came and stood beside her.

They looked at the draw together.

After a while, she said, "How much of it?"

He told her.

She stood with it. Her face did not change. She had known the shape of it before she knew the specific measurement, since morning, since looking through the window at the fence in the early light, since Vó'kêséhe's expression when he looked at her. The knowing didn't arrive in this moment. The moment just confirmed what the body had already understood.

"Martha Whitedirt's garden too," he said. "Joseph Limpy's corral."

She nodded.

They stood together in the afternoon light and looked at the draw she had named for its stillness and the garden she had put into the ground and the fence he had built in the cold of their first winter together.

"The message," she said.

"Delivered."

She looked at him.

"He said it would be passed along," Watches Twice said.

She looked back at the draw.

"Yes," she said.

* * *

She heard about Tobias the next morning.

Jane came before first light. She was one of the Cheyenne women who worked the mission kitchen, a woman who moved through the school's spaces with the specific invisibility of someone the institution had stopped seeing because she was useful and quiet. She knocked on the door and waited. Eméškeha'e opened the door and waved her in.

Eméškeha'e made tea. Jane sat at the table, held her cup, looked at it, and after a while said what she had come to say.

She said it in Cheyenne.

Eméškeha'e listened without looking away from Jane's face and did not speak, and when Jane finished, she sat with it for a moment.

Then she said, "How bad?"

Jane told her.

Eméškeha'e looked at the fire.

What Jane described was not unusual. It was the thing that happened to children who ran, the response the institution had developed for the specific problem of children who decided they would rather be home than here. It was done in front of the other children because the institution understood that the purpose of punishment was not only the correction of the individual but the education of the group. What happened to the one who ran was a lesson for the ones who stayed.

The other children had watched.

Including the ones who had worn signs around their necks. Including the ones who had leaned in to hear the story of the coot and the mud, whose lips had moved following the words.

She sat with this.

She thought about being in that room. About what she would have been able to do. What she would not have been able to do. Whether the difference between those two things would have been enough.

She did not know. She would never know. She had not been there.

She had ridden home.

Jane left before the sun was up. Eméškeha'e sat at the table in the dark and did not move for a long time.

* * *

When Watches Twice came in from tending the horses, she was still sitting there. He looked at her face and did not ask. He built the fire up, made the tea, sat across from her, and waited.

After a while, she said, "Tobias."

He waited.

"What they did to him." She looked at the fire. "In front of the others."

He looked at the fire too.

"I was not there," she said.

"No."

She did not say, I should have been. Because there was no true ending to that sentence. She could not have been both the person who refused and the person who protected him from what her refusal left him to. The institution would have done what it did regardless of whether she was in the building. The only thing her presence would have changed was that she would have been there to see it.

She looked at the fire for a long time.

"I am not going back," she said.

"All right," he said.

The fire ticked in the stove. Outside, the spring morning was coming up over the bluffs, the light moving down into the valley, the Tongue catching it along its far bank.

* * *

She found him behind the corral three days later.

He had gone out after breakfast with a shovel and begun turning the ground behind the corral, sheltered from the wind, the light coming in from the south most of the day, the earth soft from the spring thaw.

He had not told himself he was planning it. The shovel was in his hands, and the ground was there, and he began.

He heard her come out of the cabin. He heard her stop.

He kept working.

After a while, he heard her go back inside. Then she came back out. Her footsteps came around the corral, and she stopped beside him.

She had her garden tools.

She looked at the ground he had turned. She crouched down, took a handful of the turned earth, felt it, and let it fall through her fingers. She stood up.

She began to work beside him.

They did not talk about Méanôhtse. They did not discuss the survey lines or the message passed to the relevant office in Washington. They did not talk about Tobias or Jane or what had been done in front of the other children.

They turned the earth together in the spring morning and prepared the ground and did the ordinary work of people who intended to still be here when things came up.

Náhko watched from the corral fence with his chin on the top rail.

Above the river Éstávé-vóhe stood in his new leaves, pale green against the blue sky, the two leaders spreading, the branches full now, the stars traveling up through his roots in the dark as they always traveled, patient, waiting for the wind.

The survey stakes stood in the ground on the ridge above them.

The new ground was soft under their hands.

Both of them, still here.

24

Summer

Summer came to the Tongue River completely, the cold gone between one week and the next, the grass long in the draws, the river running lower and clearer than it had all spring, the days stretching until the light lasted past nine in the evening, and the nights were barely dark before the light began again.

She was at the table when he came in from the horses.

Papers in front of her. A letter half-drafted, the words in English, her handwriting careful and deliberate, not the careful deliberateness of someone uncertain about the language but of someone who understood that the language had to be exact to do what she needed it to do. The agency's own language turned back on itself. Its own logic used against its own outcomes.

He looked at what she was doing.

He made the tea. He set it beside her without interrupting and went back outside.

This was what mornings had become.

* * *

The grandmother came on a Tuesday in late June.

She came on foot from the reservation, three miles along the river road, carrying a letter she had been carrying for two weeks without knowing what it said. She was perhaps sixty, her face the face of a woman who had survived things without announcing it, her hands the hands of someone who had been working with them for sixty years and intended to continue.

She sat at the table, set the letter down, and looked at Eméškeha'e.

Eméškeha'e picked it up and read it.

It was from the agency. The allotment, her specific parcel, the hundred and sixty acres assigned to her household, the boundaries described in the numerical language of survey work that meant nothing to a woman who understood land as the place where her family's lodge had stood for four years and where her daughter's children played in the mornings. The letter also contained a discrepancy in its third paragraph. The parcel described did not match the parcel the family had been occupying. The numbers were wrong. Someone in the agency office had copied a number incorrectly from one document to another, and the error had propagated through three subsequent forms until it became official, which, in the agency's understanding, meant it was true.

The grandmother's actual land, the place where she lived, where her daughter lived, where her grandchildren ran in the mornings, was now officially assigned to a different family. The land assigned to her was three miles away, without water.

Eméškeha'e set the letter down.

She explained it in Cheyenne. Piece by piece, the way you gave someone difficult information when they needed to be able to receive each piece before the next one arrived. The grandmother listened without looking away. When Eméškeha'e finished, the grandmother sat with it for a moment.

Then she said, "Can it be fixed?"

"Yes," Eméškeha'e said. "It was a mistake. Mistakes can be corrected."

She said this with more confidence than she felt, because the grandmother needed to hear it with confidence and because it was technically true even if the agency's relationship to its own mistakes was complicated.

"Will you come with me?" the grandmother said.

"Yes," Eméškeha'e said. "Thursday."

* * *

The agent's office in Ashland was a single room in a building that smelled of paper, lamp oil, and the particular staleness of a space where windows were rarely opened. The agent was a man in his forties, efficient in the manner of men who processed many transactions daily and had developed systems for handling them without having to think too carefully about any individual one.

He looked up when they came in.

He looked at Eméškeha'e first, not the grandmother, not the person with the problem, but the one who appeared to speak English, with the assessment of a man recalibrating. He had expected one kind of interaction. He was going to get another kind.

"We're here about Agnes Limpy's allotment," Eméškeha'e said. She used the grandmother's English name, the name the agency had assigned her, the name that appeared on the forms. She had learned to use those names in these offices. The name the agency gave was the name the agency responded to.

She set the letter on his desk. She set beside it a piece of paper she had prepared with the correct parcel numbers, the correct legal description, and the documentation of the discrepancy between what the letter said and what the original survey recorded. She had spent two evenings on this paper. She had gone to the agency's own records, which were theoretically public, and found the original survey document, transcribed the numbers, and wrote a clear, specific account of where the error had occurred and what correction was required.

The agent read it.

He read it again.

His expression moved through several positions. Mild irritation, the reluctance of a man being asked to correct his own office's work, the calculation of whether this was something he could dismiss, and arrived at something that was not quite acceptance but was the recognition that the documentation in front of him was accurate and specific and would be difficult to argue with if it went further up the chain.

"I'll need to verify this against the original records," he said.

"Of course," Eméškeha'e said. "The original survey is document number forty-seven in your land records from November 1884. I've included the page and line numbers."

He looked at her.

She looked back at him with the specific quality of her look, the assessment that was quick and complete, the face of a woman who had sat across from agents and nuns and surveyors and understood exactly what each of them required in order to feel the obligation to respond.

He picked up his pen.

"I'll process a correction," he said. "Two to three weeks."

"Thank you," Eméškeha'e said.

On the ride back, the grandmother was quiet for a long time. The river ran beside them, low and clear in the summer heat. The cottonwoods along the bank cast moving shadows across the road.

After a while, the grandmother said, in Cheyenne, "You know how they think."

"Yes," Eméškeha'e said.

"That is useful."

"Yes," she said. "It is."

Word moved through the reservation, as all words moved, rider to rider, fire to fire, at the specific speed of information people needed.

She did not advertise. She did not announce. She was simply available, and the word of her availability moved, and people came.

A man whose application for additional grazing land had been denied without explanation. She read the denial, identified the regulation that had been misapplied, and wrote a response citing the correct regulation and the correct process for appeal. The appeal was partially successful. Not everything he asked for. Something.

A family whose children had been taken to the school at Busby without the parents' knowledge or consent. She wrote a letter to the agency superintendent, then to the Commissioner of Indian Affairs in Washington, and finally to a lawyer in Miles City whose name she had found in a newspaper. The children were returned. It took four months and eleven letters.

Two women whose late husbands' allotments had been reassigned to the agency's surplus pool rather than passing to the widows as the regulations specified. She found the regulations, cited them, sat across from the agent in Ashland three times in two weeks. The allotments were restored.

Not everything worked. More things didn't work than did. The machinery was large, and she was one woman with a pen, who turned the agency's own language back against it. The machinery had more patience than she did and more institutional weight than any letter she could write. There were cases she could not move. Families she could not help.

She wrote the letters anyway.

* * *

Watches Twice came home from a courier run to Miles City one evening to find four Cheyenne families in the yard. He tied his horse at the fence, looked at the yard, went inside, made tea for everyone, and brought it out on a board he carried with both hands, careful not to spill it.

He did not say anything about it.

Neither did she.

He had his own version of this.

Not the letters. Not the office visits. The connections. Years of being the reliable, quiet scout had given him access to people that access was not supposed to reach. He knew which officer at Fort Keogh had a conscience. He knew which agency official in Miles City was less corrupt than the one in Ashland and could occasionally be moved by a well-documented case.

He began delivering her letters to these people. Not officially. Not as a courier assignment. Just a man on a horse who happened to stop at a fort or an office and happened to have something in his kit that happened to find its way into the right hands.

He did not tell her he was doing this.

She did not ask.

They both knew.

* * *

Náhko was two years old and coming into his opinions.

He had always had opinions; this was Vohkoohe's son, after all, but at two, the opinions had acquired both weight and specificity. He knew what he wanted. He knew what he didn't want. He had a clear sense of which humans he was willing to negotiate with and which ones he was simply going to wait out.

Watches Twice worked with him in the mornings. Patient, unhurried, the same quality of attention he brought to everything. He understood that a horse like this one was not broken but negotiated with and that the negotiation took time and that the time was the work, not an obstacle to it.

Some mornings, the negotiation went well.

Some mornings, Náhko stood at the far end of the corral and looked at Watches Twice with the expression of a horse who had considered the day's agenda and found it unacceptable and was prepared to wait as long as necessary for a better offer.

On one such morning in late July, Eméškeha'e came out of the cabin and found Watches Twice at the fence watching the corral. Náhko was at the far end. Neither of them was moving. The standoff had the quality of something that had been in progress for a while.

She looked at this for a moment.

Then she opened the gate and walked in.

She went to Náhko without hurrying. He watched her come with the same careful attention he gave to things he was still deciding about. She stopped beside him, put her hand on his neck, and spoke to him in Cheyenne. Something brief, something that had the quality of a reminder rather than a command, the tone she used with things she expected to be understood.

Náhko put his nose against her arm.

She stood with him for a moment. Then she walked back to the gate, went out, closed it, and went back inside without saying anything.

Watches Twice stood at the fence.

He looked at Náhko.

Náhko looked back at him with an expression that had shifted, not exactly cooperative, but that of a horse who had received certain information and was processing its implications. He pawed the dirt and nickered.

Watches Twice accepted that some things about this horse would not be explained to him. He had decided some time ago that this was correct and that the correct response was patience.

He went back to work.

* * *

Vó'kêséhe came in August on his dark sorrel with the two white stockings, unhurried, the ease of a man arriving somewhere he knew he was welcome on a summer afternoon when there was no particular urgency to anything.

He came in, sat, ate, and looked around the cabin. The papers on the table. The specific purposefulness of the space, not the purposefulness of a school or an agency office, but of a place where work was being done on someone's own terms.

He looked at Watches Twice.

Something passed between them. The acknowledgment of two men who both understood what they were looking at. Not quite a smile. The thing that lived next to a smile in a man who expressed things carefully.

He stayed through the afternoon. The conversation was easy, the reservation, the summer, the horses. He told them that Joseph Limpy had repaired the section of his corral that the survey line had reassigned, and nobody from the agency had come to tell him not to, which they both understood as a small, specific victory of the kind that accumulated into something over time.

He told them his youngest, a girl, just walking, had said her first word in Cheyenne, and his wife had cried.

Emĕškeha'e smiled at this. The real smile, the one that arrived completely.

When he rose to go, he looked at her for a moment. He looked at the papers on the table. He looked at her again.

"Néheše, néhó'ëstse tsé-há'e," he said.

She received it with a slight inclination of her head.

He went out. They watched him ride until the river road took him.

* * *

That evening, she brought it up.

Not with anxiety, but with the specific practicality of a woman who had been managing difficult circumstances her whole adult life and understood that naming a problem was the first step toward solving it.

"We should talk about money," she said.

He had been waiting for this. Not with dread, with the recognition of a man who had been doing the same arithmetic in his own head for weeks and knew the conversation needed to happen.

"Yes," he said.

She told him what she had been thinking. The school money was gone. Had been gone since April. The letter-writing, the agency visits, none of it paid, not in cash, not in anything the trader in Ashland would accept. What people brought her, a jar of preserved plums, a piece of beadwork, an afternoon of labor in the garden, she received without making anything of it, but it didn't cover salt. It didn't cover the tools that needed replacing. It didn't cover the specific cash the world required, regardless of how much else you had.

He told her what the courier work still brought. Less than it had. The Army's need for Crow scouts was diminishing in ways that had been clear for two years and were now undeniable. The assignments came irregularly. The pay was the same when they came, but they came less often.

They sat with the arithmetic together.

The cabin was theirs, no rent, no mortgage, the allotment assigned in both their names. The garden was producing. They could eat through the winter on what the garden gave them, what the river gave them, and what the land around the cabin gave them if they were careful. They had been careful before. They knew how.

But the gap was there. Not large. Not immediately threatening. Present, and growing slowly in the direction of a problem.

"The horses," she said.

He looked at her.

"Náhko," she said. "When he's ready. There might be other ways."

He was quiet for a moment. He had thought about this too, the colt's potential, what he might eventually be worth without selling him. But the colt wasn't ready yet, and the gap was now, not eventually.

She looked at the fire.

"We'll manage," she said. Not as reassurance. As a statement of fact. They had managed harder things.

"Yes," he said. "We will."

Three days later, a man stopped at the fence.

* * *

Watches Twice was behind the cabin turning compost into the new garden when he heard a horse on the river road slow and stop. He came around the side of the cabin and saw the man standing at the corral fence.

He was perhaps fifty, weathered in the specific manner of men who had spent their lives outdoors in a country that had weather in it. Big through the shoulders, moving with the unhurried economy of someone who had learned a long time ago that moving carefully was smarter than moving fast. His horse was a good one, a dark bay gelding, well-maintained, the equipment on him practical and well-kept. The man himself was looking at the corral.

Not at Watches Twice. At the horses.

He stood at the fence with his hands on the top rail and his eyes moving over the three animals with the specific attention of a man who understood what he was looking at and was taking his time with it. Vohkoohe at the fence, watching him back. Néše'še-méšéne at the far end with his characteristic dignified wariness. And Náhko, the paint colt, standing in the middle of the corral with his bold irregular markings catching the afternoon light, watching the stranger at the fence with the complete attention he gave things he was still deciding about.

Watches Twice came to the fence.

The man looked up. He had the eyes of someone who read things carefully. Not the flat assessment of the agent in Ashland, not the calculating look of a man deciding what something was worth. Something different. The eyes of a man who looked at things because he genuinely wanted to understand them.

"Fine animals," he said. Not flattery. Observation.

"Yes," Watches Twice said.

They stood together at the fence for a moment, looking at the horses. The man's eyes went back to Náhko.

"Paint's yours?" he said.

"Belongs to the woman I live with," Watches Twice said. "Her mare produced him."

The man looked at Vohkoohe. He looked at the colt. He was doing the arithmetic of inheritance, what the mare had contributed, what the unknown father had contributed, how those things had combined into the specific animal standing in the corral looking back at them.

"Good cross," he said.

"Unplanned," Watches Twice said.

Something moved in the man's face. Not quite a smile.

"What's the roan?" he said.

"Néše'še-méšéne," Watches Twice said.

The man looked at him.

"River Crossing Watcher," Watches Twice said.

The man looked at the roan for a long moment. The recognition of a name that was exactly right for the animal wearing it.

"Good name," he said. "She named him?"

"Yes," Watches Twice said.

Elias looked at the corral for a moment. "The woman's Cheyenne," he said. Not a question. He had understood from the name and from something else, something in the quality of the horses themselves, the specific manner in which they were kept, the presence of three exceptional animals in one small corral on a river road in southeastern Montana.

"Yes," Watches Twice said. "Her horses. Her names."

The man nodded. He looked at the corral again. At Náhko, still standing in the middle of it, still watching him with the complete attention of a horse conducting a thorough assessment.

Then Náhko took a step toward the fence.

Watches Twice watched this. The colt that had stood at the far end of the corral and evaluated him for the better part of six months. Taking a step toward a stranger he had been looking at for ten minutes.

The man didn't move. Didn't reach. Didn't make any sound. Just stood at the fence with his hands on the top rail and let the colt come to its own conclusions.

Náhko came to the fence. He put his nose out toward Elias's hand and stood there, breathing in.

Watches Twice stood beside him and did not speak for a long moment.

"Took me the better part of six months to get him to do that," he said.

The man looked at the colt. "He's particular," he said. Not a criticism. The acknowledgment of a man who respected particularity in horses because it usually meant something worth respecting.

"His mother is particular," Watches Twice said.

The man looked at Vohkoohe, who was watching from the corner of the corral with the expression she used when something was happening that she had opinions about but had decided not to share yet.

He laughed. Quiet, brief, the laugh of a man who had known horses long enough to recognize exactly that kind of horse.

"Where are you from?" Watches Twice said.

"Deadwood now," the man said. "Blackfoot country before that. Philadelphia before that." He said *Blackfoot country* the way a man says the name of a place that has marked him, not one he has passed through. "Elias Harlan."

Watches Twice looked at him.

The name meant nothing to him. But something in Blackfoot country, the specific weight of it, did. A man who had been in Blackfoot country in the years of the Starvation Winter and was still moving through this world afterward had seen something. Watches Twice understood that without needing the details.

"Watches Twice," he said.

Elias looked at him. The name landing, understood for what it was. It was a Crow name, earned, belonging to this man specifically.

"Come in," Watches Twice said. "She'll have food."

* * *

Eméškeha'e looked up when they came in.

She read Elias in one glance, the weathered face, the careful

227

movement, the specific quality of a man who had seen things and was still standing. She looked at Watches Twice. A question in it.

He gave the slight inclination of his head that meant, this one is all right.

She did not clear the papers from the table. She set them aside but left them visible. This was her cabin, and this was her work, and a man who stayed for dinner at this table would see both.

She made food. The three of them sat.

The conversation found itself among people who were all accustomed to reading situations carefully and did not feel the need to fill the silence. Elias told them about the horse business he was doing with the Crow Agency, a negotiated arrangement, buying and selling, moving animals between the northern agencies and the ranches and forts that needed them. He told it plainly, without making himself larger in it than he was.

She told him about the allotment work. Not everything, the shape of it, what she was doing, and why. He listened completely, without hurrying. He asked one specific, practical question about the agency's appeals process. She answered it. He nodded.

He looked at the papers on the table for a moment.

"I grew up in Philadelphia," he said. "Before I went west." He said it without particular emphasis; the fact of it was placed on the table. "There were women there, church women, reform women, who had been working on Indian rights early on. Mary Bonney. Amelia Quinton. They started an organization. Women's National Indian Association." He looked at his plate. "Been sending petitions to Congress about reservation conditions ever since '79. I heard Bonney speak once, years ago. Before I left." He paused. "They'd want to know about your work. I can give you the address before I go."

Eméškeha'e looked at him.

He said it the same way he said everything, plainly, without making anything of it. Just information. Just a thing he had noticed that might be useful.

She received it without making anything of it either.

Outside, the light was going. Náhko moved in the corral. Elias looked out the window at the colt, as he had been doing throughout the meal, whenever the conversation paused, with the specific attention of a man still thinking about something.

He wrote Mary Bonney's name and the organization's Philadelphia address on a piece of paper and set it on the table. Then he stood.

At the door, he put on his coat.

He looked back at the corral one more time. Náhko in the evening light, the paint patches catching the last of the sun, the bold irregular white against the dark.

"That colt's going to be ready to cover mares in another year," he said. "Maybe less." He was looking at the corral, not quite at either of them. "A paint with that build and those markings, a man would pay good money for the right."

He left it there.

Watches Twice looked at Eméškeha'e.

She looked at him.

"We might be open to that," Watches Twice said.

Elias nodded. As if this were simply information received and filed. As if he hadn't just given them something.

"There's a rancher outside Miles City who's been looking for good paint blood," he said. "I'll mention you."

He went out.

* * *

They stood in the doorway and watched him ride north on the river road, his dark bay gelding moving steadily, until the bend took him.

She looked at the corral. At Náhko, still standing where Elias had left him, watching the road where the man had gone.

"He knew the horses," she said.

"Yes," Watches Twice said.

"He knew us too," she said. "By the end."

Watches Twice looked at the road where Elias had gone.

"Yes," he said. "He did."

* * *

That evening, she sat at the table after he had gone to sleep and wrote a letter.

Not for the agency. Not for any official. For Margaret Forsythe in Miles City, a name Elias Harlan had left on the table plainly, without making anything of it, just a thing that might be useful placed where it could be picked up.

For Mary Bonney at the Women's National Indian Association in Philadelphia, a name Elias Harlan had left on the table plainly, without making anything of it, just a thing that might be useful placed where it could be picked up.

She wrote in the specific English she had developed for these letters, precise, institutional where precision helped, personal where the personal was necessary. She told Mary Bonney about Agnes Limpy's allotment error. About the children taken to Busby without consent. About the widows whose land had been reassigned. She told it plainly, without drama, the facts in sequence, completely, without interpretation, just what was there.

She did not know if the woman would write back.

She sent the letter anyway.

Outside Éstávé-vóhe stood in his full summer leaf, his two leaders dark against the night sky, his branches moving slightly in the warm air off the river. The stars were in his highest tips, patient, waiting for the wind.

The papers were on the table.

Her handwriting on them.

Both of them, still here. Both of them, doing what they did.

25

Méanôhtse

Spring came to the Tongue River in 1889, and the reservation it returned to was not the one it had left.

The land looked the same. The bluffs still caught the morning light and went from grey to red, and the cottonwoods along the bank put out their first pale green, and the river ran high and fast with the snowmelt as it always did. But the human landscape had changed in the specific way things change when a law has time to move from paper to the ground. The survey stakes that Watches Twice had watched go in above the river had been followed by other stakes, other lines, other papers, each one a further subdivision of what had already been divided, the geometry of it becoming more specific and more final with each passing season.

The allotment papers had come the previous fall.

A clerk from the agency, young, efficient, a man with a list and a horse and no particular understanding of what the list meant to the people he was delivering it to, had ridden out to the cabin on a Tuesday in October. He had a document in his kit. He read the name from his list. He handed the document to Watches Twice and asked him to sign the receipt acknowledging delivery.

Watches Twice read it on the doorstep.

It was printed on agency paper, the heading official, the language of it dense and specific, parcel numbers, township and range designations, acreage, the legal description of the boundaries of the land assigned to them in trust for a period of twenty-five years, during which it could not be sold or alienated without approval of the Secretary of the Interior. One hundred and sixty acres. Head of household. The land was theirs in the specific sense the government meant when it said theirs, held for them, managed for them, the title not quite in their hands but close enough that the document felt like something.

Eméškeha'e came out, and he handed it to her.

She read it standing in the doorway in the October light.

She did not say anything about Méanôhtse. She did not need to. They both knew which side of the line the draw sat on. They had known since the spring that Watches Twice had sat his horse on the ridge above the river and looked down at the survey stakes.

She handed the paper back to him.

He signed the receipt.

The clerk thanked him, made a mark on his list, and rode to the next cabin.

* * *

Spring 1889. Four years on the Tongue River. The new garden behind the corral had produced three seasons now, not as large as Méanôhtse had been, not with the particular quality of light that came into the draw from the south in the long summer afternoons, but producing. The fence he had built for it was tight. The ground knew them now.

The letters had continued through the winter. Mary Bonney had written back, a careful, formal letter, the English of a Philadelphia churchwoman, but genuine in its interest and specific in its questions.

Eméškeha'e had answered every question. She had been answering questions for six months, and the correspondence had grown into something that neither of them had named, but both understood to be useful. The Women's National Indian Association had included a summary of conditions on the Tongue River reservation in their most recent petition to Congress. She had not seen the petition. She had heard about it from Vó'kêséhe, who had heard about it from someone who read newspapers.

The breeding arrangement with the Miles City rancher had worked. He had sent two mares the previous spring, a sorrel and a grey, both well-built, and Náhko had done what four-year-old stallions did when presented with mares, which was to confirm every opinion he had ever had about his own importance. The rancher had sent word that both mares had foaled. Both foals were paint. He wanted to send two more mares in the spring.

This was what Elias Harlan had seen at the fence that summer afternoon two years ago. The specific generosity of a man who left useful things on tables without making anything of them.

* * *

Elias came back in April.

He came from Miles City on his dark bay gelding with two mares on lead ropes behind him, a blood bay and a black with a white star, both belonging to the rancher, both well-traveled and calm on the road. He came to the fence, and Watches Twice came out, and they greeted each other briefly, two men who had established what they were to each other and did not need to reestablish it every time they met.

"How did the foals come out?" Watches Twice said.

"Paint," Elias said. "Both of them. Sorrel base on one, grey base on the other. Good markings. He has strong blood." He looked at the corral. "He's filled out."

Náhko was at the far end of the corral watching the mares on the road with an expression that had moved through several registers in rapid succession: alertness, assessment, a kind of urgent calculation, and had arrived at something that could only be described as decision.

"He has opinions about this," Watches Twice said.

"I imagine he does," Elias said.

They brought the mares into the corral.

Náhko was four years old and fully himself. The paint markings he had been born with now on a horse that had come into his full size, the broad chest, the long back, and the particular quality of movement that made people stop and look when he crossed a field. He was not a large horse. He was a correct horse, built as horses were built when nature rather than fashion had done the selecting, and he moved with the self-possession of an animal that had never doubted its own worth.

The mares entered the corral.

Náhko approached the blood bay with what he clearly believed was considerable dignity.

The blood bay was unimpressed.

She pinned her ears and moved away, and Náhko followed her with the expression of a horse who had expected a different reception and was reassessing the situation. The black with the white star watched from the far corner with an air of detached amusement that reminded Watches Twice of someone he lived with.

Vohkoohe was at the fence watching all of it with the expression she used when events were unfolding exactly as she had always known they would, and she had chosen not to warn anyone because they would not have listened anyway.

Néše'še-méséne had retreated to the far end of the corral and stood with his back to the entire proceedings in the dignified posture of a gelding who had opinions about the new social order but understood there was nothing to be done about it.

Eméškeha'e came out of the cabin and stood at the fence beside Watches Twice. She looked at Náhko, who was now attempting a different approach to the blood bay with marginally more success.

"He is his mother's son," she said.

"In every way," Watches Twice said.

Elias, beside them, said nothing. He was watching Náhko with the attention of a man confirming something he had predicted two years ago at a fence on a summer afternoon. His expression was satisfied without being smug, the expression of a man whose judgment about horses had once again proven correct.

The breeding fee changed hands inside, over the meal, the transaction completed in the same plain manner Elias brought to everything. He stayed through the afternoon. He saw the allotment paper on the shelf where Eméškeha'e kept documents, filed there in October without ceremony, as she filed things that needed to be kept and didn't need to be displayed.

He looked at the paper without picking it up. He set his cup down.

"Méanôhtse," she said. She did not point. She looked at the window, at the draw above the cabin, the spring green just coming into it.

"Yes," he said. He understood what she meant without being told. The draw on the wrong side of the line, the land that had been named and tended and was now legally surplus, available, waiting for whoever came to claim it.

He did not say it would be all right. He was not that kind of man.

"The rancher wants two more mares next spring," he said. "And he's told three other men about the horse. You'll hear from them."

He left in the late afternoon. They watched him ride north until the bend took him.

* * *

Jane came three days later.

She came as she always came, early, the knock of someone who knew she was welcome but respected the form of it. Eméškeha'e made tea. They sat at the table.

Jane had a cousin who traded through the Arapaho country to the south. The cousin had come through two weeks ago on his way north and had stopped at Jane's family's place, stayed two nights, and talked. He had heard something from an Arapaho man who had been west. Far west. Nevada country.

She said it in Cheyenne. Carefully, with the precision she brought to things she wanted to get exactly right.

There was a man. A Paiute man, a holy man. On the first day of the new year, the day the moon covered the sun and the world went dark and then light again, he had left his body. In the time he was gone, he had seen something. He had seen the land as it had been. The buffalo on the plains, the herds that had filled the horizon. He had seen the dead living, his own people, gone people, walking and talking and doing the things the living did. He had seen the world made new.

He came back from this vision with a message. If the people danced, a specific dance, a circle dance, men and women together, moving together, singing the songs he had been given, the vision would come true. The dead would return. The buffalo would return. The world would be restored.

The word was moving east. Rider to rider. Fire to fire.

Jane stopped speaking.

She watched Eméškeha'e's face.

Eméškeha'e sat with it for a long moment. Her hands were around her cup. She did not speak.

Watches Twice was outside, within earshot. He had stopped what he was doing when Jane began talking, not moving closer, not announcing himself, but going still with his particular stillness when something required complete attention. He heard the shape of it through the window. Enough.

He stood outside the cabin in the spring morning and looked at the draw above the cabin and thought about a woman who had walked north from Darlington and climbed cliffs in January and come to this river and named things and built something here and lost Vávàhke and Mótséhe-he'e and the draw above the cabin and was sitting at the table inside hearing that the dead would return.

He did not go inside.

He let her have it.

Jane left after a while. He heard her go. He waited a moment and then came around to the doorway.

Eméškeha'e was at the table. She was not crying. She was not praying. She was sitting with the cup in her hands, looking at something that was not the table, her face carrying the quality it had when she was not thinking about something, but inside it, submerged in it, as you were inside weather before you knew it had arrived.

He came in. He made more tea. He set it in front of her and sat.

She did not speak for a long time.

Then she said, "The dead would return."

He received this. He did not qualify it. He did not say it may not be true. He did not say these things had been promised before. He just received it, sat with it, and let her have what she needed.

After a while, she stood, went to the door, and looked out.

* * *

He saw the man in Méanôhtse before she did.

He was coming back from the river with the water bucket when he looked up and saw a figure in the draw, a man, on foot, moving with the deliberate stops and starts of a man reading land. Stopping, looking up at the rise, looking back at the stream, looking at the woodlot of cottonwood and willow on the north-facing slope. Not moving quickly. Taking his time.

He set the water bucket down.

He watched the man work his way through the draw.

The man was perhaps forty, dressed for the country, range clothes, working boots, a hat that had been rained on enough times to lose its original shape. He had a piece of paper he consulted occasionally, looking from it to the landscape and back again. He looked at the stream where it ran clearest, bent down, and examined its flow. He looked at the rise above the stream where the grass came in thick in the spring and stayed longer than the surrounding ground. He looked at the woodlot with the eyes of a man calculating board feet and cordwood simultaneously.

He did not look at the cabin.

He did not know he was being watched.

He walked the full length of the draw, the still place, the quiet place, the draw she had named Méanôhtse on a winter morning in their first year on the river, and made notes on his paper at intervals and assessed the land with the complete attention of a man deciding what he could do with it.

Then he walked back the way he came, went over the rise, and was gone.

Eméškeha'e came and stood beside Watches Twice.

He did not know how long she had been there. Long enough. She had seen.

She stood in the yard and looked at the draw.

The spring evening was coming in from the northwest, the light going golden on the bluffs, the cottonwoods along the river catching it. Méanôhtse was still and green above them, the stream running in the bottom of it, the grass coming in thick on the rise, the woodlot dark against the pale sky.

She looked at it for a long time.

She had named it the still place. The quiet place. She had walked up into it in the early mornings before anyone was awake and stood in it and let the morning happen around her. She had planted her first garden there, the one the survey line had taken. She had built the fence for the new garden behind the corral in the same motion, not replacing Méanôhtse, because Méanôhtse could not be replaced, just finding what was still available and using it.

The man with the paper had walked her draw with a rancher's eyes, water, grass, wood, shelter, and had found what he was looking for and had written it down and gone over the rise.

He would be back. She knew this as she knew all certain things before they arrived, in the body, before the mind finished the thought.

Watches Twice stood beside her. He did not say anything. He stood there, which was what she needed, what he always understood without being told.

Éstávé-vóhe stood at the riverbank below them, in his spring leaves, pale green against the evening sky, his roots deep in the riverbed where the stars began their long travel upward through the dark.

The draw above them was still.

For now, still.

26

Still There

The drums came at night.

Not every night, some nights the river was all there was, moving under its banks in the dark, the cottonwoods still, the reservation quiet in the specific quiet of a place where people had learned to be careful about what they did and when. But on certain nights, when the wind came from the southwest and the sky was clear, the drums were there, low, steady, carrying across the river bottom from somewhere up in the hills above Busby, the sound of them arriving at the cabin felt before it was heard.

Watches Twice lay still and listened.

Beside him, she was awake too. He could tell by her breathing. Neither of them said anything. They lay in the dark and listened to the drums move through the cabin walls. After a while, the wind shifted, and the drums were gone. The river was all there was again.

This had been happening since September.

* * *

Porcupine had come back from Nevada in the spring.

His Cheyenne name was Hóhkėhéso, a man the reservation knew, not a stranger, not a prophet from somewhere else, but a Northern Cheyenne from the Tongue River who had heard the word moving east through the Arapaho country and had decided to go and find its source. He had traveled from the Tongue River reservation through Wyoming to the rail line, then by train to Idaho and the Bannock agency, then further west to Nevada, to the Walker River reservation, where a Paiute man named Wovoka was living and teaching.

He came back changed.

What he brought back, the vision, the message, the dance, moved through the reservation as fire moved through dry grass in August. Not because people were desperate, though they were. Not because they had nothing left to lose, though they had lost much. But because the message was specific in the way that mattered, it named the things that had been taken and promised their return. The buffalo. The land. The dead.

The dead.

She heard it first from Jane. Then from Vó'kêséhe. Then from the women who came to the cabin with their letters and their agency disputes and their careful, exhausted faces. Each of them carried it differently. Some with the specific brightness of people who had found something to hold onto, some with the careful reservation of people who had been promised things before and understood what promises cost when they failed. But all of them carried it. It was in the reservation as the drums were in the night air, present, moving, arriving at places you hadn't expected it to reach.

She said nothing about it to Watches Twice. He did not ask.

* * *

In October, she went to see it.

Not to dance. She told herself she was going to see it, to understand what it was, what Porcupine had brought back from Nevada, what it felt like from close enough to feel it. She rode Vohkoohe out in the early evening and went south along the river road and turned up into the hills above Busby, where the fires were visible from the ridge. She stopped on the ridge and looked down.

There were perhaps two hundred people in the valley below. Men and women together, which was not how Cheyenne ceremonies had traditionally been organized, which was part of what Wovoka had brought, a new form, a circle, everyone together, no separation. They held hands. They moved in a slow circle, sidestep and sidestep, the movement deliberate and steady, not frenzied, not wild, the opposite of what the newspapers in Miles City were saying about it. The newspapers said Ghost Dance. They said outbreak. They said the Indians were working themselves into a frenzy.

What she saw from the ridge was two hundred people moving in a circle in the firelight, singing.

She sat her horse and listened.

She had been carrying specific losses for fourteen years. Vávàhke in the ground at Darlington, the fever taking her in the wrong country, far from everything she knew. Mótséhe-he'e in the school's ground three miles from her family, the institutional prayer said over her in a language her body had never fully learned. Everyone left behind on the White River plain in the January cold. Everyone who had not made it to the cliffs or over them or through what came after.

The singing carried up the ridge to where she sat.

She was off her horse and walking down before she had decided to do it. Vohkoohe came behind her, unhurried, as if she had always known they were going down.

* * *

She came home before first light.

He was awake. He had been awake since midnight, tending the fire, sitting with it. He heard Vohkoohe on the road and went out, took the reins, and looked at her face in the dark.

Her face was different.

Not transformed, she was not a woman who performed transformation. But different in the specific manner of faces after something has moved through them and left its mark. Her eyes were clear. Whatever she had been carrying in them for the past months, the weight of the man in Méanôhtse, the allotment paper on the shelf, the letters that worked and the cases that didn't, was still there, but it had been joined by something else. Something that had weight of its own kind.

He tended Vohkoohe. He went inside, built the fire up, made the tea, brought it to her, and sat.

She held the cup.

After a while, she said, "Vávàhke."

He waited.

"I thought about her. While I danced." She looked at the fire. "I could see her. Not a vision, not the way they describe the visions. Just her. How she moved. How she laughed." She was quiet for a moment. "She was alive somewhere. In this, I don't know what to call it. This place the songs were making."

He looked at the fire too.

"I don't know if it's true," she said. "What the songs promise. I don't know if the dead come back. I don't know if the world is made new." She drank the tea. "But I was there. With her. For a little while, I was there with her."

Watches Twice listened. He did not qualify it, question it, or place it inside any framework that made it smaller than she had given it to him. He just listened, sat with it, and let it be what it was.

Outside, the river moved in the dark.

The fire ticked in the stove.

Both of them, still here.

***

Vó'kêséhe came in November with news that was not good news.

He came on his dark sorrel with the two white stockings, and he came quickly, which was not how he usually came. He came in and sat, but did not eat, and set his hands on the table and looked at Watches Twice.

"They arrested Porcupine," he said.

Watches Twice looked at him.

"The agent. Upshaw. He had the Army take him in June." He stopped. "I'm sorry. I should have come sooner. I only heard last week."

"Why June?" Eméškeha'e said.

Vó'kêséhe told them. A white cattleman had been killed near the reservation, the circumstances unclear, the connection to the Ghost Dance unclear, most likely no connection at all. But white settlers had connected the two events, and the Cheyenne had feared retribution. Agent Upshaw had decided the simplest response was to remove the man who had started the dance on the Tongue River. Porcupine had been taken in. Held. The large dance he had assembled above Busby had been disrupted, people sent home, the fires put out, the Army present in the hills in a manner that made dancing something requiring a calculation about risk.

"They released him?" Watches Twice said.

"Yes. He's home." Vó'kêséhe looked at the table. "But Upshaw says if he holds large gatherings again, if he continues to spread what Upshaw calls his delusion, he'll be sent away. Somewhere else."

The table was quiet.

Eméškeha'e looked at the window. Outside, the November sky was the color of river ice. Méanôhtse was bare above the cabin, the woodlot stripped of its leaves, the draw grey and still.

"He'll dance again," she said. Not a question.

"Yes," Vó'kêséhe said. "He will."

She nodded. She had expected this. Porcupine was a man who had traveled from the Tongue River to Nevada and back to bring something home. A man who did that did not stop because an agent told him his revelation was a delusion.

The dance went underground after that. Smaller gatherings, further from the agency's eyes, at night, in places the soldiers didn't think to look because they were still thinking about what a Ghost Dance looked like from the outside, the large fires, the two hundred people in a valley, the thing that looked like a threat because it was large and unfamiliar. They didn't understand that it could also look like twelve people in a draw in the dark, holding hands, moving in a circle, singing quietly enough that you had to be inside it to hear it.

She went again in December.

* * *

The second time was different.

Not in the dance itself. The circle was the same, the sidestep and sidestep, the songs she was beginning to know. What was different was what she brought to it. The first time she had come open, not knowing what to expect, the surprise of it doing some of the work. The second time, she came knowing what it was and what it wasn't, knowing it was not proof, not certainty, not the literal return of the dead walking back into the world with their particular faces. It was something else. Something that did not have a word in English and had only an approximate word in Cheyenne and existed most fully inside the circle itself, inside the movement and the singing, inside the

246

specific act of joining your hands to the people on either side of you and moving together in the same direction.

She thought about Mótséhe-he'e while she danced.

The watchful girl. The girl who had given Tobias a person to belong to in a building designed to make belonging impossible. The girl who had died in an institutional bed while her family was three miles away. She thought about her with the specific quality of thinking the dance produced, not grief, not exactly, though grief was in it. Something that held the grief and also held something else. The girl was somewhere. Moving through something. Still watching, still particular, still herself.

She came home before dawn. He was awake. He had the fire up and the tea ready. He did not say anything, and she did not say anything. They sat together in the early morning dark.

* * *

Vó'kêséhe came back in February.

He came in the cold, the sorrel's breath coming in plumes in the February air. He came with the news that had been traveling from the Dakotas since December and had taken two months to arrive. It came with the weight of something that had happened and could not be taken back.

Wounded Knee.

December 29. The 7th Cavalry. A band of Lakota Ghost Dancers moving toward Pine Ridge under Spotted Elk, Big Foot, the whites called him, was intercepted at Wounded Knee Creek in South Dakota. The soldiers had tried to disarm them. A gun had gone off, whose gun, in what circumstance, nobody fully agreed, but the gun had gone off, and then the soldiers had opened fire on the camp. When it was over, more than two hundred and fifty Lakota were dead. Women. Children. Elders. The Ghost Dance shirts they wore, the white shirts painted with sacred symbols that were said to protect them from bullets, had not protected them from bullets.

Vó'kêséhe told it in Cheyenne, looking at the table.

When he finished, the cabin was quiet.

Emėškeha'e looked at the fire.

She had known something like this was coming. Not the specific shape of it, not Wounded Knee, not the 7th Cavalry, not December 29. But the direction of it. She had understood since Porcupine's arrest that the government's response to hope of this size and this kind was not going to be patience. The machinery had a consistent response to Native hope. She had watched it for six years from the inside of an agency office and from a desk covered in letters and from a ridge above a valley where two hundred people were dancing in the firelight. The machinery did not negotiate with hope. It processed it.

She thought about the women in the circle at Wounded Knee. Moving in the same sidestep and sidestep she had moved in, singing the same songs, wearing the shirts they had been told would keep them safe. She thought about what it meant to believe something so completely that you put it on your body and walked toward soldiers.

She did not say any of this.

She looked at the fire.

Vó'kêséhe looked at Watches Twice.

Watches Twice was sitting with his hands flat on the table, looking at nothing in particular. The look of a man thinking carefully, who had not finished thinking.

"Wooden Leg guided them," Vó'kêséhe said. Quietly. Setting it on the table as you set something down carefully because it was fragile or dangerous.

Watches Twice looked at him.

"Casey's scouts. He was with Casey. They guided the soldiers in the campaign." Vó'kêséhe looked at the table. "His own people."

The cabin was quiet.

Watches Twice looked at his hands on the table. He thought about every ridge he had sat above, every report delivered plainly without interpretation, every coin counted into his hand without the quartermaster looking at him, the specific arithmetic of being a man whose skills were useful to the people with the guns, and what that arithmetic purchased, and what it never could.

"He did what he knew," Watches Twice said.

Vó'kêséhe looked at him.

"It doesn't make it right," Watches Twice said. "It makes it — what it is. A man doing what he knew in a situation where what he knew was the wrong thing to know."

Vó'kêséhe was quiet for a moment. Then he said, "You would not have done it."

Watches Twice looked at the table. He thought about this honestly, with the same quality of attention he brought to country, reading what was there rather than what he wanted to be there.

"I don't know," he said. "I'd like to say no. But I was that man for a long time. And the man who was that man, I don't know what he would have done if Casey had given the order."

Vó'kêséhe received this. He did not argue with it or absolve it. He sat with it as it deserved to be sat with.

Eméškeha'e had not spoken since Vó'kêséhe told them about Wounded Knee. She was still inside that, still in the specific place you were inside when news of that size arrived, and you were trying to find the edges of it.

After a while, she said, "The dance continues."

Both men looked at her.

"At Wounded Knee, they danced," she said. "Here, people are still dancing. Quietly, at night, in the draws. Not because they believe it will save them from bullets." She looked at the fire. "Because it's theirs.

Because it belongs to them and the Army can arrest Porcupine and kill two hundred and fifty people at Wounded Knee, and the dance is still theirs."

The cabin received this.

Vó'kêséhe looked at Watches Twice. Something passed between them, not quite a smile, not anything light, but the acknowledgment of two men who understood that the woman at the table had said the true thing.

Vó'kêséhe left before dark. They watched him ride north on the river road until the cold took him.

* * *

That night she went out.

Not to a gathering. Not to the hills above Busby. She went into the yard, stood in the February cold, and looked up.

Éstávé-vóhe stood at the bank of the frozen river, his bare winter branches against the night sky, the bark silver in the starlight. She looked up through his branches at the stars sitting in his highest tips, patient, waiting for the wind to release them, traveling up from the deep roots through the long trunk and out into the cold air where they waited.

She stood in the yard and began to sing.

Not loudly. Not for anyone. For herself, for the specific act of making the sound in the cold air, the Ghost Dance songs she had learned in the circle, the words moving through her body and into the night. She sang for Vávàhke. She sang for Mótséhe-he'e. She sang for everyone in the ground at Darlington and on the White River plain and at Wounded Knee Creek in South Dakota.

She sang, and the stars sat in Éstávé-vóhe's highest branches. The frozen river lay patient beneath its ice, and the February night was

250

very cold and very still.

He stood in the doorway.

He watched her.

He did not go out to her, and he did not call her back, and he did not look away. He stood in the doorway of the cabin they had built together on the Tongue River and watched the woman he lived with stand in the February cold and sing into the dark, and he let her have every bit of it.

The song moved through the cold air and was gone.

She stood in the yard for a while longer.

Then she came back inside.

He stepped aside to let her through the door. She went to the fire and held her hands out to it. He came and stood beside her.

The fire moved between them.

Outside Éstávé-vóhe held his stars. The frozen river held its ice. Somewhere in the hills above the Tongue River, in draws the agency men didn't know to look in, people were dancing in a circle in the dark, sidestep and sidestep, holding hands, singing the songs Porcupine had carried back from Nevada, the songs that had traveled from Wovoka's vision through the Bannock country and the Arapaho country and the Lakota country to this river, to this reservation, to these people who had walked north from Darlington and climbed cliffs in January and come home to a country that had been surveyed and divided and was still, still, home.

The dance was out there in the dark.

She could feel it from here.

He could feel her feeling it.

Both of them, at the fire.

Both of them, still here.

Historical Appendix

THE LONG WAY HOME
Book Three of The Long Reckoning

This novel is a work of fiction set against the historical backdrop of the displacement, survival, and endurance of the Northern Cheyenne and Crow peoples in the last decades of the nineteenth century. While the characters and their personal stories are invented, the historical context, the treaties, the conflicts, the dispossession of Native peoples, and the patterns of violence and broken promises are based on documented history.

I have tried to represent these events and their impacts with respect and accuracy, while acknowledging that as a white author writing about Native American experiences, I am working from outside these communities. Any errors or misrepresentations are mine alone.

The following appendix provides historical context for readers interested in the real events that inform this fictional narrative.

Part One: Crow Language — Apsáalooke

The Crow language belongs to the Missouri Valley Siouan family and is closely related to Hidatsa. It is spoken primarily by the Crow Tribe of Montana on the Crow Reservation in the south-central part of the state. In the nineteenth century, the Crow people ranged across the Yellowstone River valley from present-day Wyoming through

Montana. Their alliance with the United States government during the Plains conflicts of the 1870s placed Crow scouts in close proximity to the events depicted in this book.

All Crow names and phrases in this novel are constructed from attested lexical items. Primary sources:

Graczyk, Randolph. A Grammar of Crow, or Apsálooke Aliláu. Lincoln: University of Nebraska Press, 2007.

Crow Language Consortium Dictionary. Hardin, Montana.

Lowie, Robert H. The Crow Indians. New York: Farrar & Rinehart, 1935.

Boas, Franz. Notes on the Crow Language. 1904.

Voget, Fred W. The Shoshoni-Crow Sun Dance. Norman: University of Oklahoma Press, 1984.

Names

Bíalish Dúua — Watches Twice

The protagonist's Crow name, earned for his practice of returning to observe what he has already seen.

bi- = 3rd person prefix (he/she)

-alish = verb root: to look, watch, observe

dúua = twice, two times

Búuwatisshish — Old Hawk

The Crow medicine man who serves as mentor and elder to Watches Twice.

búuwa = old, aged, elderly
tisshish = hawk

Bíawakshish — *Red Bear*
Watches Twice's father, killed by Northern Cheyenne warriors when Watches Twice was seven years old.
Biawá-/Biá- = red, reddish, blood-colored
-kshish/-akshish = bear

Iiláxxe Baa — Kind-Hearted Woman
Watches Twice's mother.
Iiláxxe = kind, good-hearted, gentle, generous
Baa = woman

Phrases

Daxpitcheésh awáala
Go with clear dreams / go with good vision. Old Hawk's blessing to Watches Twice before the march south to Darlington Agency, 1877.

Part Two: Cheyenne Language — Tsėhésenėstsestȯtse

The Northern Cheyenne language is spoken by the Northern Cheyenne Tribe of Montana on the Northern Cheyenne Indian Reservation in southeastern Montana. The reservation was established by executive order on November 26, 1884. The language is documented and preserved by Chief Dull Knife College in Lame Deer, Montana.

All Cheyenne names and phrases in this novel are constructed from attested lexical items or are documented historical names. Primary source:

Leman, Wayne; Fisher, Laird; and the Cheyenne Language Committee. Cheyenne Dictionary. Chief Dull Knife College & SIL International.

Additional references:

Grinnell, George Bird. By Cheyenne Campfires. New Haven: Yale University Press, 1926.

Powell, Peter. Sweet Medicine: The Continuing Role of the Sacred Arrows, the Sun Dance, and the Sacred Buffalo Hat in Northern Cheyenne History. Norman: University of Oklahoma Press, 1969.

Names

Emėškeha'e

Attested Cheyenne woman's name. No direct English translation. The protagonist of the book's second storyline: a Northern Cheyenne woman who survived the Northern Cheyenne Exodus of 1878–79, including the Fort Robinson breakout of January 1879. Her path from Fort Robinson to the Tongue River reservation follows documented routes taken by other Northern Cheyenne survivors. She is a fictional character walking real historical ground.

Intimate form: Eméshke, following standard Cheyenne nickname formation — first syllables preserved, feminine suffix dropped.

Hevávàhkema — Butterfly

Eméškeha'e's daughter, who dies of malaria at Darlington Agency, November 1877. Called Vávàhke by her mother.

hevávàhkema = butterfly (attested noun)

Sources: sesquiotic.com linguistic comparison; Cheyenne-English Dictionary, cheyennelanguage.org; Chief Dull Knife College Cheyenne Dictionary.

Vohkoohe — Rabbit

Eméškeha'e's horse, a dark bay mare of unusual intelligence. Name given for the circumstances of the horse's actions.

vohkoohe = rabbit (attested noun, CDKC)

Néše'še-méšéne — River Crossing Watcher

Watches Twice's bay roan gelding. Named by Eméškeha'e.

néše'še = river, stream (attested noun, CDKC)

méšéne = one who watches, observer (attested verb form, CDKC)

Éstávé-vóhe — Star Tree

Emëškeha'e's name for the large cottonwood at the bank of the Tongue River near their cabin. Built from attested roots consistent with Cheyenne place-naming practice.

éstávé = star (attested noun, CDKC)

vóhe = tree (attested noun, CDKC)

The legend that stars travel up from the earth through the roots of cottonwood trees and rest in the highest branches before the wind releases them into the sky is documented as Northern Cheyenne oral tradition from the Tongue River and Ashland area of southeastern Montana.

Náhko'e-vó'kòhéva — Sudden Little One

The paint colt born to Vohkoohe, spring 1885, by an unknown wild mustang. Called Náhko in daily use.

náhko'e- = suddenly, unexpectedly (attested adverb, CDKC)

vó'kòhéva = little one, young one (attested noun, CDKC)

Name constructed from attested morphemes. Consistent with Cheyenne naming practice — descriptive, event-based, built from the circumstances of birth.

Vó'kêséhe — Little Bear

Emëškeha'e's Cheyenne cousin, who appears throughout the novel's second half as a connector between the reservation community and the cabin on the Tongue River.

vó'kêse = bear (attested noun, CDKC)

-he = diminutive suffix (attested productive suffix, CDKC)

Mótséhe-he'e — Little Watcher / Watchful Girl

A nine-year-old Northern Cheyenne girl at St. Labre Mission School who dies of tuberculosis. The girl who watched quietly from across the sewing room.

mótséhe = to watch, to look carefully, to observe attentively (attested verb stem, CDKC)

-he'e = diminutive feminine suffix (attested productive suffix used in girls' names, CDKC)

Name constructed from attested morphemes. The same morphological pattern used historically for Northern Cheyenne girls' names.

Méanôhtse — The Still Place

Eméškeha'e's name for the draw above the cabin on the Tongue River — the ground she first gardens, later designated surplus land under the Dawes Act.

méanôhtse = still, quiet, calm (attested form, CDKC)

Phrases

Héšenovéhe — Alone

The opening word of the novel. Eméškeha'e's condition when Watches Twice first sees her in the trader's store, Chapter Thirteen.

héšenovéhe = alone, by oneself (attested form, CDKC)

Néheše, ného'évoomáhe — You are a good man

Vó'kêséhe's farewell to Watches Twice, Chapter Twenty-One.

néheše = you (animate, 2nd person, attested, CDKC)

né-ho'évoomáhe = you are a good man (né- 2nd person prefix + ho'é- male/man + -voomáhe good/virtuous, CDKC)

Néstahe Náhko'e vó'kòhéva néháahtse tsé-háe'ëstse

You named the Crow's horse after what he did to get you. Vó'kêséhe to Emëškeha'e, Chapter Twenty-One, after learning Néše'še-méšéne's name. Constructed from attested CDKC components.

Néheše, néhó'ëstse tsé-há'e — This is what you are

Vó'kêséhe to Emëškeha'e, Chapter Twenty-Four, after seeing the papers on her table and understanding the work she has built.

néheše = this (animate demonstrative, CDKC)

né-hó'ëstse = you are this way / this is your nature (stative verb of character, CDKC)

tsé-há'e = the way / the manner (relational particle, CDKC)

Historical and Cultural Notes

The Maheo Creation Story

The creation story Emëškeha'e tells the children at St. Labre Mission School — Maheo alone on the water, the waterbirds diving for earth, the coot succeeding where the others failed, Grandmother Turtle carrying the world on her back — is documented Northern Cheyenne oral tradition. Primary source: Grinnell, George Bird. By Cheyenne

Campfires. Yale University Press, 1926.

The detail that Grandmother Turtle is slow because she carries the weight of the world and all its people is part of the attested tradition.

Tuberculosis at St. Labre Mission School

The Washington Post's investigation of deaths at Indian boarding schools documented that in 1941, Paul Sponge, 13, of the Northern Cheyenne Tribe, died of pulmonary tuberculosis at St. Labre Indian Mission Boarding School in Ashland, Montana. The following year, his two younger siblings — 8-year-old Bertha and 10-year-old Charles — died at the same school of the same illness.

Tuberculosis and influenza were the leading causes of death at Indian boarding schools throughout the late nineteenth and early twentieth centuries. Overcrowding, poor nutrition, inadequate ventilation, and the failure to separate sick children from well children allowed communicable disease to spread unchecked. Mortality rates were so high that most schools maintained their own cemeteries. Native American children died at four times the rate of non-Native children.

Mótséhe-he'e's death at St. Labre, and the school's failure to notify her family in time for them to be present, is consistent with documented practice. Parents were frequently not informed of their children's deaths until after burial in school cemeteries.

Runaway Punishment at Boarding Schools

Runaways from Indian boarding schools faced severe punishment upon return, typically administered publicly in front of other students as a deterrent. Documented punishments included the belt line or hotline — students forced to run or crawl through a gauntlet of classmates who struck them. Beatings, solitary confinement, and restriction of food were standard. The practice of forcing peers to participate in punishment was intended both to correct the individual and to educate the group.

Sources: Washington Post investigation, December 2024; Samantha M. Williams PhD, Physical Violence at Native American Boarding Schools; American Indian boarding schools — Wikipedia.

The Women's National Indian Association

Founded in Philadelphia in 1879 by Mary Lucinda Bonney and Amelia Stone Quinton. The organization sent petitions to Congress throughout the 1880s advocating for Native American rights and documenting reservation conditions. Quinton took over organizational leadership in 1883 and remained active through the decade. The WNIA was among the earliest organized Native American rights advocacy groups in the United States and was part of the reform network that eventually influenced federal Indian policy.

Emėškeha'e's correspondence with Mary Bonney, facilitated through the Philadelphia connections of Elias Harlan (protagonist of Book One, The Rancher), is consistent with the organization's documented practice of receiving letters and reports from individuals on reservations. The WNIA's 1880s petitions to Congress cited specific conditions at specific reservations.

Part Three: Historical Figures

The following individuals appear in the novel. All are documented historical figures. Their presence in the narrative is consistent with the historical record.

Crow

Goes Ahead (c. 1851–1919)

Crow scout. One of six Crow scouts assigned to Custer's 7th Cavalry at the Battle of the Little Bighorn, June 25, 1876. Married Pretty Shield. Buried at the Custer National Cemetery at Little Bighorn Battlefield. His accounts of the battle are among the primary Crow sources for that engagement. The author has visited his grave.

Plenty Coups (c. 1848–1932)

Chief of the Crow Nation. Became principal chief in 1876. Believed that alliance with the United States was necessary for the survival of the Crow people and maintained that alliance throughout his long tenure. Traveled to Washington, D.C., multiple times to advocate for Crow treaty rights. His decision to remain allied with the U.S. government during the Plains conflicts is analyzed by philosopher Jonathan Lear in Radical Hope: Ethics in the Face of Cultural Devastation (Harvard University Press, 2006).

Northern Cheyenne

Dull Knife (also known as Morning Star, c. 1810–1883)

Northern Cheyenne chief. Led his people on the march south to the Darlington Agency in Indian Territory in 1877. Co-led the Northern Cheyenne Exodus of September 1878. Surrendered at Fort Robinson, Nebraska, October 1878. Led the Fort Robinson breakout of January 9, 1879, in which approximately 60 Northern Cheyenne were killed on the frozen Nebraska plain. Survived and reached Pine Ridge in South Dakota, where he lived among the Lakota until his death. Buried at Lame Deer, Montana.

Little Wolf (c. 1820–1904)

Northern Cheyenne war chief and Sweet Medicine Chief, carrier of the sacred Sweet Medicine bundle. Co-led the Northern Cheyenne Exodus of September 1878. Separated from Dull Knife's band in Nebraska and wintered his people in the sandhills. Reached the Tongue River country in Montana in spring 1879 and surrendered peacefully at Fort Keogh in March 1879 to Lieutenant W.P. Clark. His band's survival is the more optimistic branch of the exodus story. Buried at Lame Deer, Montana.

Two Moons — Éše'he Ohnéšeséstse (1847–1917)

Northern Cheyenne chief. Surrendered at Fort Keogh in 1877 with approximately 300 Cheyenne and remained in the Tongue River area, forming the core community around which the Northern Cheyenne Reservation was eventually established by executive order in November 1884. A signatory of the Fort Laramie Treaty of 1868. His presence and authority on the Tongue River during the early reservation period is documented. The message he sends through Watches Twice in Chapter Twenty-Three, regarding survey lines cutting through Cheyenne homesteads, is consistent with documented Cheyenne protests against the Dawes Act allotment process.

Porcupine — Hóhkéhéso

Northern Cheyenne from the Tongue River reservation. Traveled to Nevada in 1889 to meet Wovoka, the Paiute holy man who originated the Ghost Dance. Brought the Ghost Dance back to the Tongue River reservation and assembled a large dance in the hills above Busby, Montana. Agent Upshaw had the Army arrest Porcupine in June 1890 following the killing of a white cattleman near the reservation — an event the agent connected to the Ghost Dance despite unclear evidence of any connection. Porcupine was released but placed under surveillance. Upshaw recommended that if Porcupine continued to hold large gatherings, he should be removed from the reservation.

Sources: We Do Not Want the Gates Closed Between Us, nativeame ricannetworks.com; Historical documentation of Ghost Dance sup-pression on the Tongue River reservation, 1890.

Wooden Leg (1858–1940)

Northern Cheyenne warrior who fought at the Battle of the Little Bighorn. Enlisted at Fort Keogh in 1889 as a U.S. Army Indian scout, assigned to Lieutenant Edward W. Casey's Cheyenne Scouts of the Department of Dakota. Guided soldiers during the Ghost Dance campaign that resulted in the Wounded Knee Massacre of December 29, 1890. His memoir, Wooden Leg: A Warrior Who Fought Custer

(University of Nebraska Press, 1931), as told to Thomas B. Marquis, is a primary source for Northern Cheyenne history of the period. He is treated in this novel with the honesty his complexity deserves — a man doing what he knew, in a situation where what he knew was the wrong thing to know.

Standing Elk

Northern Cheyenne leader whose agreement with General Crook in 1877 authorized the removal of the Northern Cheyenne to the Darlington Agency in Indian Territory, over the explicit objections of Dull Knife, Little Wolf, and the majority of the people. His agreement committed approximately 937 Northern Cheyenne to a march south from which many did not return.

U.S. Army and Government

General George Crook

U.S. Army general. Oversaw the Battle of the Rosebud (June 17, 1876) and the removal of the Northern Cheyenne to the Darlington Agency in 1877. Promised Little Wolf and Dull Knife that if they were unhappy after a year, they could return north. Washington overruled him before the promise could be honored. Later argued, unsuccessfully, for postponing the return of Fort Robinson survivors to Indian Territory until spring, which might have prevented the January 1879 breakout and massacre.

John D. Miles

Indian agent at Darlington Agency, 1877–1885. Received the Northern Cheyenne upon their arrival in August 1877. Refused Little Wolf's and Dull Knife's repeated requests to return north. When told his people were dying, he replied that the situation was being monitored. Wrote to Washington that conditions were difficult but manageable. Washington wrote back that the situation was being monitored. Miles was either incompetent or corrupt in his management of the agency; historians have argued both.

Part Four: Historical Events

The Battle of the Rosebud — June 17, 1876

General Crook's column, including Crow and Shoshone scouts, was attacked by Lakota and Cheyenne warriors under Crazy Horse on Rosebud Creek in southeastern Montana, eight days before the Battle of the Little Bighorn. Crook held the field but withdrew without advancing, effectively removing his column from the Little Bighorn campaign.

The Battle of the Little Bighorn — June 25–26, 1876

Known to the Lakota as the Battle of the Greasy Grass. Lakota, Northern Cheyenne, and Arapaho warriors defeated the 7th Cavalry under Lieutenant Colonel George Armstrong Custer. Goes Ahead was among the Crow scouts present. The battle led directly to the intensified Army campaign against the Northern Cheyenne that ended with their surrender and removal to Darlington.

The Northern Cheyenne Removal — May–August 1877

972 Northern Cheyenne marched from Red Cloud Agency in northwestern Nebraska to Darlington Agency in Indian Territory (present-day Oklahoma) under Army escort. The march took 70 days. 35 slipped away during the journey. 937 arrived at Darlington on August 5, 1877. Within two months of arrival, two-thirds of the Northern Cheyenne fell ill. 41 died in the first winter from malaria, measles, and starvation. Medical supplies did not arrive until mid-winter. Rations were insufficient. The attending physician had no medicine.

The Northern Cheyenne Exodus — September 9, 1878

353 Northern Cheyenne under Dull Knife and Little Wolf left Darlington Agency and walked north. Less than a third of those who had arrived fourteen months earlier. The exodus became one of the most documented episodes in Northern Cheyenne history — pursued by 10,000 soldiers and 3,000 settlers through Kansas and Nebraska, fighting more than a dozen engagements, the Cheyenne moved north with a speed and discipline that repeatedly evaded and defeated pursuing forces. In the Nebraska sandhills, the two leaders separated. Little Wolf's band survived. Dull Knife's band surrendered at Fort Robinson.

Fort Robinson — October 1878–January 1879

Dull Knife's band of 149 persons surrendered at Fort Robinson in northwestern Nebraska in late October 1878. They were housed in cavalry barracks. In December, they were told they would be returned to Indian Territory. They refused. In January 1879, after the Cheyenne continued to refuse, the soldiers began withholding food, water, and wood for heat. On January 9, 1879, the Cheyenne broke out of the barracks. The Army pursued them. Approximately 60 were killed on the frozen Nebraska plain. Dull Knife escaped and eventually reached Pine Ridge. In 1994, the Northern Cheyenne reclaimed the remains of those killed and buried in Nebraska; they were reinterred on the Northern Cheyenne Indian Reservation on a hill overlooking Busby, Montana.

The Tongue River Reservation — November 1884

The Northern Cheyenne Reservation was established by executive order of President Chester A. Arthur on November 26, 1884. It consisted of 371,200 acres in southeastern Montana, bounded on the east by the Tongue River and on the west by the Crow Reservation. St. Labre Mission was established in the same year by Ursuline nuns at the request of the Northern Cheyenne, near the present town of Ashland, Montana.

The Dawes General Allotment Act — February 8, 1887

Signed into law by President Grover Cleveland. Authorized the division of Native American tribal communal lands into individual allotments of 160 acres for heads of household, held in trust by the federal government for 25 years. The land remaining after allotment was designated as surplus and opened to white homesteading. Over the 47-year life of the Act, Native Americans lost approximately 90 million acres — about two-thirds of their 1887 land base. The Act was implemented tribe by tribe; on the Northern Cheyenne reservation, the allotment process proceeded through the late 1880s. Senator Henry Teller of Colorado, among the Act's most outspoken opponents, said in 1881 that the real aim of allotment was 'to despoil the Indians of their lands and to make them vagabonds on the face of the earth.' In 1890, Dawes himself remarked: 'I never knew a White man to get his foot on an Indian's land who ever took it off.'

The Ghost Dance — 1889–1890

On January 1, 1889, during a solar eclipse, Wovoka — a Paiute holy man of the Walker River reservation in Nevada, also known as Jack Wilson — experienced a vision in which he saw the land restored, the dead returned to life, and the buffalo returned to the plains. He brought back a message and a ceremony: a circle dance, men and women together, moving in a slow sidestep, singing songs he had been given. If the people danced, the vision would come true.

The message spread rapidly east through the Plains nations. For the Northern Cheyenne, who had walked from Darlington and climbed the cliffs of Fort Robinson and come home to a reservation being surveyed and divided, the promise was not abstract. They knew specifically who they wanted back. Porcupine traveled from the Tongue River to Nevada to meet Wovoka and brought the Ghost Dance home.

The government's response to the Ghost Dance was suppression. Arrests. Surveillance. The massacre at Wounded Knee on December 29, 1890, in which more than 250 Lakota Ghost Dancers were killed by the 7th Cavalry, effectively ended the Ghost Dance as an open movement. The dance continued quietly, in the draws, at night.

Wounded Knee — December 29, 1890

The 7th Cavalry intercepted a band of Lakota Ghost Dancers moving toward Pine Ridge under Spotted Elk (Big Foot) at Wounded Knee Creek in South Dakota. The soldiers attempted to disarm them. A gun discharged — whose and under what circumstances remains disputed. The 7th Cavalry opened fire. More than 250 Lakota were killed, the majority women, children, and elders. The Ghost Dance shirts worn by the dancers, which were said to protect their wearers from bullets, did not. The Congress of the United States officially apologized for the Wounded Knee Massacre in 1990.

Part Five: Fictional Characters — Historical Notes

Eméškeha'e — Historical Note

The Northern Cheyenne who survived the Fort Robinson breakout of January 9, 1879, were scattered by the aftermath. Some were killed on the White River plain. Some were recaptured and held. A number of survivors — including Dull Knife himself — eventually reached Pine Ridge in South Dakota, where they lived among the Lakota for several years.

The Northern Cheyenne Reservation on the Tongue River was established by executive order on November 26, 1884. In the years that followed, survivors from Fort Robinson and their families made their way to the reservation — the homeland they had walked north to find in 1878 and had been prevented from reaching until the government finally acknowledged their right to it.

St. Labre Mission was established on the Tongue River near Ashland, Montana, in 1884 by Ursuline nuns. It served as a school for Cheyenne children from its founding and employed Cheyenne interpreters to bridge the language gap between the nuns and the children and families they served.

Eméškeha'e is a fictional character. Her path from Darlington to Fort Robinson to Pine Ridge to the Tongue River follows routes that many Northern Cheyenne survivors traveled. The work she does in the novel's second half — reading agency letters for families who cannot read English, accompanying people to the agency office, writing letters citing regulations, corresponding with the Women's National Indian Association — is consistent with the earliest forms of Native American rights advocacy documented in this period. The names of individuals she helps (Agnes Limpy, Martha Whitedirt, Standing Cloud) are fictional, but the types of allotment errors she corrects are drawn from documented cases in the historical record of the Tongue River reservation.

Watches Twice — Historical Note

Crow scouts served the United States Army throughout the Plains conflicts of the 1870s and 1880s. Their motivations were complex: traditional enmity with the Lakota and Cheyenne, a pragmatic assessment of where survival lay, genuine belief in alliance as the path forward for the Crow people (as articulated by Plenty Coups), and the specific skills of men who knew the country and were paid to use that knowledge.

Watches Twice is a fictional character. His role as a scout on the 1877 march south to Darlington, and again tracking the Northern Cheyenne during the 1878 exodus, is consistent with documented use of Crow scouts in both operations. His moral weight — the specific arithmetic of a man whose skills were useful to the people with the guns, and what that arithmetic purchased, and what it never could — is the book's central reckoning.

A Note on Sources and Language

The Crow and Cheyenne names and phrases in this novel were constructed with the same care applied to all other historical research in this series. No name or phrase appears without a documented linguistic source. Where a name is constructed from attested morphemes rather than appearing as a documented historical name, this is noted in the appendix above.

The Cheyenne language is complex, with phonological features — aspirated stops, voiced fricatives, whispered vowels, precise tonal distinctions — that cannot be fully represented in standard English typography. Readers wishing to learn more about the Cheyenne language are directed to:

The Chief Dull Knife College Cheyenne Language Program, Lame Deer, Montana (cdkc.edu)

cheyennelanguage.org

Graczyk, Randolph. A Grammar of Crow. University of Nebraska Press, 2007.

The author acknowledges that working with living indigenous languages as an outsider is a responsibility that requires care, humility, and the acceptance that perfect accuracy may not be achievable. Any errors in the representation of these languages are unintentional, and the author welcomes correction.

The histories of the Northern Cheyenne and the Crow people are living histories. The Northern Cheyenne Nation and the Crow Nation both maintain active cultural programs, language preservation efforts, and archives. This novel is a work of fiction set within and around those histories. It does not speak for either nation.

The Long Reckoning series continues in Book Four.